THE OUTLIERS

Also by Kimberly McCreight

For adult readers

Reconstructing Amelia

Where They Found Her

THE OUTLIERS

KIMBERLY McCREIGHT

HarperCollins *Children's Books*

First published in Great Britain by HarperCollins Children's Books in 2016
HarperCollins Children's Books is a division of HarperCollinsPublishers Ltd,
1 London Bridge Street, London, SE1 9GF

The HarperCollins website address is: www.harpercollins.co.uk

1

Text © Kimberly McCreight 2016

ISBN 978-00-0-811506-7

Kimberly McCreight asserts the moral right to be identified as the author of the
work.

Printed and bound in England by Clays Ltd, St Ives plc

MIX
Paper from
responsible sources
FSC C007454

FSC™ is a non-profit international organisation established to promote
the responsible management of the world's forests. Products carrying the
FSC label are independently certified to assure consumers that they come
from forests that are managed to meet the social, economic and
ecological needs of present and future generations,
and other controlled sources.

Find out more about HarperCollins and the environment at
www.harpercollins.co.uk/green

FOR HARPER AND EMERSON,

THE BRAVEST OF THE BRAVE

K.M.

PROLOGUE

Why are the bad things always so much easier to believe? It shouldn't be that way. But it is, every single time. You're too sensitive and too worried, they say. You care too much about all the wrong things. One little whisper in your ear and the words tumble through your head like you're the one who thought them first. Hear them enough and pretty soon they're etched on the surface of your heart.

But right now, I've got to forget all the ways I've come to accept that I am broken. As I sit here in this cold, dark room, deep in the pitch-black woods, staring into this lying stranger's beautiful eyes, I need to think the opposite about myself. I need to believe that I am a person I have never known myself to be. That in my deepest, darkest, most useless corners lies a secret. One that just might end up being the thing that saves me. That saves us.

Because there is a lot that I still don't understand about what's going on. So much, actually. But I do know this: despite all the fear in this woman's eyes, we need to convince her to help us. Because our lives depend on it. And on us getting out that door.

CHAPTER 1

My dad's phone vibrates loudly, shimmying a little across our worn dining room table. He reaches forward and switches it off.

"Sorry about that." He smiles as he runs a hand over his thick salt-and-pepper hair, pushes his square black glasses up his nose. They're hipster glasses, but that's not why he bought them. With my dad, any hipness is entirely accidental. "I thought it was off. It shouldn't have even been on the table."

It's a rule: no phones in the dining room. It's always been the rule, even if no one ever really listened—not my mom, not my twin brother Gideon, not me. But that

was before. Things are divided up that way now: *Before.*
After. And in the dark and terrible middle lies my mom's
accident four months ago. In the *after*, the no-phone rule
is so much more important to my dad. Lots of little things
are. Sometimes, it feels like he's trying to rebuild our
lives out of matchsticks. And I do love him for that. But
loving someone isn't the same thing as understanding
them. Which is okay, I guess, because my dad doesn't
understand me either. He never really has. With my mom
gone, sometimes I think no one ever will.

My dad can't change who he is—a hard-core nerd-
scientist who lives entirely in his head. Since the accident,
he says, "I love you," way more than he ever used to and
is constantly patting me and Gideon on the back like
we're soldiers marching off to war. All of it is weird and
awkward, though, and it just makes me feel worse. For
all of us.

But he is doing his best. He's trying to be everything
my mom was. It isn't his fault that he's going about it
all wrong. He hasn't had a lot of practice with warm and
fuzzy. My mom's heart was always big enough for the both

of them. Not that she was soft. She couldn't have been the kind of photographer she was—all those countries, all that war—if she hadn't been tough as hell. But for my mom, feelings existed in only one form: magnified. And this applied to her own feelings: she bawled every time she read one of my or Gideon's homemade welcome home cards. And how she felt about everyone else's feelings: she always seemed to know if Gideon or I were upset before we'd even stepped in the door.

It was that crazy sixth sense of hers that got my dad so interested in emotional intelligence, EI for short. He's a research scientist and professor at the university, and one tiny part of EI is pretty much all he's ever studied. It isn't the kind of thing he'll ever get rich from. But Dr. Benjamin Lang cares about science, not money.

And there is one legitimate upside to my dad being the Tin Man. He didn't fall apart after the accident. Only once did he start to lose it—on the phone with Dr. Simons, his best friend/only friend/mentor/surrogate dad. And even then, he yanked himself back from the edge pretty fast. Still, sometimes I wonder whether I wouldn't trade my dad totally losing it for a hug so hard I can't breathe. For a look in his eyes that says he understands how ruined I am. Because he is, too.

"You can answer your phone," I say. "I don't care."

"You might not care, but I do." My dad takes off his glasses and rubs at his eyes in a way that makes him look so old. It tears the hole in the bottom of my stomach open a little wider. "Something has to matter, Wylie, or nothing will."

It's one of his favorite sayings.

I shrug. "Okay, whatever."

"Have you thought any more about what Dr. Shepard said in your phone session today?" he asks, trying to sound casual. But he's for sure been waiting to talk about this one thing since we sat down. Me ditching the home tutor and finishing up my junior year at Newton Regional High School is my dad's favorite subject. If we ever aren't talking about it, that's because he's biting his tongue in half trying to keep his mouth shut. "About starting back for the half days?"

My dad is afraid if I don't go back to regular school soon, I might never. My therapist, Dr. Shepard, and he are on exactly the same page in this regard. They are perfectly aligned in most things. Probably because the two of them have been exchanging emails. I said they could after the accident. My dad was really worried about me, and I wanted to seem all cool and cooperative and extra sane. But their private chitchat has never actually been okay with me, especially not now that they're both on team get-Wylie-back-into-regular-school. I don't think it's helped that Dr. Shepard and I had to switch to phone appointments three weeks ago because I can't get myself to leave the house anymore. It kind of proves her point that me avoiding school is just the tip of a very dark iceberg.

Really, Dr. Shepard barely signed off on the home tutor in the first place. Because she knows that my problems with regular school didn't start that day, four months ago, when my mom's car spun across a sheet of ice and got sliced in two.

"I'm concerned about where this might lead, Wylie," Dr. Shepard said in our last face-to-face session. "Opting out of school is counterproductive. Giving in to your panic will only make it worse. That remains true even in the midst of your very legitimate grief."

Dr. Shepard shifted in her big red armchair, which she always looked so perfect and petite sitting in, like Alice in Wonderland shrunk down to nothing. I'd been seeing Dr. Shepard on and off—mostly on—since middle school, almost six years, and sometimes I still wondered whether she really was a therapist at all; someone that small and young and pretty. But she had made me better over the years with her special therapy cocktail—breathing exercises, thought tricks, and lots and lots of talking. By the time high school started, I was pretty much just a regular kid on the nervous side of normal. That is, until my mom's accident cracked me open and out oozed my rotten core.

"Technically, I'm not opting out of school, just the school *building*." I forced a smile. Dr. Shepard's perfectly tweezed eyebrows pulled tight. "Besides, it's not like I didn't try to stay in school."

In point of fact, I'd only missed two actual days of school—the day after my mom's accident and the day of her funeral. I even had my dad call ahead to be sure no one treated me weird when I went back right away. Because that was my plan: to pretend nothing had happened. And for a while—a whole week maybe—it worked. And then that Monday morning came—one week, one day and fourteen hours after the funeral—and I started throwing up and throwing up. It went on for hours. I didn't stop until they gave me antinausea medicine in the ER. My dad was seriously freaked. By the time we were leaving the hospital, he had agreed to the home tutor. I think he would have agreed to anything, if there was a chance it might make me okay.

But even with Dr. Shepard working her best magic, I wasn't getting much better. And how could I without my mom around to help me see the bright side? *My* bright side. "You're just sensitive, Wylie," she'd always say. "The world needs sensitive people." And somehow I had always believed her.

Maybe she'd just been in denial. After all, my mom's mom—my grandmother—had died sad and alone and in a psychiatric hospital. Maybe she didn't want to believe

I was history repeating itself. Or maybe she honestly thought there was nothing wrong with me. Someday my mom might have told me. Now I'll never know for sure.

I look down at my plate, avoiding my dad's stare as I push some perfectly cooked asparagus into a sculpted mound of couscous. In a rough patch, my appetite is always the first to go. And since the accident, life is basically one long rough patch. But it's too bad I'm not hungry. My dad's cooking is one of the few things we've had going for us—he's always been the family chef.

"You said I could decide when I was ready to go back to school," I say finally, even though I'm already sure that I will *never* be ready, willing, or able to return to Newton Regional High School. But there is no reason to break that to my dad, at least not yet.

"When you go back to school *is* up to you." He's trying to sound laid-back, but he hasn't touched his food either. And that little vein in his forehead is standing out. "But I don't love you bumping around alone in this house day after day. It makes me feel—it's not good for you to be by yourself so much of the time."

"I enjoy my own company." I shrug. "That's healthy, isn't it? Come on, you're the psychologist. High self-esteem and all that."

It's crazy how much less convincing my smile feels each time I force it. There is even a part of me that knows it would be better if I finally lost this argument. If I was forced, kicking and screaming, back inside Newton Regional High School. Because one thing is for sure: being home isn't making me any better.

"Come on, Wylie." My dad eyeballs me, crosses his arms. "Just because you like yourself doesn't mean that—"

There's a loud knock at our front door then. It makes us both jump. *Please, not Gideon*—that's what I think, instantly. Because the last time an unexpected knock came, one of us was ripped away. And Gideon—my opposite twin, my mom used to joke, for how insanely different we are, including that Gideon is a science and history whiz and I'm all about math and English—is the only one of us left who's not at home.

"Who's that?" I ask, trying to ignore the wild beating of my heart.

"Nothing to worry about, I'm sure," my dad says. But he has no idea who's at the door, or what there might be to worry about. That's obvious. "Someone probably selling something."

"No one sells things door-to-door anymore, Dad." But he's already tossed his napkin on the table and started through the living room toward the front door.

He's got the door open by the time I round the corner.

"Karen." He sounds relieved. But only for a second. "What are you—what's wrong?"

When I can finally see past him, there's Cassie's mom, Karen, standing on our porch. Despite the sickly yellow glow of our energy-efficient outdoor bulbs, Karen looks as coiffed as always—her brown, shoulder-length hair perfectly smooth, a bright-green scarf knotted neatly above her tailored white wool coat. It's the beginning of May, but we're locked deep in one of those mean Boston cold snaps.

"I'm sorry to just show up like this." Karen's voice is all high and squeaky. And she's panting a little, her breath puffing out in a cloud. "But I called a couple times and no one answered, and then I was driving around looking for her when I saw your light on and I guess—God, I've looked everywhere." When she crosses her arms and takes a step closer, I notice her feet. They're completely bare.

"Looked everywhere for who—" My dad has caught sight of them, too. "Karen, what happened to your shoes? Come inside." When she doesn't move, he reaches out and tugs her forward, gently. "You must be freezing. Come, come."

"I can't find Cassie." Karen's voice cracks hard as she steps inside. "Can you—I hate to ask, Ben. But can you help?"

CHAPTER 2

In the living room, my dad guides Karen to a nearby chair. She drops down, body stiff, face frozen. Nothing at all like I've ever seen her. Because it's more than Karen's clothes that are always perfect. She is always perfect, too. "The Plague of Perfect," Cassie actually calls her—so thin and so pretty, always with a smile and never a hair out of place. And *thin*. It's worth saying that twice. Because according to Cassie, someone's weight matters to Karen twice as much as anything else. And that could be true. Karen's never been anything but nice to me, but there is something about the way she talks to Cassie, a sharp edge buried inside her smooth voice. Like she loves her daughter, but maybe doesn't like her very much.

"Wylie, can you get Karen a glass of water?"

My dad is staring at me. He's worried about this—whatever it is—upsetting me. The last thing I need is to be more upset; it's not a totally unfair point. So he's dismissing me for my own good. As if keeping me from the room could ever keep me from worrying about Cassie now. I've already heard enough.

"Water would be great," Karen says, but like she couldn't want anything less. She's just following my dad's lead. "Thank you."

"Wylie," my dad presses when I stay put, staring at the carpet.

But I have to be careful. If I seem like I'm losing it, he'll make me go upstairs for good. He might even tell Karen to leave before I find out what's going on. And I need to know. Even after everything that's happened between us, even though this isn't exactly my first-ever Cassie-related emergency, I still care about what happens to her. I always will.

I can tell by the look on my dad's face. He wants to wrap this up ASAP and send Karen on her way. He'll do that, too, no matter how much he likes Karen and Cassie. Since the accident, he's drawn a lot of new lines in the sand—with my grandparents, teachers, doctors, neighbors. Anything to protect Gideon and me. More me, it's true. Gideon has always been the "more resilient" one. That's what people say when they think I'm not listening. And if they're my grandmother—my dad's mom—they even say it to my face. She cornered me at the house right after my mom's funeral and told me all about how I should really try to be more like Gideon. That was right before my dad asked her to never visit again.

The truth is, my grandmother never liked me. I remind her too much of my mom, who she also never liked. But she was right about Gideon. He does bounce back more easily than me. He always has. Feelings, especially the bad ones, roll right off him—probably something having to do with that huge computer brain of his—while on me they get stuck, forever trapped in my gooey, inescapable mess. Don't get me wrong, Gideon's definitely been sad. He misses our mom, but he's mostly stoic like my dad. I'm more like our mom. Except if her feelings were always cranked up to full volume, mine have blown out the speakers.

"Okay, water, fine," I say to my dad, who's still eyeballing me. "I'm going."

Cassie and I became friends in a bathroom. *Hiding* in the bathroom of Samuel F. Smith Memorial Middle School, to be exact. It was December of sixth grade and I'd headed to the bathroom, planning to crouch up on a toilet through all of homeroom if I had to. It didn't occur to me that someone else might have the same idea when I banged hard on the door in the last stall.

"Ow!" came a yelp when the not-locked door swung back and banged into someone. "What the hell!"

"Oh, sorry." My face flushed. "I didn't see any feet."

"Yeah, that's kind of the whole point." The girl sounded pissed. When she finally opened the door, she looked it, too. Cassie—the new girl, or newish girl—was squatting up on the toilet, fully clothed, just like I had planned on doing myself. She stared at me for a minute, then rolled her eyes as she shifted to the side, freeing up some of the seat for me. "Well, don't just stand there. Come on. Before someone sees you."

Cassie and I knew of each other—our school wasn't that big—but we weren't friends. Cassie didn't really have any friends yet. And I felt bad about the way some kids picked on her. It was her snug sweatpants or her short, knotted curls or the fact that she was bigger than the other girls—both her boobs and her belly. No one cut Cassie a break because she was a sports star either. She might have single-handedly made our soccer team decent for the first time that fall, but all they cared about was that she didn't look the part. I did feel bad, but it wasn't like I could be Cassie's defender or something. Not when I was barely hanging on myself.

"So what brings you to the bowl of shame?" Cassie asked once our knees were touching over the open water of the toilet.

There was no way I was going to tell her anything. Except then suddenly, all I wanted was to tell her everything.

"All my friends hate me," I began. "And they're all in my homeroom."

"Why do they hate you?" Cassie asked. I was glad she hadn't tried to talk me out of them hating me straight off the bat. People love to talk you out of your bad feelings. (Believe me, I am an expert in this phenomenon.) Instead, she just seemed curious. "What happened?"

And so I told her all about how Maia, Stephanie, Brooke, and I had been a foursome since we were eight years old, but lately it had felt like the rest of them were in on some joke that was mostly about me. I'd still been hoping it was my imagination, though, right up until that Saturday night at the sleepover when they started interrogating me about my therapist. Maia's mom volunteered in the school office and must have seen the note about me having to leave early for my first appointment with Dr. Shepard. And then had apparently decided to tell Maia, which I still couldn't believe.

"Come on, Wylie. Tell us," they'd chanted.

By then I was sweating already. Suddenly, the room began to spin. And then, it had happened.

"I didn't even realize that I'd thrown up until after I'd heard the screams," I said to Cassie. And I could still hear them ringing in my ears: "Oh my God!!" "Ew!!!"

"Oh, that sucks," Cassie said. Like what I'd told her was

important, but not really that alarming. "My basketball coach showed me his stuff yesterday. You know, Mr. Pritzer. He drove me home after practice and then he just whipped it out. And unfortunately, he's my homeroom teacher."

And she said it like her getting flashed wasn't so terrible either, just kind of unfortunate.

"Oh," I said, because I couldn't think of what else to say and it made me embarrassed just imagining Mr. Pritzer doing that. "Ew."

"Yeah, ew." Cassie frowned and nodded. Now she looked sad.

"Did you tell your parents?"

"My mom won't believe me." Cassie shrugged. "That's what happens when you lie a lot."

"I believe you," I said. And I did.

"Thanks." Cassie smiled. "And I'm sorry you lost all your friends." She nodded, pressing her lips together. "Good thing you've got a new one now."

Out in the kitchen, I move fast, not waiting for the tap to run cold before sloppily filling a glass of water for Karen.

The truth is, I've been waiting for a long time for the "big one" to happen where Cassie is concerned. Rescuing her has always been a thing—playing a human shield so she didn't get beat up for talking shit about some huge eighth grader, bringing money down to the Rite Aid so she didn't get reported for shoplifting a lipstick (Cassie doesn't even wear lipstick). Harmless, *stupid* kid stuff.

This fall, though, things did take a dark turn. Cassie's drinking was the biggest problem. And it wasn't just how much (five or six beers in a single night?) or how often (two or three times a week?) that got me worried. That was kind of excessive for anyone, but for someone with Cassie's genes, it was a total disaster. Once upon a time, she said herself that she should never drink. Because she loved her dad, but the last thing she wanted was to end up like him.

But then it was like Cassie decided to forget about all that. And boy, did she not like me reminding her. By a couple months into this year, our junior year, she was unraveling so fast it was like watching a spinning top. And the more worried I got, the angrier she became.

Luckily, Karen is still talking when I finally get back out to the living room. I might still catch some details that matter.

"Yeah, so . . ." She glances up at me and then clears her throat before going on. "I came home to see Cassie after school and she wasn't there."

The glass is definitely warm as I hand it to Karen. When she takes it, she doesn't seem to notice. But she does finally notice my hair. I see the split second it happens. In her defense, Karen recovers pretty well, steadies her eyes before looking all the way shocked. Instead, she takes a sip of that bathtub water and smiles at me.

"Couldn't Cassie just still be out then?" my dad asks. "It's only dinnertime."

"She was supposed to be home," Karen says firmly. "She was grounded this whole week. Because she—well, I don't even want to tell you what she called me." And there it is. The tone. The I-hate-Cassie-a little-bit, maybe even more than she hates me. "I told her if she wasn't home, I really was going to put a call into this boarding school I'd been looking into—you know, one of those therapeutic ones. And no, I'm not proud of that threat. That we've sunk as low as me shipping her off. But we have, that's the honest truth. Anyway, I also found this."

Karen fishes something out of her pocket and hands it to my dad. It's Cassie's ID bracelet.

"She hasn't taken that bracelet off since the day I gave it to her three years ago." Karen's eyes fill with tears. "I didn't even really mean it about that stupid school. I was just so worried. And angry. That's the truth. I was angry, too."

My dad looks down quizzically at the bracelet looped over his fingers, then at Karen again. "Maybe it fell off," he says, his voice lifting like it's a question.

"I found it on my pillow, Ben," Karen says. "And it wasn't there this morning. So Cassie must have come back at some point and left again. It was meant as a sign—like a 'screw you, I'm out of here.' I know it." Karen turns to me then. "You haven't heard from her, have you, Wylie?"

Back when things were still okay between us, Cassie and I wouldn't have gone more than an hour without at least texting. But that's not true anymore. I shake my head. "I haven't talked to her in a while."

It's been a week at least, maybe longer. Being at home, it's easy to lose track of the exact number of days. But it's the longest stretch since the accident that we've gone without talking. It was bound to happen eventually: we couldn't be pretend-friends forever. Because that's all we were really doing when Cassie came back after the accident: pretending.

The accident happened in January, but Cassie and I had stopped talking the first time right after Thanksgiving. Nearly two long months, which, let's face it, might as well be a lifetime when you're sixteen. But the morning after the accident, Cassie had just showed up on our doorstep. My eyes had been burning so badly from crying that I'd thought I was seeing things. It wasn't until Cassie had helped me change out of the clothes I'd been dressed in for two days that I began to believe she was real. And it wasn't until after she'd pulled my hair out of its ragged, twisted bun, brushed it smooth, and braided it tight— like she was arming me for battle—that I knew how badly I needed her to stay.

I don't know what Cassie has told Karen about our best-friend breakup and our temporary get-back-together. And it ended anyway a few weeks ago. But I can bet it's not much. The two of them aren't exactly close. And it's not like the reasons we stopped talking reflect so well on Cassie.

"You haven't talked to Cassie in a while?" my dad asks, surprised.

My mom knew about Cassie and me having a falling-out back when it first happened. She apparently just never told him. It is possible that I asked her not to—I don't remember. But I do remember the day I told my mom that Cassie and I weren't friends anymore. We were lying side by side on her bed, and when I was done talking, she said, "I would always want to be your friend."

I shrug. "I think the last text I got from her was last week? Maybe on Tuesday."

"Last week?" my dad asks, eyebrows all scrunched low.

The truth was, I really wasn't sure. But it was the following Thursday now. And it was definitely at least a week since we'd spoken.

"Oh, that long." Karen is more disappointed than surprised. "I noticed that the two of you hadn't been talking as much, but I didn't realize . . ." She shakes her head. "I called the police, but of course because Cassie's sixteen and we've been fighting they didn't seem in a big rush to go after her. They filed a report and they'll check the local hospitals, but they're not going to start combing the woods or anything. They'll send a car out looking, but not until the morning." Karen presses her fingertips against her temples and rocks her head back and forth. "Morning. That's *twelve* hours from now. Who knows who Cassie will be with or what shape she'll be in by then? Think of all the horrible— Ben, I can't wait until morning. Not with the way she and I left things."

I'm surprised that Karen seems to know even partly how out of control Cassie has gotten. But then, without me to help cover for her, Cassie was bound to get busted eventually. And this scenario Karen has in her head— Cassie well on her way to passed out somewhere—isn't crazy. Even at that hour, just before seven p.m., it's possible.

"Nooners," the kids at Newton Regional called them. Apparently getting totally wasted in the middle of the day was what all the cool kids were doing these days. The last time I rushed out to help Cassie back in November, it was only four or five in the afternoon. I had to take a cab to pick her up at a party at Max Russell's house, because she was way too drunk to get home on her own. Lucky for her, my mom had been traveling, my dad had been, like always, working at his campus lab on his study, and Gideon was still at school, working late on his Intel Science Competition application. I slipped out and we slipped back in with no one ever the wiser, Cassie bumping into walls as she swayed. After, I held her hair back over the toilet when she threw up again and again. And later I called Karen to say she had a migraine and wanted to stay the night.

I told Cassie the next morning that she needed to stop drinking or something terrible would happen. But by then I wasn't her only friend. I was just the one telling her the things she didn't want to hear.

CHAPTER 3

"Are you okay, Wylie?" My dad is staring at me. And he's been staring at me for who knows how long. I realize then why. I've got myself pressed hard up against the back wall of the living room like I'm trying to escape through the plaster. "Why don't you sit down?"

"I'm fine," I say. But I do not sound fine.

"Oh, honey, I'm sorry." Karen looks at me, seems again like she might cry. "The last thing all of you need is my, is our—" She forces a wobbly smile, looks even closer to falling apart. I stare down. If I see her really start to lose it, I will too. "Cassie will be fine, Wylie, I'm sure. The police are probably right that I'm overreacting. I can have a bit of a short fuse for this kind of . . ."

She doesn't finish her sentence. Because of Cassie's dad, Vince, that's what she means. Cassie's parents were already divorced when we met, but Cassie told me all about life before. And Vince was never a quiet drunk. Fights with neighbors at summer barbecues, calling home to be rescued from whatever latest bar he'd been tossed out of. But the final straw was the second DUI, the one where he'd crashed his car into a mailbox downtown. Karen is as afraid of Vince's history repeating itself in Cassie as I've been. When I glance up from the carpet, my dad is still looking at me.

"I'm fine," I say again, but too loud. "I just want to help find Cassie."

"Wylie, of course you want to help," my dad starts. "But right now, I don't think you—"

"Please," I say, willing my voice to sound determined, not desperate. Desperate is not my friend. "I need to do this."

And I do. I don't realize how bad until the words are out of my mouth. Partly because I want to prove to myself that I can. But also, I do feel guilty. I didn't agree with the things Cassie was doing, was scared about what might happen to her if she didn't stop. But maybe I should have made more sure that she knew I'd always love her no matter what mistakes she made.

"It was so selfish of me to come here." Karen rests her forehead against her hand. "After everything all of you have been through—I wasn't thinking clearly."

My dad's eyes are on mine. Narrowed, like he's assessing some tricky quadratic equation. Finally, he takes a deep breath.

"No, Wylie is right. We want to help. We need to," he says. And my heart soars. Maybe he *can* hear me after all. Maybe he does understand a little bit of something. He turns back to Karen. "Let's back up. What exactly happened this morning?"

Karen crosses her arms and looks away. "Well, we were rushing around getting ready, and Cassie and I were snapping at each other as usual, because she wouldn't get out of bed. She's missed the bus *five* times in the last two weeks. And I had to be somewhere this morning and I couldn't—" Her voice tightens as she pulls a crumpled tissue out of her pocket. "Anyway, I totally lost my patience. I—I screamed at her, Ben. Completely let her have it. And she called me the most horrible word. One that I won't repeat. A word that I have never in my life said out loud. But there was Cassie calling me *that*." Her voice catches again as she stares down at her fingers, twisting the bunched tissue between them. "So I told her I was finally going to call that boarding school and have them cart her away. So they could scare some sense into her."

My dad nods like he knows exactly what Karen means. Like he's yelled the exact same kind of thing at me countless times. But the only time I can remember him ever yelling at me about anything was one Fourth of July at Albemarle Field when I was barefoot at the fireworks and almost stepped on a broken chunk of bottle.

"The worst part is that what started it—my big rush— wasn't even about a work meeting or an open house or a prospective client. Nothing I needed to do to put food on our table. Nothing that actually mattered." Karen looks up, toward the ceiling. Like she's searching for an answer up there. "It was a *yoga* class. *That's* why I lost it." She looks at my dad like maybe he can explain her own awfulness.

"I fought Vince through the entire divorce for Cassie to live with me, so I could be there for her, and now—I am so selfish."

Karen drops her face in her hands and rocks it back and forth. I can't tell if she's crying, but I really wish she wouldn't. Because I am worried about Cassie. But not *that* worried. Ironic that I—of all people—would ever be *less* worried than anyone else. Makes me feel like maybe I'm in denial. And whatever it is could definitely be bad. Would any of the people Cassie hangs out with these days really call for help if she needed it? Would they stay to make sure she didn't vomit in her sleep, that no one took advantage of her while she was passed out cold? No. The answer on all fronts is no.

"Karen, you can't do this to yourself. No one is perfect." My dad steps toward her and leans in like he might actually put a hand on her back. But he crosses his arms instead. "Was Cassie absent from school?"

"There was no message from them. But I guess—" Karen twists her tissue some more. "Cassie could have deleted it when she came back to leave the bracelet. She did that a couple weeks ago when she skipped school. I was going to change the school contact number to my cell, but I forgot."

Cassie's been skipping school, too? These days there is so much about her I don't know.

"Why don't you try texting her now, Wylie?" my dad suggests. "Maybe hearing from you—you never know."

Maybe she's just not answering Karen. He doesn't say that, but he's thinking it. And after Karen threatened her with that boarding school boot camp, Cassie might never talk to her again. But then if she's avoiding her mom, she'll probably avoid me, too, for the exact same reason: we both make her feel bad about herself.

"Okay, but I don't know . . ." I pull my phone out of my sweatshirt pocket and type, *Cassie, where r u? Your mom is freaking.* I wait and wait, but she doesn't write back. Finally, I hold up my phone. "It can take her a minute to respond."

Actually, it never does. Or never did. The Cassie I knew lived with her phone in her hand. Like it was a badge of honor to respond to every tweet or text or photo within seconds. Or maybe it was more of a life vest. Because the skinnier and drunker and more popular Cassie got, the more desperate she seemed.

"Can you think of anywhere Cassie might be, Wylie?" Karen asks. "Or anyone she could be with?"

"You tried Maia and those guys?" I ask, hating the feel of her name in my mouth.

The Rainbow Coalition: Stephanie, Brooke, and Maia—still best friends after all these years. All except me. They started calling themselves the Rainbow Coalition freshman year because of their array of hair colors. (And they seemed not to care that their all being white made their nickname totally offensive.) More beautiful than ever, they'd also gotten much cooler. By junior year, Maia, Brooke, and Stephanie had clawed their way to the top of the Newton Regional High School popularity pile. Cassie had always hated the Rainbow Coalition for what they'd done to me, right up until they reached down and invited her to climb up and join the pile.

"Maia and those girls." Karen rolls her eyes. "I honestly don't know what Cassie sees in them."

That they see her, I want to say. *In a way you never did.* But then, I'm hardly one to talk. At the beginning, Cassie tried to hide how proud she was that she'd been invited to join the Rainbow Coalition at one of their "hangouts." Not "parties," because that would be "so basic." (And yes, they actually talk like that.) She pretended that she was doing it for research purposes only. It was at the very first Rainbow Coalition "hangout" that Cassie met Jasper. And after that, she seemed to care a whole lot less about pretending anything.

It was exciting for her. I did get that part. But I also thought Cassie would get over it pretty fast, that she'd come to her senses. Instead, she just got more and more drunk at more and more parties. More than once, I played back to her what she had always told me about her dad: that she never wanted to end up like him. I told her again and again that, as her friend, I was worried. But what did she need me for when all I did was make her feel bad about herself? She had the Rainbow Coalition to fill her days and, at night, she was falling in love, hard. I could see it, but I was trying hard to pretend it wasn't happening. Because Jasper Salt didn't lift Cassie out of the gutter the way a real friend would, the way someone who really cares about you does. No, he grabbed Cassie's hand and leaped with her right down the drain.

"You know, Jasper really is a good person, Wylie," Cassie had started in the Monday after Thanksgiving. "You need to get to know him."

We were eating lunch at Naidre's, the one coffee shop near school where upperclassmen were allowed to go off campus. Soup and a sandwich for me, a dry bagel for Cassie, which she was busy tearing into small pieces and rearranging on her plate so it seemed like she was eating.

We'd only been together five minutes after not seeing each other for four days and already we were back in a fight. But really, things had been off between us since Cassie came home from fitness summer camp at the end of August. "Fat camp," Cassie had called it when her mother had forced her to go the summer before eighth grade. But this time had been Cassie's idea. Even though it was hard to see how she had any more weight to lose. When she got home, she was absolutely skeletal, a comparison that delighted her.

It wasn't just the weight loss, either. Cassie also had new hair, longer and blown straight, and stylish clothes. It was hard to believe she was the same person who'd hunched over that toilet with me. I wasn't surprised weeks later when the Rainbow Coalition had come knocking or even that somebody like Jasper—popular, good-looking, an athlete (and an asshole)—had noticed Cassie. I just couldn't believe how much she'd liked them back.

"I know everything about Jasper that I need to know," I said, then burned my mouth on my tomato soup.

Rumor was he had knocked some senior out with a single punch his freshman year. In one version, Jasper had broken the kid's nose. I still couldn't figure out why he wasn't in jail, much less still in school. But I hadn't liked Jasper even before I'd heard about that punch, and maybe some of those reasons were shallow—his body-hugging T-shirts, his swagger, and his stupid, put-on surfer lingo. But I also had proof that he was an actual asshole. I had Tasha.

Tasha was our age but seemed way younger. She hugged people without warning and laughed way too loud, always wearing pink or red with a matching headband. Like a giant Valentine's Day card. But no one was ever mean to Tasha; that would have been cruel. No one except for Jasper, that is. A couple of weeks after he and Cassie started hanging out—the beginning of October—I saw Jasper talking to Tasha down at the end of an empty hall. They were too far away to hear, but there was no mistaking Tasha rushing back my way in tears. But when I told Cassie about it afterward, she just said Jasper would never do something mean to Tasha. Which meant, I guess, that I was lying.

"Jasper might not be perfect, but he's had a really hard life. You should cut him a break," Cassie went on now, readjusting her bagel scraps. "It's just him and his mom, who's totally selfish, and his older brother, who's a huge asshole. And his dad's in *jail*," she added defensively, but also kind of smugly. Like Jasper's dad being a criminal was somehow proof that he was a good person.

"In jail for what?"

"I don't know," she snapped.

"Cassie, what if it's something really bad?"

"Just because Jasper's father did something doesn't mean there's something wrong with *him*. It's actually really messed up that you would even think that." Cassie shook her head and crossed her arms. The worst part was that she was right: it was pretty awful that my mind had jumped there. "Besides, Jasper understands me. That matters more than his stupid dad."

I felt a flash of heat in my chest. So here it was, the real truth: *Jasper* understood her and I did not.

"Which you, Cassie?" I snapped. "You have so many faces these days, how can he even keep track?"

Cassie stared at me, mouth hanging open. And then she started gathering her things.

"What are you doing?" I asked, my heart beating hard. She was supposed to get angry. We were supposed to have a fight. She wasn't supposed to disappear.

"I'm leaving," Cassie said quietly. "That's what *normal* people do when someone is awful to them. And in case you're confused, Wylie"—she motioned to herself—"this is normal. And *you* are awful."

***

"Anyway, I did speak to Maia and the other girls," Karen goes on. "They said they last saw Cassie in school, though none of them could seem to remember exactly when."

"Have you talked to Jasper?" I ask, trying not to sound like I've already decided that he is—in spirit if not in fact—100 percent responsible for every bad thing that has ever happened to Cassie.

Karen nods. "He exchanged texts with Cassie when she was on the bus on her way to school, but that's the last time he heard from her. At least, supposedly." She squints at me. "You don't like Jasper, do you?"

"I don't really know him, so I'm not sure my opinion means anything," I say, even though I think just the opposite.

"You're Cassie's oldest friend," Karen says. "Her only real friend, as far as I'm concerned. Your opinion means everything. You don't think he would hurt her, do you?"

Do I think that Jasper would actually *do* something to Cassie? No. I think many bad things about Jasper, but I have no reason to think that. I do not think that.

"I don't know," I say, being vague on purpose. But I can't even half accuse Jasper of something that serious just because I don't like him. "No, I mean. I don't think so."

"And Vince hasn't heard from her either?" my dad asks.

"Vince," Karen huffs. "He's hanging out with some new 'girlfriend' in the Florida Keys. Last I heard he was going to try to get his private detective's license. Ridiculous."

The insane part is that Cassie might actually call her dad. Cassie is crazy about Vince, despite everything. They email and text all the time. It's their distaste for Karen that unites them.

"You should probably try to reach him," my dad suggests gently. Then he heads over to the counter, picks up his wallet, and peers at the little hooks on the wall where we hang our keys. "Just in case. And you and I will go out looking for her."

Karen nods as she looks down at her fingers, still working them open and closed around the mostly shredded tissue.

"He's going to blame me, you know. Like if I wasn't such a hateable hardass, Cassie would still be—" Karen clamps her hand over her mouth when her voice cuts out. "And he'll be right. That's the worst part. Vince has problems, but he and Cassie—" She shakes her head. "They always connected. Maybe if I—"

"Nothing is that simple. Not with kids, not with anything," my dad says as he finally finds his keys in a drawer. "Come on, let's stop back at your place first. Make sure there's no sign of Cassie there. We'll call Vince on the way. I'll even talk to him if you want." My dad steps toward the front door but pauses when he notices Karen's feet. "Oh, wait, your shoes."

"That's okay," she says with an embarrassed wave of her hand. Even now, trying to reclaim a small scrap of perfect. "I'll be fine. I drove here this ridiculous way. I can get back home."

"What if we end up having to stop someplace else? No, no, you need shoes. You can borrow a pair of Hope's."

Hope's? So casually, too, like he didn't just offer Karen a sheet of my skin. Of course, it's not like he can offer Karen a pair of my spare shoes. After a panic-fueled anti-hoarder's episode after the funeral, I only have one pair of shoes left. The ones I'm wearing. But it's the way my dad said it: like it would be nothing to give away all my mom's things.

Sometimes I wonder if my dad had stopped loving my mom even before she died. I have evidence to support this theory: their fight, namely. After an entire life of basically never a mean word between them, they had suddenly been at each other constantly in the weeks before the accident. And not really loving her would definitely explain why he hasn't seemed as broken up as me in the days since she died.

Don't do it, I think as he moves toward the steps for her shoes. *I will never forgive you if you do.* Luckily, he stops when his phone buzzes in his hand.

He looks down at it. "I'm sorry, but this is Dr. Simons." Saved by my dad's only friend: Dr. Simons. The one person he will always drop everything for. That never bothered me before. But right now, it is seriously pissing me off. "Can you take Karen upstairs, Wylie? See if there's something of your mom's that will fit her?"

I just glare at him.

"Are you okay?" he asks, when I still don't move. His face is tight.

"Yeah," I say finally, because he'll probably use me being angry as more proof that we shouldn't be helping Karen. "I'm awesome."

But the whole way upstairs, I still try to think of an excuse not to give Karen the shoes. One that doesn't seem crazy. One that my mom would approve of. Because my mom would want me to give Karen whatever she needs. *You can do it,* she'd say if she was there. *I know you can.*

Soon enough, Karen is behind me in my parents' room as I stand frozen in front of their closet. We're only *lending* them, I remind myself, as I pull open the closet door and crouch down in front of my mom's side of the closet. I close my eyes and try not to take in her smell as I feel around blindly for her shoes. Finally, my hands land on what I think are a pair of low dress boots that my mom only wore once or twice. But I feel sick when I open my eyes and see what I've pulled out instead. My mom's old Doc Martens, the ones she loved so much she had the heels replaced twice.

"I know Cassie misses you," Karen says while I'm still bent over my mom's Doc Martens like an animal protecting its last meal. "Because I still know how she *really* feels. Even if she thinks I don't. And I know that right now, Cassie's totally lost and what she really needs is a good friend. A friend like you."

Karen comes over and kneels next to me. I feel her look from me to the boots and back again. Then she leans forward and reaches into the closet herself. A second later, she pulls out a pair of bright-white, brand-new tennis shoes. The ones that my grandmother—my dad's mom—gave to my mom years ago, probably *because* my mom always hated tennis.

"What about these instead?" Karen asks.

Yes, I would say if I wasn't so afraid my voice would crack. *Those would be much, much better.*

"Do you think Cassie at least knows how much I love her?" Karen asks, rocking back to sitting, her eyes still on the sneakers. "Because things haven't been easy between us lately. Let's face it, they've never been easy. And I know I've made a lot of mistakes. I could have done so many things, so much better. But I was always trying. And I really do love her. She knows that, right?"

Cassie has said so many awful things about her mom—selfish, self-involved, fat-shaming, judgmental, superficial. But the thing that Cassie said most often was that she didn't think Karen loved her. Not in the way a mom should.

"Yeah," I say, before I wait too long and it sounds like the lie that it is. "Cassie knows that, definitely."

"Thank God." Karen sounds so relieved that it kind of breaks my heart for her. "That's really—that's good."

Karen puts the sneakers down, then reaches over to take my hand in hers, rubbing my knuckles in a mom-ish way that makes my throat squeeze tight. Her other hand moves to the hacked remains of my wavy brown hair, her fingers drifting away before they reach its most jagged ends.

The night before I'd glimpsed myself in the hallway mirror and for a second—one fucked-up second—I thought I *was* her. My mom. That she was there, warm and alive and well again. With my hair longer, I was starting to look exactly like her. And last night I needed not to. I needed to know I'd never again mistake myself for her. Never again would I believe for one awfully beautiful moment that she had come home.

So I grabbed the scissors and leaned over the bathroom sink to cut my hair. So that it, that I, looked nothing like her. I nailed the different part. That's for sure. I'd been avoiding mirrors ever since, but I could tell it was bad from the freaked-out look that had passed over my dad's face when he first saw me. But even worse, actually, was the way Gideon—always up for making me feel bad—didn't say a word.

When I look up at Karen, she smiles, her eyes glistening as she wraps a hand gently around my head and pulls it to her neck. And I'm pretty sure it's because she needs to be holding someone. Even more, maybe, than I need to be held. She strokes my hair. *Don't cry,* I tell myself as my eyes start to burn. *Please don't cry.*

"You're going to be okay, you know," she whispers. "Not now, but someday."

CHAPTER 4

When Karen and I get back downstairs, my dad is just hanging up the phone. But instead of putting it down, he keeps it gripped in his hand, so tight his fingers are white at the edges. Something is wrong. Something new. Something bad on top of whatever is wrong with Cassie.

"What did Dr. Simons want?" I ask, because it was the conversation with him that freaked my dad out apparently.

Dr. Simons was my dad's professor at Stanford. He's a psychologist and a professor like my dad, but he studies peer pressure, not EI. Similar enough, I guess. And he has no family of his own anymore, so my dad is like his surrogate son. He's always off teaching this place or that—England, Australia, Hong Kong—which is why we haven't seen him since we were super-little kids. Lack of geographical proximity is probably part of what my dad likes about Dr. Simons. They are as close as two people, forever thousands of miles apart, can possibly be.

"He was just calling back to answer a question, something about my new data." My dad waves a hand: *nothing for you to worry about*. And I so want to find that believable. But it is not. At all. My dad forces a bigger, even less convincing smile as he turns to Karen. "We ready? Wylie, just be sure to lock up once we're gone, okay?" He says it casually, like it's an ordinary, everyday request.

"Lock up?" I ask.

My dad has never thought to lock a door in his entire life. If it hadn't been for my mom, he would have left for our annual two-week vacation on the Cape with our front door hanging wide open.

"Wylie, please," my dad snaps, like he's fed up with me and my obsessing, and fair enough, I guess. "Just lock the door. Until we know what's happened to Cassie, I just— we should exercise all due care."

That explanation would be a lot more believable if he didn't look so freaked out. He hasn't looked that spooked in ages. Not since the day the first baby came.

We were at the breakfast table a couple of days after Halloween when my mom found the first one. It was sitting there on our front porch when she went out to get the newspaper.

"I guess they get points for creativity," my mom said as she came inside, holding up a plastic baby doll. Her nose crinkled as she peered at the red splattered all over it, which one could only hope was paint. "Much more vivid than the usual emails. I guess that's the price you pay for page one. I should probably call Elaine and see if she got one, too."

Elaine was the journalist my mom had been working with on a story about a coalition bombing in Syria. It had run that day on the front page of the Sunday *Times*, and it was my mom's photographs of a bombed-out school that had stolen the show. She had always gotten her fair share of hate mail. A couple of times even left at our house. But nothing like a plastic baby.

"Why are you even touching that!" my dad shouted. And so loud. "Put it back outside!"

"It's not contagious, honey." My mom smiled her beautiful, mischievous smile and raised an eyebrow. She was going to let the shouting go, apparently. She'd been doing that a lot lately—letting everything with my dad go—but I could tell she was starting to get annoyed. "You've got to keep your sense of humor, Ben. You know that."

And my dad *did* used to have a sense of humor. He used to be really, really funny actually. In a way, that was even funnier, because of his whole stiff science-guy thing. But these days, he was so wound up. First, because he'd been working around the clock at the university trying to finish his study, then I guess his results were kind of disappointing. It wasn't going to be officially published until February, but it was already finished. The icing on the cake, though, was him having to fire his favorite postdoc, Dr. Caton, because—according to my dad—he'd let "personal bias cloud his judgment." Whatever that meant. We'd never met Dr. Caton—my dad wasn't big on socializing—but from the day he hired him, he'd talked about the supposedly very young Dr. Caton (twenty-four and already with a PhD) like some kind of precious, unearthed jewel. I didn't care, but it drove Gideon—our other resident science boy wonder—totally crazy. He was delighted when Dr. Caton got the ax.

My mom shrugged as she stepped over to pick up her half-eaten toast. She took another bite, the doll still gripped in her other hand, then placed the toast back down delicately, brushing the crumbs from her fingers as she walked back toward the foyer with the baby. She opened our front door and calmly tossed the doll outside. We all heard it go thud, thud, thud down the front steps. Gideon and I giggled. So did my mom. My dad did not. Instead, he headed for the phone.

"Who are you calling?" my mom asked.

"The police," he said, like this should have been self-evident.

"Come on, Ben," my mom said, crossing over to where he was standing. "I can give you one definite. You calling the police is exactly what they want: attention."

"I can't deal with this, Hope," my dad said quietly,

sad almost, as my mom took the phone from him and hung it up. Then she wrapped her arms around him and whispered something in his ear.

"You don't have to deal with it," she said as they separated, but loud enough that it seemed like she was saying it for my benefit. And weirdly, she did not even seem mad at my dad for making something that had happened to her all about him. "That's why you have me."

After my dad and Karen are gone, I sit on the living room couch in the dark, staring out our large bay window overlooking Walnut Hill Road, waiting for the lights from Gideon's ride home from track practice. Neither of us even have our learner's permits yet, though we've both been legally allowed to for two months now. Nothing like your mom dying in a car accident to kill your thirst for the open road. Gideon will probably learn to drive eventually. Bur I already know that I never will.

I peer again down the road for any sign of headlights. What is taking Gideon so long? He should have been home—well, just a few minutes ago, but still. Tonight, a few minutes feel like hours. It's weird to be waiting on Gideon. His company is so prickly lately. But right now, I'd choose anything over being alone.

I did lock all the doors after my dad and Karen left, then checked them twice. And then a third time. Because you don't have to tell me twice to worry. I checked the locks and then I checked anything and everything else that could even potentially jump out, burn up, or otherwise turn on me.

I've also checked my phone a dozen times for an answer to one of my texts to Cassie. I've sent four so far, and called her twice. But there's been nothing. I would have sent more texts, but each one that goes unanswered makes me feel worse. Makes me more worried that this time, Cassie has finally gotten herself sunk into something so dark and deep that even I won't be able to yank her back out, no matter how hard I try.

"Why are all the lights off?"

A voice behind me. When I spin around, heart racing, there's Gideon, coat and backpack still on. He's wearing sweatpants, his blond, shaggy hair damp against his forehead as he chews on what's left of a Twizzler.

"Why did you do that, Gideon!"

"First of all, calm down." He takes another bite. "Second of all, do what?"

"Sneak up on me, you stupid jerk!"

"Um, wow." He holds up his hands like I'm pointing a gun at him, the half-chewed Twizzler flopping around in his fingers. He loves to point out whenever I'm acting nuts. Which, let's face it, is most of the time lately.

Gideon is perpetually annoyed at me because he thinks it's unfair that he gets less attention for being more normal. Like with the home tutor, for instance. Gideon is an insanely smart kid (though even he would admit I could easily *crush* him on any math test anywhere, any day), but he hates school even after moving to Stanton Prep so they could better accommodate his über-genius science needs. He thinks he should get to opt out, too. My dad had shut him down so fast, it had made *my* head spin.

"Did Stephen drive you home?" I look back out the window. Did I somehow miss the car? Am I now not seeing things right? "I didn't see him."

"We came the back way. We stopped at Duffy's for fries with some of the other guys." He shrugs: *hanging out like all the normal kids with lots of friends do.* That's what the shrug says. He so bad wants to be that kid. But I know that only Stephen is Gideon's friend, sort of, and that the rest of the guys on the track team mostly put up with him because he's willing to run everyone's most-hated race, the two-mile, without complaining. Friends have never come so easily for Gideon, maybe because of how smart he is. Maybe just because of how he is period. "I came in the back door."

"You should go take a shower." I turn back to the window. I want him to go, leave me alone, not pick a fight.

"Who died and left you in charge?" When I look back at him, he puts a hand over his mouth and opens his eyes wide in fake shock. "Oh snap. Get it? *Who died*? You gotta admit, that was pretty funny." I scowl at him. Gideon always tries to make jokes about our mom being gone. It makes him feel better. And it makes me feel worse. My mom was right, we really are opposite twins. Forever repelling each other, like the wrong sides of a magnet. "Come on, it was."

"It wasn't funny."

"Fine, whatever." Gideon shrugs as he turns toward the stairs. Does he actually look hurt? It's so hard to tell with him, but I know there's a heart in there somewhere. And these days he's just trying to survive. We both are. "When is Dad going to be back? I have to ask him something about my chem homework."

Having exhausted all of Stanton Prep's AP offerings, Gideon now takes science classes at Boston College. I don't know if he really likes science or if it's just a way to get closer to our dad. It's not the worst call. One surefire way to get more attention from our dad is to somehow get mixed in with his work. I wouldn't say our dad loves his work more than us, but sometimes it does feel like we're neck and neck.

"I don't know, maybe a couple hours," I say.

I should have been more vague. Since the accident, our dad never goes out that long. It's only going to lead to more questions. And I don't want to talk to Gideon about Cassie. He'll end up saying something rude. Gideon has never liked Cassie. Or, more precisely, he has always *really* liked her, but she never gave him the time of day. So he decided to hate her instead. Right now, I can't take him insulting her down to a more manageable size. Or worse, trying to make me worry more just for the fun of it.

"A couple hours? Where did he go?"

"To help Karen."

"Help her with what?"

Ugh. Too late. He's already too interested. "She doesn't know where Cassie is." I shrug. No big deal.

For a split second, Gideon almost looks worried for real. But then his mouth pulls down into his fake-thoughtful frown. "Huh. Now I get it," he says.

I hate it, but I'm going to have no choice but to play his game. "Get what, Gideon?"

"Why Cassie was acting all freaky when she came by here," he says, like I should know what he's talking about. "I mean I don't know *exactly* why. But it makes sense that she'd be acting weird if she was about to take off."

"Wait, Cassie came here?" My heart skips a beat. "When?"

Gideon rubs his chin, then looks up at the ceiling. "Um, I think it was—let's see." He counts on his fingers like he's measuring the days or even weeks. "Yesterday. Yup, that's it, in the afternoon."

Jerk.

"Yesterday?" I say, trying not to get mad. Gideon wants to get under my skin, that's the whole point. "Why didn't you tell me she was here?"

"She didn't want me to." He shrugs. "She just wanted to drop off the note."

"What *note*, Gideon?" I'm up off the couch now. "You didn't give me any note."

"Huh," he says again, nodding. Like he's confused, even though he obviously isn't. Then he starts patting around his sweatshirt pockets and digging in his jeans. "Ah, here it is." He pulls out a folded page and holds it up into the air, pulling it farther away when I grab for it. "Oh wait, now I remember why I didn't give it to you. I knocked on the bathroom door to tell you about it, and you yelled, 'Go away, jerk!'"

He's right. I did that. Screamed it, actually. Since the accident, my anxiety has been back with such Technicolor vengeance. Each day is mostly a thing I survive. But some are even crappier than others. And yesterday was one of the super-crap ones. By the time I got into the shower, hoping it would help me calm down, all I wanted to do was scream—at myself, at the world. I definitely couldn't deal with Gideon. If I thought apologizing to him wouldn't just make things worse, I would have. And I am kind of sorry. Deep down, Gideon doesn't mean to be a jerk. But the sweet part of him is buried so deep these days, it won't be able to keep the rest of Gideon from kicking me when I'm down.

"Give me the note, Gideon. Please."

He lifts his hand and the note even higher in the air. I've always been on the tall side, but Gideon is pushing six feet. There's no way I can grab it. "Maybe *I* should read it," he says. "You two aren't even really friends anymore. Probably because Cassie got tired of everything being all about you and your *problems* all the time."

"Gideon, if you don't give me that note, I'm going to tell Dad I saw you smoking pot with Stephen the other day."

It's true—out in our small square of a backyard, next to the shed. From the look of it, it was Gideon's first time. He's got his issues, but drugs aren't one of them. But even if it was just a one-off, I'll still use it if I have to. The color has gone out of Gideon's face. And there's this look in his eyes. Like now he really, really hates me. I want not to care. But I do. I always do.

"Whatever," he says finally, throwing Cassie's note at me. It hits the wall over my head and drops to the floor. "But if I was stuck with a messed-up best friend like you, I'd run away, too."

And with that, Gideon turns and walks out of the living room, headed for the steps. I wait until he's gone before I pick up the note.

I'm sorry, it reads in Cassie's bubbly letters. *You were right. About everything, I just wasn't ready to hear it. But I'm ready now. For whatever happens. Xoxo C*

For whatever happens? I read the words again, my fingers gripping the paper. My heart is thumping in my chest. I do not like the sound of that—like Cassie has made peace with something. Like people do before they— Cassie wouldn't *do* something to herself, would she? No, I don't think so. In the past few months, *I've* thought about putting an end to things, an end to me. But Cassie is not like me. She's like a giant rubber ball. She always bounces back. It's what defines her as a human being. She's just out having one too many Smirnoff Watermelon Ices again. She has to be.

My stomach twists tighter as I read the words again. What was I "right" about exactly? That Cassie needed to stop drinking, put on some weight, take better care of herself? That Jasper wasn't a person she should trust? That he would hurt her eventually? I don't want to be right about any of those things anymore. Not when me being right could mean something awful for Cassie. And the truth is, I don't know what she's capable of anymore.

I pick up my phone to send Cassie yet another text. It might be worth saying I'm sorry, too. I was right to try to get her to stop drinking. I had good reason to be worried. But I did mix that up with other things that didn't matter nearly as much, like the Rainbow Coalition and Jasper.

Just got your note. I'm sorry too. I should have been a better friend. Come home. Please. Whatever is going on, we'll fix it together.

CHAPTER 5

I'm still staring down at my phone, willing a response from Cassie, when there's a knock at our front door. Or did I imagine it? I'm hoping I might have when it comes again. Cassie? But the knock is harder and louder even than before with Karen. A bigger fist maybe, a heavier hand? *Keep the doors locked.* But I have to at least check to make sure it's not Cassie.

I make my way over carefully to the foyer. I can hear the shower upstairs. Gideon can't hear a thing. Not even if I scream. I suck in some air, tucking myself to the side so I can peek out the window without being seen.

There on our porch, with his hands shoved deep in his pockets, huge shoulders hiked up toward his perfect ears, is the very last person I want to see: Jasper Salt. He has on one of his trademark skintight T-shirts—short-sleeved, despite the cold—and slouched-just-right jeans. He's staring down at his black Nikes, rocking back and forth like he's freezing, but pretending *it's all good, man.* Because that's the way Jasper talks. Even though *no one talks like that*, not even in Long Beach, California, where Jasper's from.

Jasper was already a sophomore when we started at Newton Regional High School, and he stood out from the start. There was the inhuman way he looked, of course, like he just walked out of a Gap ad, with glowing skin, bright-green eyes, and six-pack abs that you could detect even when he was wearing one of his baggy football or ice hockey jerseys.

The first time Cassie and I saw him was in the cafeteria at his usual table with all the other football players, all wearing their stupid jerseys for the first game. They were huge and loud, deliberately trying to draw attention to themselves. All except Jasper, their starting quarterback even as a sophomore, who never moved fast or raised his voice. He didn't make threats, or hassle anyone. He was the calm and quiet sun around which the rest of them revolved.

But there was this energy underneath all that calm, tight and wound. Like inside he was a coiled spring no one wanted to see snap. Or snap again. Because Jasper had exploded at least once already. With that one legendary punch.

All the freshman girls couldn't have cared less about Jasper's supposed assault and battery, though. Actually, I think it might have made them love him even more. "He's from L.A.," they said. "I heard he has a movie agent." "I heard his whole family moved here so he could play ice hockey." "I heard he slept with twelve girls last year. All of them seniors."

Twelve girls. One punch. What an asshole. That's what I'm thinking as I step over to the door. Because I already know that Jasper showing up on my doorstep isn't some kind of accident. It's proof enough for me that he had something to do with what's going on with Cassie. Where she is. What she's up to. Or maybe why she left.

But I hesitate once my hand is on the doorknob. Maybe he's here fishing for what other people know. I should play dumb. See what Jasper says first, let him dig himself a hole deep enough I can kick him into it later.

"Oh, hi." Jasper looks surprised when I finally open the door. And, annoyingly, up close he is even better-looking than I remembered. He's not my type, too pretty and too perfectly imperfect. And thinking about it now, I can only imagine how Cassie must feel with his attention fixed on her: special. The way she always wanted to feel. "I didn't, um, think that anybody was home."

Jasper's eyes flick up to my hacked hair then. They snap right back down. He's pretending not to notice the disaster that is the top of my head, which, I guess, is one tiny point in his favor.

"Well, here I am," I say. I force myself to loosen my grip on the doorknob, hoping it might help relax the rest of me. "What's up?"

"Can I come in?" Jasper asks, looking around behind him like there might be someone out there in the dark, watching him. "I'd rather explain inside."

No. But I can't say that while pretending I don't know why he's here.

"All right." I step to the side but keep him blocked into the foyer. "What?"

I don't want him any farther in the house, or my life. I just want him to tell me what he knows about Cassie and then be on his way. Because the longer Jasper stays, and the more it seems like he's stalling, the tighter my chest is getting. And I am really not interested in having one of my episodes in front of him.

Jasper crosses and uncrosses his arms, lifts his shoulders even closer to his ears. Now he officially looks guilty. I press my lips together and swallow hard. He didn't do something *to* Cassie, did he? I am not a member of the Jasper Salt fan club. I think he is a bad influence with a mean streak that everyone, for some reason, pretends doesn't exist. But when I told Cassie's mom that I didn't think he would hurt her, I meant it.

"Cassie's missing," he begins finally. "And I, um, got a call a couple hours ago from her mom asking if I'd talked to her. But I haven't since yesterday." Well, there's lie number one: Jasper told Karen that he'd texted with Cassie this morning. "Oh, wait, I mean, I guess we texted this morning." Okay, fine. Back to zero lies, that I know of. But we are just getting started.

"She wasn't in school?"

Jasper somehow walks right past me, uninvited, into my living room. That's the kind of guy he is: convinced that he's welcome everywhere.

"I don't know for sure. We were in a fight," he says, and kind of defensively. "I texted her this morning, but I was still kind of pissed. So I dodged her at school. Later Maia told me Cassie must have bagged school anyway. Have you seen her, or heard from her or anything?"

So the Rainbow Coalition lied to Karen about seeing Cassie in school.

"I haven't talked to Cassie in days," I say. And he must know that. "Why would you think I'd have heard from her?"

"Because I got this." Jasper digs his phone out of his pocket and hands it to me. There's a text from Cassie open on the screen: *Go to Wylie's house.* That's it. That's the whole message. "You have no idea why she'd tell me to come here?"

"Me?" It actually sounds like he thinks *I'm* the one who's hiding something. "I have *absolutely* no idea. Did you tell her mom that you got this?"

"I was about to, but then—" He motions for his phone back and moves his finger up a little on the screen before handing it back to me. "I got this one."

Don't tell anyone you heard from me. Especially my mom.

"Okay, but—"

He reaches for the phone again, tapping in search of yet another message. He holds up the phone a third time.

I messed up again. If you call my mom, she'll call the police. And you know what will happen. Please, just go to Wylie's. More soon.

"What the hell is going on?" I ask, and I sound angry. At Jasper. But I am sure this is somehow at least a little bit his fault.

"I have no idea what's going on. I came here because that's what her text said to do," Jasper says, and now he sounds angry at me. "But who knows? Cassie has been acting weird lately."

"What does that mean: 'weird'?"

"Are you asking me the definition of the word 'weird'?"

I just glare at him. At least it's obvious now. He doesn't like me either.

"Like distant or whatever," he goes on. "I don't know why."

"And what does she mean about the police: 'you know what will happen'?"

"I can't tell you," Jasper says.

"So you can come here and pump me for information, but not give any away?"

"It's just—she was really embarrassed about some stuff that went down," he says finally. "She wouldn't want you, of all people, to know."

Fuck you, Jasper Salt, I want to shout. *You don't know anything about me. And you don't know anything about the real Cassie, the awesome person she was before you helped destroy her.* But I can't tell him off yet, not when he knows things that I don't. Things that might help find Cassie.

"Trust me, I know lots of embarrassing things about Cassie," I say. "We have been friends a really long time."

And there are definitely secrets I know that Jasper does not. Things that Cassie would have been way too embarrassed to tell him. For instance, maybe Cassie peed her bed again, but this time her mom caught it. She did that after one of her first "hangouts" with the Rainbow Coalition before she and Jasper started talking.

She was really freaked out about it, especially because she'd also blacked out at the party. Didn't even remember getting home. Blacking out had been one of her dad's signature moves. Cassie was convinced he didn't remember half the messed-up things he'd done. It was how Cassie managed not to hate him. Anything he didn't remember didn't get held against him. But even blacking out didn't scare Cassie straight the way I'd hoped it would. Instead, the next time it happened, she decided it was funny.

"I know you guys are close, but—" Jasper looks down at his hands, presses his fingertips together. "She specifically said she didn't want you to know this one thing. She was worried you'd look down on her, I guess. And I have to respect that, right?"

"You cannot be serious," I laugh. Or sort of laugh.

Jasper holds up his hands. "I'm not saying you would look down on her." But I can tell from the way he says it that he totally *does* think that. "That's just what Cassie was afraid of. She's not always the best judge of people." *Him* saying that to *me* makes me want to spit. "Anyway, I think the part that matters is that she's done something her mom would be seriously, seriously pissed off about. And she was already talking about sending Cassie to some crazy boot camp boarding school." He takes a deep breath. "Anyway, I guess Cassie having done something wrong is at least better than someone having kidnapped her or something."

"Kidnapped?" That had not even occurred to me. "What do you mean kidnapped?"

My phone vibrates loudly on the coffee table before Jasper can explain whether he's got some actual reason to consider kidnapping, or if he was just throwing that out there. Because now Cassie getting snatched off the street is all I can think about. As I reach for my phone, I feel like it might bite me.

Please, Wylie, I need your help, the text reads. *I messed up big. I need u to come get me. I sent Jasper so he can drive. But the person I really need is you. More soon.*

I take a shaky breath. At least she's okay enough to text. That's something. And "messed up big" does not sound like being kidnapped. And even after everything between us, I have to admit there is a tiny part of me that likes that Cassie feels like she needs me specifically.

"What does it say?" Jasper asks, peering over my shoulder.

"'I need your help. I messed up big,'" I say, feeling this sadness sink over me. Like I'm finally realizing that Cassie might never be okay. "Can you drive? I don't have my license."

Of course, there is one additional, teeny-tiny problem with this plan. A problem that I'm trying not to think about. Or really less of a problem, because that sounds like the kind of thing that can be worked around. This is more of a brick wall.

There is no way I'm going to be able to get myself to leave the house. Haven't stepped outside in three weeks. It started with not being able to get myself to school, then having a hard time running errands in the car. Then just taking a walk was pretty uncomfortable. Like Dr. Shepard had feared, the home tutor was the top of a very steep hill and I've already rolled fast to the bottom. I am a full-on agoraphobic. Only three weeks in the making, but I am here to report that three weeks is plenty long enough for something to feel like the way you always were. At some point during this Project Rescue Cassie discussion, I am going to have to give this problematic little tidbit some thought.

"Come get her where?" Jasper asks. "What happened?"

"She messed up, that's all it said. Like the text you got."

"This is so fucked," he says. "How do we even know that's really her texting? It could be anybody. Maybe somebody stole her phone."

Of course, he's right. And him being suspicious like that definitely goes down in his not-guilty column. But I'm not ready to let him off the hook completely. Not until I know what's really going on. I turn back down to my phone.

"What are you writing?" Jasper asks as my fingers fly over my phone's touch screen.

"A question," I say. "To make sure it's really Cassie."

Are you pulling a Janice? It's the first inside joke that popped into my head. An oldie, but a goodie. It makes me miss Cassie just thinking about it.

Jackie Wilson—not Janice Wilson—was a tiny sprite of a girl who came to Newton Regional High School at the beginning of freshman year. She only stayed three short months before her parents moved on again, but Cassie and I had both really liked her. We had specific conversations about Jackie turning our twosome into a threesome. That was, until we realized that Jackie lied about *everything*. Including stupid pointless things like the color of the socks *she had on*. It was hard not to feel bad for her. She must have really needed all those lies for something. Anyway, after she left, Cassie and I started using "Jackie" as shorthand for lying: pulling a Jackie. But I'd written the wrong name now—Janice—on purpose. Otherwise, even if it wasn't Cassie, the person on the other end still would have had a 50 percent chance guessing right—yes or no. If it is really Cassie, she'll mention me using the wrong name.

It takes a little longer for the reply this time.

U mean Jackie? No, not pulling a Jackie. Please, for now head north on 95. Then take Route 3 to 93 north. More details 2 come. Hurry, Wylie. Please, I need you.

"It's her." And saying it makes me feel much, much worse. "Definitely."

"Okay," Jasper says. "So what do we do?"

I could call Karen, tell her that Cassie has gotten herself into some mess again. I could be the reason Cassie is sent someplace where she's forced to march for fifty miles in the burning desert to teach her respect or whatever. Or I could be the friend that Cassie has asked me to be: someone she can trust.

I look up from my phone and straight at Jasper. "We go."

CHAPTER 6

Supplies. It's what I think of next. We'll need supplies. And yes, that is mostly my way of delaying the inevitable: the outside. But also, supplies couldn't hurt.

As I head upstairs toward my bedroom, Jasper follows. Uninvited again. Though I didn't specifically ask him to wait downstairs, because it didn't occur to me he'd come. But him hovering is the least of my problems. The outside is looming larger and larger with each passing second. With each step, my feet feel heavier on the stairs, my lungs stiffer.

"What exactly are we doing?" Jasper asks as we continue up the stairs.

I realize now that he probably followed because I started marching upstairs without an explanation.

"I need to get some stuff. It might be cold," I say. "You didn't have to come."

That is true. It might be cold. *North on 95 and north on 93.* That's what Cassie said. It's cold still in Boston even though it's May. Who knows how much colder it could get. Or how far north we may have to go.

A change of clothes, warm things—socks, boots, sweaters. And that is partly me being paranoid. But it can't hurt to be prepared. That's one thing the Boy Scouts and my mom could agree on.

Once she finally had some marching orders from Dr. Shepard—help build Wylie's confidence—my mom was all over it. By then I was in seventh grade and I'd been seeing Dr. Shepard for nearly a year. And my mom was desperate to help, to do something.

To her, building confidence meant one thing: adventure. My mom had learned all her outdoors skills from my grandfather, the original Wylie, when she was my age. Wylie the First—an actual, real-life explorer always in search of some relic in a far-off land—had to return home for good once my grandmother was hospitalized. After that, he'd take my mom to the woods often, teaching her to build a fire or navigate by the sun, and out there, surrounded by all that wild, they'd both try to forget my grandmother's untamable mind.

Those trips with my grandfather had always been fun for my mom. For me? Not so much. They were too terrifying to be considered fun. The second time I ever rock climbed I got stuck halfway up, convinced my mom would have to call the National Guard with a helicopter. But she didn't. She didn't rush to rescue me at all like I thought she would. Like I kept begging her to. Instead, she just kept telling me that I could do it. Again and again and again. *You can do it. You can do it.* Not a shout or a yell or a cheer. Just quiet and steady and sure. Like a promise. *You. Can. Do It. Of course you can.* And so I closed my eyes and pretended I believed that until eventually—two hours later—I made it to the top of that rock. And for someone bawling, I did feel pretty awesome. I wasn't cured and I wasn't exactly having fun, but that trip and others did give me hope. And I needed that more than anything.

I also loved every minute alone with my mom. Couldn't get enough of listening to her explain how best to pitch a tent in the rain or how to get a foothold on a steep sheet of rock. And I'll never forget what she looked like out there in the woods in the glow of a rising sun. Like a goddess. Or a warrior. A warrior-goddess. In my memory, that's who she'll always be.

When Jasper and I reach the top of the steps, the bathroom door flies open and Gideon bounds out on a cloud of steam, a towel wrapped around his waist. He ends up nose to nose with Jasper.

"Who are you?" Gideon asks. He looks small suddenly compared to Jasper, who has only an inch of height on him, but many pounds of muscle.

"Jasper." He holds out a closed fist, but instead of bumping it with his own knuckles like a normal teenager, Gideon tries to shake it awkwardly and upside down as he struggles to keep up his towel.

"Jasper is Cassie's boyfriend." I wave for Jasper to follow me down the upstairs hall.

Gideon squints at Jasper. He's jealous, of course. He thinks *he* should be Cassie's boyfriend, though he would never, ever admit this.

"Hey, wait!" Gideon calls after us. "Does that mean Dad found Cassie?"

I flinch as I continue on down the hall, hoping Jasper won't put two and two together and realize that I must have known that Cassie was missing when he got there. That I played dumb when I answered the door. But as soon as we're in my room, I can tell by the look on Jasper's face that he didn't miss a thing. No one actually ever said he was stupid.

"You pretended not to know Cassie was gone?" He doesn't sound angry, only seriously confused.

I shrug and look away. "I wasn't sure what you knew."

His eyes open wide, then squint shut. He's not confused anymore. He's pissed. "Wait, do you think *I* had something to do with what happened to her?"

"I didn't say that." But I'm also not going to say that I

don't think it's possible. I'm not going to lie to make this less uncomfortable. I'm used to uncomfortable. It's the only way I know how to be.

"But then why would she text me to come get her?" he asks.

"I didn't say you *did* something to her." Because there are other ways to be responsible. "And I can't drive, you know. If she wanted me to come, she'd have to figure out a way for me to get there. Anyway, Cassie has gotten herself into stuff before, but nothing as bad as this. She has kind of fallen apart, you know, since you two started dating."

"And that's *my* fault?" Jasper's eyes are wide and bright.

"I didn't say that." Though I do kind of mean it. I cross my arms. "Anyway, do you really want to do this? To waste time having some kind of *situation* between the two of us? You don't like me and I don't like you. But we both care about Cassie, right? What matters is getting her out of whatever mess she's in."

"How can I not like you?" Jasper blinks at me. Like that was the only important part of what I just said, the part about him. "I don't even know you."

I'm relieved when my phone vibrates in my hand again, saving me from saying something I shouldn't. But it's not Cassie. It's my dad: *Be home in ten minutes.*

Shit. The time for stalling is over. We have got to get going. And I have to get myself out the door.

Any sign of Cassie at her house? I write back.

Not yet. But I'm sure she's fine. Don't worry.

Am I really going to do this? Not tell him or Karen that I've heard from her? I don't want to keep it from them, but I don't feel like I know enough to overrule Cassie. At least not yet. Besides, it's not like we can't change our minds. We'll wait for more details. Once we know exactly what kind of mess Cassie's in and how deep it goes, then we'll decide who needs to know.

"Listen, we have to go. My dad will be home soon." I grab my small duffel bag and start tossing things inside: a change of clothes, sweatpants, one of my bandannas. The bandanna reminds me of my hacked hair that Jasper has still been doing a decent job of pretending not to notice.

"Does your dad or brother maybe have a sweatshirt or something I could borrow? I ran out to come here when I got Cassie's text." Jasper looks down at his short sleeves. "If we stop back at my place, my brother will never let me leave again with his car."

"Sure, yeah," I say, feeling a little guilty that I'd assumed he was showing off his bare arms on purpose. "I'll see what I can find."

My mom's Doc Marten boots are still sitting in the middle of my parents' carpet. I stand in front of them for a minute, staring down. Finally, I push my feet in and jerk the laces tight—they're a size too big, but not terrible. I also grab my mom's favorite sweatshirt off the back of the door. It's not an accident that it's been hanging there for the last four months, right where she left it. But right now, I need it more than my dad does. Besides, he was the one who didn't care about her shoes.

The last thing I take is from my mom's nightstand. Her Swiss army knife. A gift from my grandfather when she was sixteen, it has her initials on it. *Good for everything,* she always said. I turn it in my fingers, feeling its weight in my palm.

When my hands start to tremble, I jam it deep in my front pocket.

Back in my room, Jasper is walking around looking at my photographs. Black and white, they're hanging from a string that runs around the edge of my room. It's been so long since I've even noticed them, probably since the day of the accident. Once upon a time I lived with my fancy, birthday-gift digital camera in my hands, seeing more of the world through that lens than with my own eyes. My mom always said I had this way of capturing the real person hidden inside, the mark of a true photographer, she assured me. Now, I can't imagine taking a picture of anyone ever again.

"They're kind of—" Jasper searches for a word, his eyes on a photo of an old woman sitting on a park bench near Copley Square with a big plaid bag next to her. She's staring straight up at the camera, not smiling, a pile of crushed saltines between her feet. "Depressing."

I hate how naked I feel. Because they are depressing. *I'm* depressing. But Jasper didn't actually have to say that to me, either. I wonder if that was him being clueless or if he was trying to be rude. With him, it's kind of hard to tell. But either way, I want him to stop looking at my pictures. I want him out of my room.

"Come on." I shove a long-sleeved shirt and a fleece of my dad's at him. "We need to go."

Amazing how confident I sound. Like this outside thing is a real, legitimate possibility. Like it hasn't been three weeks since I've stepped out the door. Sure. Right. No problem.

Once we're downstairs, I try to stay in the moment like Dr. Shepard has taught me. Not to get ahead of myself to where the dread lies. I feel the scratch of the fabric as I pull the heavy coats from the closet, the cool metal of the doorknob. Those things are real. Everything else is in my head. But the panic monster—*Outside! Outside! Outside!*—is still screaming. And my heart is beating so fast it feels like it's going to explode.

"Here, take this." I shove my dad's parka at Jasper.

Already, he's studying the side of my face as I turn

toward the garage. Jasper has noticed there's something wrong with me, of course he has. He'd have to be a total idiot not to. For all I know, Cassie's told him all about my "issues" anyway. And they've gotten way worse than even she knows.

I suck in a mouthful of air as I pull open the door to the garage. As I step out, the air is so thin and sharp. Like we just entered outer space. And that's with the door to the outside still closed. I put one hand on a nearby shelf for balance and catch sight of my mom's camping gear. The stuff I will never let anyone ever give away. I'll take some of that gear too. I need to suddenly. I grab one of the compact tents, a plastic tarp, a sleeping bag, some flares, a compass, the water purifier. I stack half on the floor; the rest I clutch against me.

When I turn, Jasper is staring at all of it.

"Um, did Cassie say something about us camping somewhere?"

We don't need it, part of me wants to confess. *I* do. To get me out the door.

"You never know," I manage, then motion for Jasper

to grab up what's left on the floor. I point to the button on the wall next to him. "Can you press that? It opens the garage door."

I twitch when the door grinds up loudly, squeezing my supplies so tight that they cut into my ribs. The pain is weirdly reassuring, though. Before I pass out always comes the numbness and then the tunnel to blackness. And I don't feel any of that, not yet. Just deep underwater, the pressure crushing my skull.

As the door rattles the rest of the way up, maybe Jasper says something, maybe he doesn't. Because I can't hear anything but the roar of that door. Can't feel anything but the thumping of my own heart.

There's a rush of cold air on my face as the night sky finally rises before my eyes. I can see the house across the street, the front yard I played in so many times as a little kid. The side yard that was once my shortcut to school. Memories now from someone else's life. The air smells good, too, like wood smoke and snow. Safe. And yet all I feel is more afraid.

Jasper is already out on the driveway, marching toward

his car like the totally normal person he is. Loading up his trunk with the rest of my useless supplies. A second later he's back, standing next to me, staring. But even with the shame of Jasper's eyes boring into me, the pain of knowing that I could be wasting Cassie's time, my feet still will not move.

There's only one way out of this garage: to believe that I can. *You can do it. You can do it.* I hear my mom's voice in my head. I can feel her fingers crossed as I inch my way for hours up the side of that stone. It got me up that stone. It's what will get me out that door.

"Give me your arm," I say to Jasper without looking at him. He hesitates, then holds a bicep out toward me. I wrap a couple of fingers around his bare elbow, which was supposed to feel less weird than actually holding his muscular arm. But does not. "I just need you to walk me to your car. Don't ask why, please. I'm not going to tell you anyway."

And then I close my eyes. Because pretending I'm not actually doing this couldn't hurt either.

"Okay," Jasper says, almost like a question.

My eyes are still closed tight as we walk forward through the garage. Still, I can feel the darkness rush in around me when we finally step outside. *Breathe*, I tell myself as we make our way down what I'm guessing is the driveway. I don't open my eyes until I feel the cool metal of the car in front of us. Finally, I suck in some air, dropping Jasper's elbow and opening my eyes only long enough to dump everything inside the open back of his old Jeep. I squeeze my eyes shut as I feel my way over to the passenger door. Behind me, I hear Jasper close the trunk.

I climb into the car, heart pounding. But for the first time it's a rush of something good: I made it. I almost don't believe it, looking down at myself sitting in the Jeep. I brace myself for all the questions Jasper will have when he finally slides into the car next to me. The ones I told him not to ask. And I can feel him staring at the side of my face again for a long minute, like he's considering.

"Okay, then," is all he says when he turns the key. Like maybe he thinks I'm a little crazy, but has decided to be polite and keep it to himself. And I can accept that. I'll have to.

Instead of starting, Jasper's car makes a loud coughing sound. "Don't worry. It does this. It'll catch eventually."

And I'm so relieved when it finally does turn over. Because if I have to go back inside, there's zero chance I'm ever coming back out. And then a second later we're pulling out of the driveway, and another second more and we're already halfway up the street. We're really going. *I'm* really going. And I am almost starting to—well, not relax. No, that would be a *huge* overstatement. But nothing is getting worse. I haven't passed out, haven't thrown up, which in this case—in my case—just might count as better. That is, until I see headlights at the top of our street: my dad coming home.

I feel an unexpected stab of guilt. He's going to be so worried when I'm not there. He wanted me to lock all the doors, and instead, I leave? And my note: *Be back soon?* It's not like it explains anything. He's going to freak.

It's true my dad isn't my mom and he never will be. He doesn't get me. And sometimes I feel like he doesn't miss my mom enough. Like maybe they had fallen apart for good before the night she died. But he is trying his best now. I have no doubt about that.

Still, I duck down as we roll past my dad's car, moving fast in the opposite direction. I again choose protecting Cassie's secret—whatever it is—over waving him down and telling him everything. Right now, I am Cassie's friend first, a daughter second. And I could pretend that's about me doing what's right for her, but the dark truth is it feels a whole lot more selfish. Like it's a lot more about proving her wrong about me.

On cue, my phone vibrates in my hand, and I brace myself for a text from my dad, begging me to come home. But the text isn't from him. It's from Cassie. And it says so very little. But also way more than I want it to.

Hurry.

CHAPTER 7

We do as Cassie has told us. Jasper and I drive briefly north on 95, then to Route 3 and onward north on 93 for almost an hour. The lights of Boston fade out behind us quickly and soon we pass out of Massachusetts and into New Hampshire. The highway is still wide, but pitch black on either side. Jasper and I each text Cassie again, more than once, hoping she'll tell us something. *How far north on 93? What next after that? What town are you in?* Anything that might get a response. *Are you okay? Please, answer us.* But Cassie hasn't. Not a single time.

The only person I have heard from is my dad. He's

already sent half a dozen texts, all of which sound pretty much exactly the same as the one that just came through: *Please, Wylie, tell me where you are. Please come home. I'm worried.* He's called a couple of times, too. Left a message once, though I haven't been able to bring myself to listen to it.

Not surprisingly, my dad found the *Be back soon* note I left in our kitchen lacking. But he's trying so hard not to freak out. To even act like he's also kind of proud of me for making it outside. To be honest, I felt pretty good about it, too. For a whole twenty minutes after we pulled away from the house, I was on an actual I'm-cured high.

Now, that prison-break rush is gone, but I still feel better than I have in months. Like being in the middle of this actual emergency is exactly the cure I've been searching for. Or maybe it's just harder to hear all the alarms sounding in my head now that they match reality. Because there I am, hurtling north to an unknown destination for an unknown reason to save a friend whom I love, but whom I also know cannot be trusted—and I feel calmer than I have in months.

Jasper and I don't talk much as the miles pass except "Are you cold?" and "Can we change the station?" Pretty soon almost every alternative on Jasper's old-school radio is static, except some talk-radio program about the evils of psychiatric drugs and teens, which under the circumstances—my circumstances—feels pretty awkward.

Luckily, it's hard to hear much of anything anyway over the roar of Jasper's car. Riding in the worn Jeep feels like being a stowaway in a cargo plane. Like I'm in a space not meant for passengers. And the farther north we go, the colder it gets. Soon, my toes are almost numb, despite the fact that Jasper keeps turning up the heat. As I check the time on my phone—almost eight thirty p.m.—I'm starting to worry that the cold and the noise might be a sign something is dangerously wrong with the Jeep. I peer over toward Jasper's feet, where the sound and the wind seem to be coming from.

"There's a hole." Jasper points down.

"In the floor?" I ask, squeezing the door handle so hard my hand starts to throb.

"Don't worry. It's not dangerous or anything," Jasper goes on. "It's nowhere near the pedals. My brother should fix it. It's his car. But he never thinks about anything, except getting laid and beating the shit out of people." Jasper looks like he's going to say something more. Instead, he half smiles. "Like me, for instance, when he realizes I took his car."

"Oh," I say.

"Whatever. It's fine. He's big, but seriously slow. I can usually outrun him. Once I didn't." He points to a scar next to his right eye. "Pushed me into the corner of our coffee table. Only five stiches, but the blood was insane. Luckily, my mom is a nurse, so she was pretty calm about it. She did have to replace part of the carpet afterward, though."

"That's terrible." I wince. "She must have killed him."

Jasper glances over at me. "Yeah, not so much. In my house, it's survival of the fittest."

This must be the "hard-knock life" Cassie told me about. "Oh," I say again, because I have no idea what I'm supposed to say.

"Yeah, my mom only gets involved in my life if it's going to have a direct effect on her wallet." He smirks like he doesn't care, but I can tell he does. "She's got high hopes about my future as a human ATM."

"That sucks." And it does.

"Yeah," Jasper says quietly. "There are worse things, I guess."

My phone buzzes in my hand again then. *Wylie, please don't do this. Answer me. Right now.*

"Cassie?" Jasper asks hopefully.

I shake my head. "My dad again."

"Is he pissed?"

"Worried, I think mostly."

"That's nice," he says, like my dad being worried is proof that I've got it so much better.

"Yeah, I guess," I say, staring down at my phone. And maybe it should feel nice, but it doesn't. Probably because the more texts he sends, the more it feels like it's about him getting me to do what he wants instead of how much he loves me.

Jasper holds up a hand. "Sorry, I hate when people say that kind of crap to me. 'Your mom loves you, I'm sure. She's your mother.'" And now he sounds pissed—a little bit like a guy who could punch somebody in the face. "My mom is living proof that life is full of messed-up options."

He shakes his head. Shrugs. "Maybe your dad's an asshole. How would I know?"

I don't feel like I know either. But I do think the time has come that I answer, tell my dad something that will calm him down.

We heard from Cassie. She's totally okay. She just got mixed up in something and needs us to come get her. We'll be back soon! Xoxo

I hit send, staring at my totally unconvincing *x*'s and *o*'s. Even the exclamation point was overkill. But it's not a lie. Not completely.

NO, comes my dad's response almost instantly. *You should NOT be doing that. Tell Karen where she is NOW and she will go get her.*

"He wants me to tell Karen where Cassie is," I say, staring at his all caps, which are digging under my skin.

"You think we should tell him?" Jasper asks. I can't tell if he sounds judgmental or I'm just hearing it that way.

"And you don't?" I ask. Because the truth is I'm not sure what I think. It does feel vaguely insane that this—of all situations—is when I suddenly decide to do what

Cassie wants, the way I used to. But then again, me feeling worried about something isn't actually a very good indication of whether it's the right course of action.

"Technically, we don't know where she is yet," Jasper says. "Can't we wait? See what she says next? You could pretend you didn't see his message yet or something."

"Lie."

"Buying us some time to think, I'd call it. But sure, lie is another word for it," he says, like I'm the jerk. "I'm okay with a little misdirection, as long as he's not a cop or something."

My stomach pulls tight. Why is Jasper worried about cops? "No, he's a scientist. Why?"

"I dated this girl once and her dad was a probation officer," he says. "I didn't find out until after he caught us together. He had one of his friends lock me up in a holding cell overnight." He shakes his head and almost laughs. "She and I were both kids. It's not like it was a crime or something. But man did her dad scare the crap out of me. I didn't go near another girl for weeks."

I stare at the side of Jasper's face. Does he actually think his girlfriend's best friend is going to enjoy hearing about his sexcapades?

"Anyway." He clears his throat and looks confused when I keep scowling at him. "What kind of scientist is your dad?"

I put my phone facedown on my lap, trying to pretend I'm actually interested in this conversation instead of just buying myself time before I answer my dad's text like Jasper suggested. But it does feel like the best I can do for Cassie is wait to find out what's going on before I decide to rat her out.

"Live Conversation and Emotional Perception: Implications for the Integrative Approach to Emotional Intelligence," I say, repeating the title of my dad's study, trying to make it sound like something Jasper would never understand.

"Right," Jasper says with a thoughtful frown. "I mean—I don't have any idea what integrative whatever emotional perception is. Am I supposed to?"

I shrug. "I wouldn't if my dad didn't talk about it nonstop. He set up this test to look at this one small part of 'perception,' which is this one small part of this one approach to emotional intelligence—that's the 'integrative' part. Anyway, my dad started studying emotional intelligence, which is basically like IQ but for feelings, after he met my mom and got totally convinced she was psychic because she always knew what he was thinking. I think she was the only person who ever really understood him."

I was passing through the foyer on my way upstairs to bed when I spotted the green flyer on the floor. It was in front of the mail slot, tucked under yet another Wok & Roll menu.

The Collective, it read in big black letters across the top, and beneath it the details of some kind of lecture: *The Spirituality of Science, Seven p.m., December 18! Explore the intersection between freedom, faith, and science.*

"Huh," my mom said, appearing behind me and reading over my shoulder. She twisted her wavy hair into a knot at her neck. "Life in a college town—the good, the bad, the vaguely fanatical. Sometimes I love it, and sometimes I wish the flyers were all about garage sales."

She was trying to make like the flyer just happened to have been slipped under our door. She did the same thing the time I met her at work and someone had stuck a collage of the Middle East under her windshield wiper. It had a skull and crossbones over it.

"Is this about your story?" I asked, thinking, of course, about the baby dolls. Almost a month and a half after the first one, another had been delivered three separate times.

"Oh, I don't think so," she said, like the possibility had honestly not occurred to her.

"And what's 'The Spirituality of Science'?"

"Who knows?" she said, a hint of humor back in her voice as she wrapped an arm around my shoulders and squeezed. "More proof it's a free country. And thank God for that."

"And so it's nothing to worry about?"

"No, definitely not. It's just more proof that you cannot control the world," she said, taking the flyer from my hands. She folded it crisply into a small, sharp square and slipped it into her back pocket, then kissed the top of my head. "Luckily, you don't need to. Now, your dad didn't see the flyer, did he?"

I shook my head.

"Then let's not tell him," she said. "After the baby dolls and Dr. Caton's plummet from Mount Olympus"—she rolled her eyes—"I think his head might explode from even something as innocuous as this."

"Why did Dad fire him anyway?" I wasn't as curious about Dr. Caton's fall from grace as Gideon, but the whole thing had seemed so weird and out of the blue and dramatic when it had happened a couple of months earlier, especially for my dad, Captain No Emotion. And my dad had still refused to talk about it.

"Dr. Caton was so used to getting his own way, he wouldn't listen to your dad, who is not only a very gifted scientist and a very smart person, but also *his boss*," my mom said. "I'm sure it's hard to be well adjusted when you graduate high school at fifteen. From what your dad's told me, Dr. Caton also came from an extremely wealthy family, who didn't exactly take the time to socialize him down to size. Always getting what you want can make people extremely shortsighted. Which just makes me more glad that we've kept Gideon with his peer group."

"I wouldn't exactly call Gideon socialized."

"Well, we are trying." My mom laughed. "The point is sometimes it's not *what* you believe that's the problem, it's *how* you believe it."

"Break it down for me, then," Jasper says, startling me back to the Jeep and the dark with his pseudo-surfer-boy twang. It reminds me of all the reasons I don't like him.

"Break what down for you?"

"Your dad's stuff."

"His 'stuff'?"

"Yeah, his research. We've got time. And I actually like science—you know, the dumb-jock version." Now Jasper is mocking me. He thinks that's why I don't like him, because he's a "jock"? I stare hard at the side of his face until he holds up a hand. "Too soon for jokes, I see that now."

I don't feel like talking about my dad's work, but if I don't distract myself, who knows where my mind will wander. Conversation about anything is a good thing. And my dad's study is for sure a lot safer topic than Cassie and Jasper's relationship.

"He's done lots of studies about EI, but in this one he wanted to prove that with the part of emotional intelligence that is reading other people's feelings, 'perception,' some people do it not just by looking at people's faces or listening to their voices—which is how most people do it."

He shrugs. "I wouldn't say I'm exactly badass in that department. But I get that it's a thing some people can do."

"It's like this tiny sub-thing in EI, not exactly something the world is holding their breath waiting to find out. Anyway, my dad ran his test trying to see if people could read feelings differently or better, I guess, if they were watching a live conversation between two other people instead of by looking at pictures of people's faces, which is how they usually test it."

"And?" Jasper asks, like he's waiting for the big reveal that the study showed something amazing. He's going to be disappointed, just like my dad.

"It's not that exciting," I say. "He learned some small things. But it's not like he cured cancer or something."

"Ouch," Jasper says. "Way to take a man down at the knees."

And he's right. That was harsh. But that is the way

I feel: annoyed. More than I realized. Even if he didn't know it at the time—couldn't have—my dad wasted the little time he had left with my mom. Instead of being with her and being happy, he was obsessed with yet another stupid study that no one is ever going to care about. And now she's gone. And now, no matter what he does, he can never make up that lost time to her. Or us.

I shrug. "It's important to him, I guess." I can feel Jasper still staring at me, and I want him to stop. I want to change the subject before I start bawling my face off. "I just wish other things had been as important."

My phone vibrates again in my hand then. I brace myself for another message from my dad. But it's Cassie, finally. *Take Exit 39C off 93. Onto Route 203. More soon.*

My heart picks up speed as I type a response. *Are you okay?? What's going on?*

Can't talk now. Not safe. It's an answer, at least. Just not the one I was hoping for.

"What is it?" Jasper asks.

"She wants us to get off at Exit 39C." I check the GPS on my phone. "It's about forty minutes away."

"And that's it? She didn't tell you anything else?" That anger is back in his voice. He's not shouting or anything, but it's there. Beneath the surface. Makes me wonder how deep it goes.

"'More soon,' she said. And that it's not safe to write more right now."

"So that's it?" he asks. "We just keep driving?"

"Do you have a better idea?"

He's quiet for a minute. "No," he says finally, his voice beaten down. "I do not have any better ideas. I don't know what the hell we should be doing. Sometimes, I don't even feel like I know her anymore."

He sounds like me now, which I find both comforting and suspicious. "Yeah, I know what you mean."

"I do think Cassie really misses you," he says. "She wouldn't admit it. You know how she is, stubborn like that." And I do know, but it feels weird that Jasper does, too. "But she was sort of lost without you." He almost sounds hurt or jealous or something, and I try not to be too happy about that.

"I wasn't the easiest person to be friends with lately." And I'd rather just pretend that's why she and I aren't talking. Anything else is going to lead straight back to the truth and to how little I really think of Jasper.

"I don't know," Jasper says. "Isn't that what best friends are for? To hang in there when the going gets rough?"

Wait, did Cassie tell him *she* couldn't deal with *me* anymore? Did she say that was why we're not friends anymore? Was that the way she really felt? Because here I've been thinking all along that *I'd* drawn my line in the sand about Cassie's behavior. That *that* was why we were no longer friends. But maybe the real truth is that Cassie got tired of me long ago? My cheeks flush when Jasper looks over at me like he wants to hear my side of the Cassie debacle. But I've gone too fast from self-righteous to dumped to talk any more about anything.

"What was your fight about anyway?" I ask, deflecting. There is still plenty Jasper is to blame for. "Maybe that has something to do with this?"

"I hope not." Jasper sounds guilty again. "Anyway, it wasn't even really a fight. It was more me yelling and Cassie crying." He shakes his head, frowns. "Even while it was happening, I felt like it had to be someone else standing there in front of the Mobil station, screaming at his girlfriend. Has that ever happened to you? Where you can see yourself doing something, like, from the outside?" Jasper glances over at me. This is apparently a real question he wants an actual answer to.

"Everyone feels that way sometimes," I say, even though I don't like the feel of letting him off the hook for something that sounds potentially so messed up. "Anyway, I'm not exactly an expert on normal."

Immediately, I wish I hadn't said that second part out loud.

"Well, only an asshole keeps on yelling when the other person is standing there crying—no matter what she did. The crazy thing is that the whole time I was yelling, I was thinking, 'This is the kind of thing my brother does. It's the kind of thing my—I don't do this.'" He shakes his head. "I never used to, anyway."

Why is Jasper confessing this to me? It's obviously not going to make me like him more. Unless he's sharing this little bad thing to cover up for something much bigger and badder.

"Why were you yelling at her?" I ask. "You said she did something?"

"She's been cheating on me," he says, quiet and sad. "For a while now. I'm ninety-nine percent sure."

"There's no way," I almost laugh. Because *that* is ridiculous. Being with Jasper was a total prize for Cassie. Complete validation of her worth. As much as I hate knowing that, it's true. Why would she cheat on him? "Why do you think that?"

"A feeling." He shrugs. "I might not be the best at reading people, but Cassie was texting somebody all the time and hiding it. But that wasn't the only reason I lost it on her. She's also gotten way out of hand lately. I was trying to get her to dial it back. And she *freaked out*. Said I was trying to control her. And I felt like, screw you, I'm trying to help you."

"What do you mean, 'out of hand'?"

"You know, partying and whatever," he says.

"Partying?" I say, like I have no idea what that could mean. Like I haven't been worried about the exact same thing.

"Cassie was getting way too wasted, way too often."

"And you're morally opposed?" I try not to sound snide. And totally fail. I go on, trying to pretend that's not what I meant. "I mean, you go to parties all the time."

"Yeah, going out and being *out of control* are two totally different things."

"And Cassie was out of control?"

I want to hear him say it. Like it'll be some key. Because if Cassie turned on Jasper for telling her the exact same thing, doesn't that prove I was right?

"Cassie was *way* out of control," he says. "And it was scaring the crap out of me. Didn't you see that?"

He sounds confused now, like he's afraid maybe he imagined Cassie going off the deep end. And as much as I kind of like us going back to a world where Jasper gets that I know Cassie better than he ever will, this doesn't seem like a good time for that kind of lie.

I nod. "I saw it. And it scared the crap out of me, too."

CHAPTER 8

We drive on in silence, for what feels like the whole of the length of New Hampshire, the exits slowly clicking up to 39C. And the whole time, I try to decide whether Jasper agreeing with me about Cassie being off the rails makes me more worried or less, while trying hard not to think about how long it will be before my emergency exception escape valve suddenly stops working and my anxiety floods back, waterlogging my lungs. Somewhere, a clock is ticking down. The only real question is what will happen when it reaches zero.

At its worst, there is no keeping my panic private. These days, the throwing up is mostly a bullet I've learned to dodge. But the passing out is still always a messed-up possibility.

The first time it happened was in a diner on a family road trip to the Four Corners the summer before eighth grade. That summer, restaurants were my panic button du jour. Stepping inside one was hard enough, forget about eating. The second we were in the breezy Gloria's Café in Chinle, Arizona, I could feel something wasn't right. But it wasn't until I got up to go to the bathroom that I realized how bad off I was. I'd only gotten a few steps when the floor pitched hard to the left and the world went full-on black. I wasn't out long. But passing out was freaky and embarrassing, and I'd worked hard to avoid a repeat performance. Still, there have been at least a half-dozen times in the years since that I've failed. I'm not looking for lucky number seven to be when I'm with Jasper.

The Exit 39C sign finally appears up ahead.

"Now what?" Jasper asks.

We're at Exit 39C. Where now? I type.

Luckily, Cassie answers right away.

Get off onto Route 203 and wait. Trying to figure out address. More soon.

Cassie, you have to tell us something. What is going on? Who are you with?

I wait. But there is no other reply.

"What's up?" Jasper asks.

"I told her she had to tell us something."

"Good," he says. "She does."

Finally, another text. *They don't—got2g*

"What did she say?"

"'They don't,'" I read. "And 'got to go.'"

"What the hell does that mean?" Jasper looks over at me, his eyebrows bunched.

"Maybe she was kidnapped." And I feel much worse once I've said it out loud. "I mean, she's obviously with somebody, more than one person, it sounds like."

I imagine some kind of roving band of hippies that Cassie joined up with. Maybe now that she's with them at their commune, they have turned vaguely creepy. Cassie would want to keep things friendly. She'd be smart enough to seem game until she makes a run for it. I try to keep picturing this, instead of the many terrible alternatives, like a group of tattooed men with Cassie tied up somewhere.

"That does not sound good," Jasper says as we pull to a stop at the bottom of the steep exit ramp. "'They' does not sound good. Not good at all."

The only sign of life in the pitch-black distance is the glow from a gas station up the hill to the right: Clark's Auto and Freshmart. At least it looks open. Good news at almost nine thirty in middle-of-nowhere New Hampshire. *If* we're even still in New Hampshire anymore. I didn't see any sign that we'd crossed into Maine or Vermont even, but it's possible that I missed it.

"Let's go wait there," I say. "Cassie will have to give us an address eventually if she wants us to find her."

"*If* she really wants us to find her," Jasper says quietly. He glances in my direction as he turns right at the stop sign.

"What do you mean?"

"Listen, I'd take her cheating on me at this point as long as she's okay, but don't you think all of this is just a little suspicious?" he asks. "Especially with her being kind of, just coincidentally, pissed off at *both* of us already? And now, here we are. Together in the middle of freakin' nowhere? Maybe she just wants us to look and look for her. Until we're the ones who are lost."

"She wouldn't do that," I say, even as my heart speeds up. "And she's not mad at *me*. We're not in a fight."

At least I didn't think we were. Obviously things weren't normal even when Cassie came back after the accident. Ours was a zombie friendship then. It looked kind of right from a distance, but up close the wrongness was obvious. And yeah, Cassie did just kind of drift away again a few weeks ago without any explanation. But to be honest, I was kind of relieved. It was a lot of pressure after the accident trying to pretend that she was making me feel better. No one ever could have.

"We weren't in a fight," I say again. I don't even know why, except it feels important to emphasize.

"Great, but I'd rather have the truth be that she's messing with us," he says. "Because I do not have a good feeling about any of this."

I'd been hoping that was just me. Because my bad feelings don't usually mean a thing.

As we head up the road toward the gas station, my phone rings again. When I look down, it says *Dad* on the caller

ID. What if I am putting my dad through this all for some game that Cassie is playing? He doesn't deserve that. And we're far enough away now, too far away for him to stop me. Besides, nothing good is going to come from him getting more and more freaked out. Once he hears I'm fine, he'll calm down at least some.

"Hi, Dad." I try to sound casual. I do not. "Did you find anything at Cassie's house?"

"Where are you, Wylie?" He's trying to sound calm, too, but he's doing an even worse job than me. "Gideon said that Cassie's boyfriend Jasper was here and that you left with him? Your text said that the two of you had heard from Cassie. That she asked you to come get her?"

Crap. I forgot that I told him that. I'd done that to calm him down, too, which obviously hadn't worked. I never should have written that, never should have answered the call. Of course, he's going to ask *where* she is. And, of course, nothing I say is going to make him feel that much better, certainly not the truth, which I still don't want to tell him anyway.

"Yeah, it's no problem. Jasper's driving. We'll be home soon," I say, like the whole thing is totally normal and no big deal. If he keeps pushing for details, I'm going to probably have no choice but to hang up and pretend the call got dropped.

"And so you went out? Just like that?" He sounds confused and kind of suspicious, which is fair considering that my suddenly leaving the house makes no sense whatsoever, because I've left out the whole part about Cassie saying she was desperate for help, my help specifically.

"I thought you wanted me to go out."

"I did want you to go out, Wylie. You're right." My dad's voice has a new, different edge to it, one that I don't recognize. Not exactly angry, but seriously intense, maybe kind of insulted even. I didn't consider that. After all, he's been trying so hard to get me to leave the house, to go to an actual in-person appointment with Dr. Shepard, to go back to school. And here I am driving around with some boy he's never met because Cassie asked me to? "I'm extremely concerned and I would feel much better if you were here, instead of out there. Karen and I can go get Cassie. Tell us where she is and we'll leave right now. But I'd like you to turn around and come home, Wylie."

I'm guessing it wouldn't make him feel better to know that we can't actually do that because we have no idea where Cassie is, specifically. Also, there's no way he realizes how far away I already am.

"It's fine. We're already, like, halfway there. Cassie will explain everything to Karen once she's home," I say, trying to sound cooperative and like this really isn't my situation anyway. It's Cassie's. But I'm still going to keep her secret for now. And the angrier my dad gets, the more sure I am of it. "I'll be home in a—"

"You'll come home right now." It's an order, an angry one. His voice is actually shaking.

"Dad, I will, just as soon as we—"

"Now, Wylie!" he shouts so loud this time that I have to pull the phone away from my ear. "Right this minute!"

My heart is pounding and my throat feels tight. "Dad, why are you screaming at me?"

Jasper glances over my way as he pulls into the gas station's brightly lit, mostly empty parking lot. The only other car in sight is parked at the pumps. Jasper rolls past it, the gravel crunching under our tires, until he comes to a stop at the back of the lot. Like he wants to give me privacy. Except he's still sitting right next to me. And I feel like I might cry as I stare at the wall of tall evergreens, glowing white in our headlights.

My dad takes a loud breath, like he's trying to calm himself down. "I'm sorry, Wylie. I didn't mean to yell." At least he does sound like he feels bad. "But we're worried about Cassie and now I'm worried about you, too. In your condition, I don't think you should be—"

"Wait, my what?" He didn't just say that, did he? "Condition," like I am diseased. Defective. Is that what he thinks? My mom never would have talked to me like that. She never saw me that way. My eyes are burning as I grip the phone and stare hard at the trees. I can't speak, can't say another word. If I do, I will definitely start bawling.

"It's too early for me to report you missing," my dad goes on like that bomb he just lobbed didn't obliterate the earth between us. "But Dr. Shepard can contact the police. And under the circumstances, I'm sure she will agree that's a good idea, especially after I tell her about what you did to your ha—"

"You cannot be serious." My cheeks are stinging with anger and shame.

"Of course I'm serious. If you won't come home, what choice do I have? And if Dr. Shepard reports you as a danger to yourself or others, the police will come looking for you immediately, Wylie. And when they find you, which they will, they won't bring you home. They'll take you straight to a hospital. You know that as well as I do."

Yes, I know that. And my dad knows that being committed is one of my greatest fears. My grandmother dying strapped down in a psychiatric ward has haunted me since I was a little kid. It was the whole reason I hadn't wanted to start seeing a therapist in the first place, convinced it was step one down a slippery slope that would dead-end in a straitjacket.

"Dad!" I shout, because I can't even think of where to start. But he has to stop. Wake up. Take it all back.

"Believe me, I don't want to call Dr. Shepard, Wylie. It's the last thing I want to do. Come home, tell us where Cassie is, so I don't have to."

He'll do that—break my heart, betray me, shame me—just so he can get me to do what he wants? Suddenly, my brain is swimming, with rage.

"If you call Dr. Shepard, I will never come home," I say. And I mean it. I will hate him forever. Maybe I already do. Because now all I want to do is hurt him, the way he just hurt me. "You know what else, Dad? You know what I really wish? That it had been you who went out for milk. That you had been driving the car that night."

I tap the button on my phone, ending the call before he can respond, then stare down at it, trembling in my hand. I switch off the ringer and a second later it's vibrating, *Dad* flashing on the screen. I wait until it says missed call, then buzzes with a voice mail. My dad calls back two more times, right in a row. I ignore both.

"That went well," Jasper says after another minute of silence. He's smiling a little, trying to make me feel better. I don't.

"Yeah." My voice sounds numb. And I feel hollow. Like someone cracked open my chest and scooped out my insides. "Awesome."

"Do you want me to try to say something that might make you feel better?" Jasper offers halfheartedly. "Because I can if you want me to."

I shake my head, then turn to look at him. "If you haven't lied to me yet, don't start now."

Jasper nods as he puts the car in reverse, then pulls slowly toward the gas pumps. He parks across from the only other occupied car, a new-looking Subaru station wagon with New York plates. Black and shiny, it has carefully arranged lefty stickers on the back—*Hillary for America, One Million Moms for Gun Control, Green and Mainstream*—the kind my parents might have had, if my dad hadn't always been too anal for stickers on even his old, crappy car.

"I think I'm going to go inside." I motion toward the Freshmart. It's a place to go, a destination. And I need air, movement. I need to get out of Jasper's Jeep. "You want anything?"

Jasper shakes his head. "I'm good."

My phone vibrates with another text as I'm getting out of the car. Not my dad, luckily. It's Cassie.

Still trying to figure out where exactly I am. Where are you?

We got off at 39C like you said. We're at a gas station on Route 203.

OK. Can you wait there for a minute? I'll tell you where to go as soon as I can.

We'll wait, I write back, trying to hint that we're not going anywhere again without at least that. *Who are the people you're with?*

Not who I thought they were.

CHAPTER 9

A cold gust cuts into me as I type a response to Cassie. I need to get something more from her. Something useful. *Are the people you're with dangerous? Where did you meet them? How many are there?*

I stand in the freezing cold, waiting for an answer. Any answer. But nothing comes. Finally, I put my phone away and wrap my arms around myself, pulling my shoulders up as I step toward the door.

"Brutal, isn't it?" When I turn toward the voice, there's a woman standing in front of the Subaru. She's smiling at me, a baby buried under the blankets cradled against her chest. "It was so much warmer when we left Brooklyn."

She is pale with long, reddish hair gathered loosely at her neck and startling blue eyes. She's beautiful, but fragile-looking, like a long-limbed bird. She looks up at my hacked hair, but her eyes linger as she sways gently from side to side. Unafraid, unashamed on my behalf. When she finally does meet my eyes again there's this look, like she gets it. Like she's done that exact same thing to her own hair a bunch of times. Though looking at her, so normal and pretty, that's seriously hard to believe.

I smile at her and nod, but my mouth feels glued shut. It's the kindness in her eyes and all that mom-love pulsing off her. If I did speak, my words would surely be a soupy mess. This beautiful, blue-eyed baby-lady reminds me of my mom, of course. If my mom had been there, she never would have let my dad threaten me. He wouldn't have had to. Because I would have trusted her with the whole truth. I would have told her where I was going. I smile harder at the baby-lady, my eyes filling with tears as I turn away from her and toward the Freshmart.

"I still have to feed the baby, Doug," she calls out to her husband as I drift away. "Maybe I should go inside.

It's too cold out here and too cramped in the car. Right, baby?" she says, her voice rising. "Way too cold."

As I continue alone across the frozen parking lot, holding myself tight against another brutal gust, I hear that graceful bird-woman begin to sing to her little baby. And what's left of my heart finally turns to dust and disappears with the wind.

Inside, the Freshmart is weirdly warm and cheerful, more like a country store than a rest stop on the side of a highway. Nothing like those grimy gas stations near Boston where the bulletproof glass in front of the register is so smeared with handprints it looks like a herd of zombies went for the cashier. There's even a bulletin board near the register with photos of happy customers and cheerful thank-you notes pinned one over another. The tall man with thick gray hair and a perfect smile behind the counter looks like the hearty type who might have built the place with his bare hands.

"Cold enough for you?" he calls as I step inside.

Careful. That's my first thought. I need not to seem

suspicious. I'm still trying to believe that my dad was just threatening to have Dr. Shepard call out the dogs, but I can't know that for sure. I don't feel like I know anything for sure anymore where my dad is concerned.

"Yep," I say, smiling harder and more guiltily before ducking fast down the nearest aisle, which of course is not suspicious at all.

Halfway down the aisle I stop and turn to face all the perfectly laid-out snacks—Pringles, Honey Braided Pretzels, beef jerky. Twizzlers. They make me think of Gideon, which, surprisingly, makes my gut twist. But I do feel bad imagining him home with my dad obsessing about me, *again*. And what if my dad is even right? What if I am too crazy to be out here trying to help Cassie? I squeeze my fists closed, then open, like maybe I can pump my doubt out through my fingertips. Because what I need is not to let what he said get to me. What I need to do instead is to get busy proving him wrong.

I hear the door to the Freshmart open again, brace for the woman and her baby to head down my way.

"Cold enough for you?" the man behind the counter calls again in the exact same cheerful way. It's creepy, the second time. Like he is something less than human.

"Yeah, definitely," Jasper answers. I step back so I can see him near the door, blowing on his hands. He has on my dad's black coat. The dark color makes his green eyes glow. "This can't be normal for May?"

"Too hot, too cold, too wet, too windy. Always seems too much of something around here."

"You have a bathroom?"

"Sure thing. All the way down in the back."

Jasper pushes his hands in his pockets as he heads for me. And I wonder if I've let my guard down too quickly, been too easily won over. He is more likable, more genuine, and even smarter than I expected. But none of that means he is more trustworthy. None of the bad things I know about him have gone away—his temper, Tasha, that punch, and most of all the part he played in the mess that is Cassie now.

"Maybe we should buy a map in case we lose our phone signal," he says when he reaches me. He grabs three off a nearby rack—Maine, New Hampshire and Vermont—then motions to the snacks I'm still staring at. "You getting something?"

"Um, yeah." I grab a bag of pretzels, though the thought of food makes me want to gag. "Just this."

"I'll meet you up there," Jasper says. "I'm going to go to the bathroom."

"Big trip?" the man asks when I put the maps and the pretzels I don't actually want down on the counter.

My body tenses even though I know he's just making friendly conversation. I just wish he'd make less of it.

I shrug. "Visiting my aunt. She lives up here." His face brightens instantly. What a stupid lie.

"Oh yeah? What's her name?" Of course he was going to ask. "Aren't enough of us around here for anyone to be a stranger."

"Oh, well, she lives farther north, way farther," I say, praying he doesn't ask where exactly. I'm not even sure exactly which state is north.

Luckily, before I have to tell him anything else, Jasper appears right next to me.

"We've got to go." His mouth is up close to my ear. His voice is a wound, wild whisper. "Now."

He has his phone in one hand, an unused coffee cup crushed in the other. His eyes are wide and unblinking. He grabs the maps and my pretzels, even takes my change out of the old man's hand.

"Come on, Wylie, now!" Jasper shouts as he steps toward the door and I remain motionless at the counter.

He comes back, grabs my arm, and yanks me toward the door. I wait until we're outside, away from the old man's prying eyes, to jerk away.

"Jasper, let go!" My heart is racing, my arm throbbing. "What's wrong? What happened?"

He doesn't answer. Instead, he tosses his phone back at me and keeps on toward his car, past the pretty baby-lady, who's watching him. Watching us. She's without her baby now, fussing with something tied to the roof of their car. I look away from her worried face and down at the message on Jasper's phone as he climbs back into the Jeep. The headlights flick on as I read.

I'm at Camp Colestah near a town called Seneca. It's in Maine. Hurry. I think they're going to hurt me.

Whatever is going on, it's not Cassie playing some game. Even she wouldn't go this far.

"Wylie, come on!" Jasper shouts out his window. He's worried and he's losing it. "Let's go!"

"Are you okay, sweetheart?" the baby-lady asks me. Her voice is so soft and sweet, like a lullaby.

"Yeah, yes," I say, looking away from her as the tears rush again into my eyes. I can't help it. It's that mom thing about her that just makes me want to cry my face off. "I'm fine."

"Honestly, you don't seem fine," she says, and when I turn, her bright-blue eyes are serious. "Do you need help?"

She's choosing her words carefully. Like maybe it's been her job before to help women *not* get back in the car with the men they shouldn't. And she might not even be wrong.

"Sweetheart?" the woman goes on, sounding more concerned. "Does your mother know where you are? I think maybe you should call her."

Right. Call her. What a simple thing. Tears, fast and hot, are actually running down my cheeks now. I wipe them away as I walk on. "I'm okay," I say. "But thanks."

Of course, I do not sound okay. Because I am not okay.

I've only taken a couple more steps when Jasper goes to turn on the Jeep. It makes that same awful whirring sound it did in my driveway. But this time there's a sharp screech to cap it off that makes even the nice woman jump. Then silence again when Jasper kills the engine. A second later he tries the key again, and the coughing and whirring pick right back up. Then that terrible metallic shriek a second time. I watch Jasper through the windshield rest his forehead against the steering wheel as he begins to turn the key again and again. I watch his body wind tighter, like any second he's going to blow.

The woman steps closer. "You know, you don't have to get back in the car with him. We could take you somewhere." She looks around. "Or wait with you while you call someone."

I look again at Jasper, still collapsed over his steering wheel. He's got a temper, that's for sure. But he's desperate to find Cassie, that much is real. No one is that good of an actor. And in that moment I have two totally incompatible thoughts. *Something terrible will happen if you go with him. Something worse will happen if you do not.*

"He's just worried about our friend," I say to the baby-lady, and that does feel absolutely true. Still, I don't meet her eyes. "We're looking for her." Was it a mistake to say even that much? *Does your mother know where you are?* This nice woman might call the police herself. People like her do that—they get involved. "I mean, our friend isn't *missing* missing. She's at some camp in Maine. She just needs us to come pick her up, and now the car . . ."

"Okay." The woman eyes me with a mix of concern and sympathy. Then she steps forward and rests her fingertips against my shoulder. *I've been there,* the look says. *No judgments. But I do know you're lying.* "As long as you're sure."

"I am." I nod too much. "Definitely."

Suddenly, Jasper pounds hard on the steering wheel. Once, twice, three times, like he's trying to rip it off. Then he rests his head back down against his hands. *If you are trying to change my low opinion of you,* I think, *you are not doing yourself any favors.*

"Hey, maybe Doug can help with your car. Keep the stress level down for everyone's sake," she says. "In the meantime, why don't you go inside and see if they have a mechanic here?"

When I look over at Jasper again, he's staring at me, jaw flexed, nostrils flared. A temper, there's no doubt about that.

"Okay," I say. "I'll go inside and ask about a mechanic."

I turn toward the Freshmart, and the baby-lady opens her car door and ducks her head inside. I can only hear bits and pieces—"Help them . . . won't start . . . Come on, honey." As I walk away, her husband says something back. I can't make it out, but he sounds annoyed. Like he doesn't want to help us. And one look again at Jasper, angry and panting, who in their right mind would?

"Everything okay out there?" the man at the counter almost shouts as I step inside. He tugs on a small white baseball cap like he's about to spring into action and zoom to the rescue. But that's all he does: put on the cap. He doesn't even come out from behind the counter.

"Our car won't start. Can you take a look at it?"

He sucks in some air through clenched teeth. "I could try my mechanic, Jimmy," he says, but doubtfully. Checks his watch. "But it's past nine thirty. He's already playing cards for sure. House could be on fire and Jimmy would burn along with it if he's in the middle of a game. He'll never even notice the phone."

"And you can't, maybe, fix it yourself?"

"Afraid it's gas only at night." He sounds a little defensive. "I'm a decent owner, but a lousy mechanic." He holds up a trembling hand to demonstrate—arthritis, Parkinson's maybe—but I get the sense he'd be a bad mechanic regardless. "Jimmy comes in at the crack of dawn, though. And there's a motel a stretch down the road. Maybe those nice folks out there could give you kids a lift?"

A motel? Cassie said hurry, come now. She's scared they, whoever they are, are going to *hurt her*. We can't wait until tomorrow. We can't wait at all.

"No, no, you don't understand," I say. Like anything will suddenly make this man able to do something he can't. "We have to get where we're going right now."

"Well, there's a car rental place next town over." He frowns as he looks down at his watch again. "But I doubt they'd be open at this hour either."

And we're not old enough to rent a car anyway. I look out toward Jasper's Jeep. The hood is up now and a man, the baby-lady's husband he must be, is bent over it. He's even bigger than Jasper, and with his full beard and cool plaid shirt hanging over his worn jeans, he's an actual hipster, not an accidental one.

"Looks like maybe you won't need that mechanic after all."

When I get back outside, the baby-lady's husband is still bent over our car. Jasper's arms are crossed tight as he stands next to him, watching so intently that it looks like something in his head might pop. When Jasper sees me coming, he takes a couple of steps away from the car and waves me over.

"Listen, I'm sorry," he says, when we're somewhat alone. My own arms are crossed now. "I shouldn't have yelled at you and I definitely shouldn't have grabbed your arm. I just—I'm sorry." He rubs a hand over his head, looks away. Confused, worried, sad. Jasper is still all those things, but the anger is gone. "This whole thing has got me—" When he turns back to me, his eyes are glassy. "You know, I think I'm actually in love with her. I didn't realize that until right now. I've never been in love with anyone before. If something happens to her—"

"It won't," I say, more for my benefit than his. "It's not going to." Jasper and I stare at each other because we both know I have no idea whether that's true. We don't know anything. "Maybe we should call the police now. I know Cassie doesn't want us to. But there are worse things than some boarding school boot camp."

"Like jail, for instance?" Jasper asks. "Because that's what she's worried about. That's why she doesn't want us calling the police. Cassie was arrested right after Thanksgiving."

"Arrested?" Cassie and I were still talking after Thanksgiving, at least for a week. She got *arrested* and never mentioned it? "For what?"

"Buying pot downtown with Stephanie," he says. "Out of the back of some waffle truck. I guess you order some special kind of waffle, you get an eighth as a booster." He shrugs like he would have no idea about such things. "So stupid. Anyway, Stephanie and Cassie both got a CWOF."

"What's that?"

"Continuance Without a Finding," he says like he is well versed in such things. "Basically, if Cassie stays out of trouble for a year, her arrest gets erased. But if something else happens, it'll definitely go down on her permanent record. Maybe even get her sent to a halfway house or something."

"Oh," I say, feeling embarrassed that Jasper knows yet more details that I don't. I feel more worried for Cassie, too. Arrested, permanent record, halfway house? Things are even worse than I feared.

"Sorry," Jasper says. *Sorry she didn't tell you herself,* that's what he means. He's trying to be nice, but him apologizing on Cassie's behalf only makes me feel worse. "Anyway, maybe we should ask her again about telling the police or her mom. Push her a little, you know? Make sure she's thinking clearly. There are more important things even than her permanent record."

"Yeah, maybe," I say, but I'm really not convinced that Cassie is thinking clearly.

I know u said not to call the police or your mom, I type. *But Jasper and I really think we should. Your being safe is more important than anything else.*

But Cassie's response comes instantly. And settles it once and for all. *Don't call my mom or the police. These people will kill me if you do.*

The baby-lady smiles over at me when Jasper and I return. Her husband is still leaning inside the open hood.

"I'm Lexi, by the way." She holds out a delicate hand. "We're from Brooklyn, but we were just up in the White Mountains. And we're on our way now to Acadia National Park." She rolls her eyes playfully. "The out-of-our-way-mountain detour was for me. Acadia is for Doug. He's an astronomer, and there's a meteor shower that we're headed to see. Or *he's* going to see. Let's face it, the baby and I will probably be sound asleep in some motel."

She smiles and hitches her head in the direction of her husband. "And don't worry. Doug will get it started. You'd never think that someone who grew up in Manhattan would be so good with cars, but he's an absolute whiz."

"Yeah, not this time," Doug says when he pulls himself out from under the hood. He has a wrench in his thick hand, and his sleeves are rolled up over his muscular forearms. He's more solid and scruffier up close. Older, too, definitely older than Lexi. And with the beard and the plaid shirt, he looks like he should be chopping wood somewhere. A lot of it. "You're going to need a new starter. Any actual mechanic would have one. But I can't do anything for you without the part."

Damn it. My heart pumps harder in my chest. *These people will kill me if you do.* We have to go, now. When I look over at Jasper, he's staring at me with this expression: *tell me you have an idea.* I look around the gas station, at all that darkness and all those trees. This nice woman and her little baby and her Paul Bunyan astronomer-husband are it. They are our only option.

"Can you take us?" I blurt out. "Please."

"Take you where, honey?" Lexi asks. She's trying not to sound nervous, but she's pressed a protective hand against the window behind her, where her baby is probably snuggled inside.

Doug doesn't look happy either. He's leaned back against our car with his big arms crossed, glaring at the side of his wife's face. *Don't you dare*, that's what the look says. My dad used to use it on my mom all the time, right before he ended up doing whatever it was she wanted.

"Somebody took our friend to this camp near some town named Seneca. It's in Maine," I say, trying to make the situation sound pressing, but not actually dangerous and not totally inconvenient. I tap on my phone to see how far away that really is. "It's in the direction of Acadia. I mean, I guess depending on which way you were going. Or maybe you could take us part of the way and we could hitch another ride?"

Hitch another ride? Like that's a totally reasonable possibility. Lexi is still looking at Doug with her head tilted to the side now, smiling like a little girl trying to talk her parents into a treat. And it's a look she must give

Doug a lot, because he's doing his best to avoid it. Finally, he exhales loudly and shakes his head.

"This is a job, Lexi, not a hobby. You know that, right? I have a paper to write. An actual deadline."

"Honey, we have two whole days until the meteor shower. And look at them, don't they remind you of us when we were their age? It's good karma to help them. I know you like to plan your driving routes in advance, but it doesn't even sound like it'll take us much longer." She grins as she bounds over to kiss him. Already, she knows she's won. "Besides, I'll spend the rest of the week making it up to you."

Doug exhales, exasperated, as he heads back toward their car. "Fine."

"We can throw your stuff up top. We've got plenty of space! I'll help you grab it," Lexi calls happily as she goes around to open our trunk. "Wow, you have a *lot* of stuff in here. Were you really planning to camp in this weather?"

"No," I say, like the suggestion is totally absurd. Still, I step toward Jasper's car, already planning to still dig out as much as I can on the sly: compass, matches, tablets to purify water. Bandages, naturally.

"Are you sure about this?" Jasper asks, as I dig around the trunk.

"Which part?"

He motions to them, their car. Going with these people we don't know, not calling the police, he means.

"Any of it?"

"No, I'm not," I say, as I pull my backpack out. "But then, I'm never sure about anything."

CHAPTER 10

Doug and Lexi's car is nothing like Jasper's Jeep. It smells clean and looks brand-new, with a dashboard that's a computerized touch screen and an engine so quiet it's hard to tell it's even on. It's so much warmer, too, the front windshield fogging only for a second as the heater burns off the damp cold.

"Are you guys okay back there?" Lexi asks over her shoulder. With the baby's car seat taking up all of the driver's side of the back, Jasper and I are squished awfully close together. "There's not much space. Sorry about that."

"We're fine." Jasper sounds like he actually thinks we are. Like he doesn't find the whole length of our thighs touching the least bit awkward. And why would he? The dozen seniors he's slept with might just be a rumor, but he's surely had sex with lots of people (Cassie included). Sitting close to a girl is nothing for him. But up until now, my thighs have only pressed against one other boy's.

Trevor and I met in yearbook club sophomore year, and for a couple of months we hung out after school. I liked Trevor even if he was way too skinny and his chin was kind of nonexistent. He was sweet and funny and strange, but in a good way. He was obsessed with Houdini, and he knew all these random stats from World War I, which meant he was happy to do most of the talking.

Mostly we'd study and talk on those Wednesdays, but occasionally we made out. Sometimes even a lot. It was nice. And so normal that even Cassie was impressed. I felt like it was a sign, too, that I was finally out of the deep, dark woods.

But then, all of a sudden, Trevor called it quits.

"It's not because you don't want to have sex," he'd said, though I had been stalling for about a month. "I wanted to wait, too, which I realized was weird because, you know, I'm a guy." And the way he said it: like he was some ideal specimen. "And then I was thinking about *why* I wanted to wait, and I realized: I can't take the pressure. I like you, Wylie, but being with you, it's too much"—he searched for a new word and came up empty—"pressure. Like if I do something wrong, you might freak out and have a breakdown or something."

I nodded at him and prayed I wouldn't cry. Later, I would for sure. And I could live with that. Just not in front of him. "Yeah, that's okay. I understand."

And actually that was the worst part: I understood completely.

I try to shift a little closer now toward the car seat, hoping that eases the pressure of my leg against Jasper's. It doesn't, not really. The seat is facing backward with the hood down, so that all I can see are the blankets gathered around the baby's feet. I pray he'll sleep the whole way, because I'm not sure I'll be able to take Lexi cooing at him up close. I watch him for a couple more minutes, but still he doesn't make a peep.

"He's so quiet," I say, sounding like some kind of creepy baby-stalker that you shouldn't ever let near your child.

"She," Lexi corrects without turning around. Of course it has to be a girl—mother and daughter. Two peas in a pod. They probably look alike, just like my mom and I did. "I'm hoping she'll sleep the whole way. Are you really sure you're okay back there, sitting on top of each other? Not that we have a lot of better options, I guess."

"We're fine," I say. I'm certainly not going to complain. If we annoy Doug, he could change his mind, overrule Lexi and toss us out. "Thanks again for the ride. We really, really appreciate it. Our friend will too."

"Not a problem," Lexi says, putting her hand over Doug's, which is resting on the gearshift.

He links his fingers through hers but keeps his eyes on the road. He'll forgive her, but not yet. And there they are again, my mom and dad. At least like they always were, up until those few weeks before my mom died when all they did was bicker.

I look away from their hands to the shadowy outlines of the buildings passing in the darkness. A farm equipment rental store, a shuttered ice cream shop, a hardware store, a meat market. All of them are dark and deserted at this hour. Some of them shut for good or the season maybe. Past them is the motel, long and low, its small parking lot glowing eerily under a single streetlight. A TV flashes on and off in one of the rooms, but the rest are all pitch black. I've never been to this part of New Hampshire before, far away from the seaside resorts and the beautiful national parks, but it's creepier than I would have thought. I shudder hard, which makes Jasper turn. I avoid looking back at him and instead stare down at my phone. Already, my chest feels tighter, and so does my stomach.

U OK? I write to Cassie as we drive on. *Car trouble slowed us a little. But we're back on the road. B there as soon as we can. No police.*

I wait for an answer. But there's nothing.

??? I type.

Wait again. Still no answer. Maybe I shouldn't have even mentioned the car trouble. I look up and feel worse when I meet Jasper's eyes. He's worried, too. Not as worried as me, maybe—that would be stiff competition—but more worried than I want him to be. I look back to the window. The buildings are gone, so I try instead to count the trees. Focus on the details, the little things. But soon, it's so dark. The woods are just a thick and shapeless mass. There is nothing left for me to hold on to. Had I really convinced myself that an actual emergency meant my anxiety had been banished? What stupid, wishful thinking. My anxiety has always had a mind of its own. And that mind is exceptionally tenacious.

"What's the meteor shower you're going to see?" Jasper asks.

Good. Yes, talking. Something to think about other than my insides twisting themselves into a knot.

Doug's eyes flick up to the rearview, then narrow. Is he annoyed by Jasper's question? I can't tell. "You familiar with astronomy?"

Be careful, I want to say. *Don't push our luck.* But Jasper doesn't notice. His eyes are locked outside on the darkness.

Jasper shrugs. "Does having a telescope when I was seven count?"

"Big Dipper?" Doug asks.

"Come on, man," Jasper says with a genuine smile. "Give me some credit. Orion's Belt. And Cass-something. I can't remember."

"Cassiopeia," Doug says, his voice softening a little. "Not bad for a seven-year-old."

"We lived on this hill near the beach." Jasper sounds like he misses it. A lot. "The sky went on forever."

"We're going to see the Eta Aquarids," Lexi says, her hand moving to the back of Doug's neck. "If you don't believe in God after seeing something like that, you never will."

"So you just go there and, what? Watch it?" Jasper asks.

"*Just?*" Doug asks, and with an edge again. *Shut up, Jasper,* I want to say. This is not the time for his aw-shucks, stereotype-defying curiosity.

"I meant, what are you looking for?"

"You always wanted someone to mentor, Doug," Lexi says playfully. "Sounds like you have a budding astronomer back there."

"Not exactly. I like astronomy, but I'm going to law school. Public defender," Jasper says, because he can't just be polite and go along with anything, apparently. "My dad's in prison for something he didn't do because he had a terrible lawyer."

"Oh, wow," Doug says, looking over at Lexi like: *what the hell did you get us into?* We are in the backseat with his baby, after all. "What was he convicted of?"

"You're not supposed to ask that." Lexi swats at him. "It's none of our business."

"That's okay," Jasper says. "Aggravated assault. Like I said, he didn't do it. His lawyer didn't call half the witnesses he should have. Really basic stuff."

"Well then, I'm especially sorry," Lexi says, sweet, but a little awkward. "I'll keep him in my thoughts."

"Are you saying you'll pray for him, Lexi?" Doug asks sharply. "Sounds like he needs a good appellate lawyer, not some Hail Marys."

"Forever the rationalist," Lexi says.

This is their shtick. She's the mystic. He's the scientist. Like they want to show off how great their relationship is despite being so different. Almost like maybe their relationship isn't so great after all. But I'll play along if what they want is an audience. I'll do whatever they want me to, as long as they keep on getting us closer to Cassie.

"I have a religion," Doug says. "It's called science."

"Also known as sucking the joy out of life." Lexi wags a finger at him. "The vast complexities of human experience reduced to dots on a graph."

"My dad's kind of like that," I say, without fully meaning to. "He doesn't believe in anything without evidence."

"Sounds like my kind of guy." Doug looks at me in the rearview. He seems genuinely pleased. "Scientist?"

"Psychologist." I consider mentioning my dad's research, but I feel like it will diminish him in Doug's eyes.

And I hate that I've thought of my dad. Because my *condition* is the next thing I think of. And I feel so embarrassed and alone all over again. I can't believe he really said those things. *Your condition.* That's just not the kind of thing you can forget. No matter how much you want to.

It is even darker now when I look out the window,

like we've driven off the edge of a cliff. And it feels like that is what we're doing. Because what exactly is our plan now that we don't even have a car? We were supposed to swoop in and save Cassie. Now we're going to walk in on foot? We're going to need another car, that's the bottom line. I look at Lexi in the front seat, wonder how far she would go to help us. Would she rent us a car? Then I look at Doug. There's no way he's going to go for putting his name on a car we might never return.

I need to stop thinking about this. Because not having a solution is winding me tight. My eyes drift instead down to the car seat and that little baby's feet wrapped so snug and safe in her pale-green blanket.

It's weird that her feet haven't moved *once* since we got into the car. Isn't it? Lexi said she was supposed to sleep the whole way. Okay, fine. But don't babies move a little even when they sleep? Maybe she's wrapped too tight, covered in too many blankets? Was I expected to be keeping an eye out for that kind of thing? Because sometimes people expect things of you with no warning. What if she's stopped breathing or something? Lexi is so nonchalant, but none of us have any way of being sure anyone will ever be okay. Not really. And I may think about that way more than your average person, but that doesn't make it any less true.

"How about some music? We've got satellite—a million options even in the middle of nowhere," Lexi says, but like that kind of disgusts her a little bit. She leans forward to fiddle with the radio. "We've probably never heard of whatever you guys listen to these days. That's how old we are now, sweetheart, we don't even know what kind of music the young people listen to."

My heart is beating hard as Lexi turns the radio past one song to the next, rejecting each. No matter how hard I try not to, all I can think about is the baby and her breathing now, or maybe lack thereof. Because something is wrong. I can feel it. There's a hollowness in that car seat next to me. A huge sucking emptiness.

"Hey, speak for yourself," Doug says. "I'm not old. *And I definitely still have good taste in music. Use one of my Spotify playlists."

"Ugh, you're not going to make me listen to Wilco, are you?" Lexi asks. But she sounds so far away now. Like her voice is muffled through a wall. "You know a little piece of me dies every time you do."

My heart is beating harder now. I try to *center myself in the present*, like Dr. Shepard says. The seat is under my legs. My hands are resting on my legs. But my palms are sweating so much, and all I can think about is how babies do stop breathing suddenly. They die of SIDS with no explanation. And no warning. They do that all the time.

But I'm afraid to ask again about the baby. Lexi has already said once that she's fine. Mentioning it again could sound like I think Lexi is a bad mother. Instead, I could just check on the baby myself. All I need to do is feel her warmth, or squeeze her toes a little and make sure they move. If she starts to cry, God forbid, I'll snatch my hand right back before anyone knows what happened. Yes, that's what I am going to do. Even though I know that it might be a very bad idea. Even though I know the baby isn't the real reason there's so much pressure in my chest. I still believe that knowing she's okay might release it a little bit.

I keep my eyes on the rearview, as I inch my hand slowly over to the car seat. Lexi and Doug are still talking about Doug's playlists—Lexi trying to decide which one she thinks is the least bad.

"I don't know, I kind of like Wilco," Jasper offers, his eyes still on the window.

And my hand is so close now, only an inch or two more and I'll have my answer. I'll have my relief. Because the crazy thing about being so worried all the time, and having worked for so many years with Dr. Shepard, is that there's this whole part of me that knows that the baby isn't the point. She isn't what I'm actually freaking out about. I'm worried about Cassie being okay, who my dad has become, surviving this, and above all else, surviving my mom being gone. That's the way anxiety works. It's a decoy. Because I can't do anything about those big things, I worry about something else. I worry about this baby next to me, who is definitely, totally fine. But maybe, just maybe, might not be.

Already my fingers are on the baby's seat, then the edge of her blankets. Crawling across the folds. But it's not as easy to find her toes as I imagined. Not easy at all. When I move my hand around, all I feel are blankets and more blankets.

Too many blankets, actually, the more I think about it. So many that it doesn't seem right. *Boom, boom, boom*, goes my heart as I push my hand one last time, deep into the center of the car seat.

And inside, I do not find the warm body of a baby. But I do not find a cold baby either. Inside, I find nothing at all.

CHAPTER 11

Stop! Your baby is gone!

The words shoot to my lips, but my mouth stays shut as my pulse surges and my brain gets fuzzy on the rush.

No, don't say that, I think. *Don't say a word.*

Instead, I look over at Jasper. His eyes are closed, head resting against the window. I wonder for a second whether he's asleep. But when I push one of my knuckles hard into the side of his leg, he lifts his head and turns.

I shake my head a tiny bit, widen my eyes before he can ask what's wrong. I point a low finger at the car seat, then mouth the words: "No baby." I hope that will be enough for him to get what I mean, but not ask questions.

Because as soon as Doug and Lexi know—that *we* know—we will have lost the only thing we have going for us: the element of surprise. And what is it that I think I know? There's no baby in the seat, but I don't know why or what that means. *We* asked *them* for a ride, I remind myself. Doug didn't even want to take us.

Maybe these are just the people you run into in the middle of the night, in the middle of nowhere. People running from something. People with something to hide. For all we know, they stole this car with all its warm and fuzzy bumper stickers and its empty car seat. I don't want to know. Lexi and Doug can keep their secrets, thank you very much. We just need to get the hell out of their car.

I quietly pull in a mouthful of air, but I am already so light-headed. My eyes are off, too, like the filter has been switched to antique, everything a little too soft and the tiniest bit yellow. At least there is no dark tunnel yet and I haven't started to go numb. But if I can't keep it together, it will only be a matter of time before the lights go out.

Lexi glances at me over her shoulder, then smiles like she has so many times since I first saw her swaying back and forth next to her car. A minute ago that smile seemed so sweet and warm. Now it lifts the hairs on the back of my neck. I press my fingers against my thighs. Dig in my nails as I smile back at her.

But whatever Doug and Lexi are up to, it has nothing to do with us. It started before we ever pulled into that gas station. Maybe they're friendly neighborhood outlaws, environmental terrorists, or conscientious political protesters on the run for some crime of principle, and the pretend baby is cover. Not wanting to be found doesn't necessarily mean you're a bad person. I know that firsthand. And yet I still have such a bad, bad feeling.

"So your friend—" Lexi asks, finally settling on a song. "Wait, what did you say her name was again?"

I turn to Jasper, shake my head again. *Don't tell her anything else. Not another thing,* I try to say with my eyes. Jasper squints at me for a second.

"Victoria," Jasper answers finally. His lie is all the proof that I need. He gets it. "Her name is Victoria."

I tap open my phone map, to see if we've veered off course. But the little blue dot that is us is still headed on Route 203 toward Seneca. Lexi and Doug could have something to hide but still be doing us a favor. This could be more of an unfortunate coincidence, a less dangerous disaster. My chest loosens a tiny bit. Yes, maybe. But we still need to get out of the car.

When I look down, I have only one bar of signal left on my phone. Soon even that might be gone. I am angry at my dad, of course. It feels like he actually may have permanently broken us. But I am still way more afraid of Lexi and Doug than I am angry at him.

I open my texts and type out a quick message to my dad.

Jasper's car died off 93, Exit 39C in New Hampshire. Headed toward Maine on Route 203. In a black Subaru station wagon with New York plates and a Hillary 2016 sticker on it. We need help. Not safe maybe. I am trusting you. Don't mess it up.

"Victoria, that's a pretty name," Lexi goes on, and with this tone—like she knows quite a few Victorias herself. Like the name says everything you need to know about this friend of ours. "Does she get herself into a lot of situations like this?"

"Sometimes," I say, but way too high and way too loud. *Be normal. Just talk about Cassie. She is not a lie.* "She gets caught up and one thing leads to another and then she's in over her head." *Like you guys. See, we get it. No hard feelings.* "It's not the first time she's asked me to come get her. We're just trying to bring her home to her mom."

She has a home. She has a mom. They are good people. We are good people. And you should let us go.

"That's good of you to do, especially more than once," Lexi says, sounding wistful, as she turns to look out the window. "The two of you must be really close."

"We are," I say. "We are really, really good friends."

The acid is kicking high in my stomach, trying to make its way up my throat, when I spot a little blue sign up ahead: a gas pump next to a crisscrossed fork and knife. Food and gas, an excuse to stop, to get out. To run. I rub my palms against my jeans, then squeeze my fingers tight.

"I'm sorry, but I have to go to the bathroom." I point to the sign. "Could we stop? I'll be really quick, I promise."

I turn and look at Jasper. He nods. He may not know exactly what is going on, but he'll follow my lead.

"Sure, no problem," Doug says, and so easily, like I've imagined the danger. Or maybe like things are even worse than I thought.

The turn signal ticks like a metronome, the light flashing slow and steady in the darkness. The world has slowed. Every sound is amplified, every motion exaggerated. Doug's eyes are on the road. Lexi's are on her phone. It all looks so normal, which only makes me more convinced that none of it is.

"Wow, can't miss that, can you?" Lexi says, pointing.

Floating high in the sky is a huge neon sign that reads *Trinity's Diner*, with two red race cars and a checkered flag. It's way too big, an eyesore out here in the woods. Especially when the restaurant itself is a smallish, rectangular metal trailer. Not the kind of place that's going to be easy to lose Doug and Lexi inside. Once we start trying to get away, things could definitely get messy. I need to text Cassie, warn her that we could be out of touch for a while.

Ran into trouble. You should text your mom just in case. More important that you're safe. Just tell her not to call the police. She'll listen. I know she will. At least I hope.

It isn't until I've hit send and closed out of that message that I see the red exclamation point next to the one I'd sent to my dad. *Failed to deliver* reads the red message next to it. My signal was already gone. All those choices I'd been mulling over about who to tell what about Cassie—they were no longer mine to make.

As we pull into the parking lot, I turn to Jasper, holding up my phone. I shake my head. *No signal.* He immediately looks down at his own phone. His face brightens for only a split second before he shakes his head, too. He doesn't have a signal either.

"I should probably go in also, just in case," Jasper says as we pull into the parking lot. *In case?* "I mean, so we don't have to stop again later."

Inside, Jasper and I will decide what to do. We can tell someone in the diner or we could ask to use the landline. Inside, there will be safety in numbers. And, after a while, when we don't come back out, Doug and Lexi will probably drive away with their secrets, and without us. Happy to be gone, to be rid of us. We are a complication they didn't ask for. Relieved, yes. There's no reason to think they won't be. Except as the gravel crunches loud under our tires, I do not believe that. Not at all.

Doug parks in a spot under the glow of the diner windows, next to a brand-new pickup with tinted windows, shiny hubcaps, and some kind of rack on top. For guns probably, given all the stickers: *Maine Bears Arms, Terrorist Hunting Permit*, an NRA emblem. There's also a green tarp lashed to a back shelf, the tip of a hoof poking out from underneath. Not exactly who I was hoping to be asking for help.

But when I look up at the table in the diner window above, there are three girls about my age sitting in a booth, eyes locked on the one boy sitting opposite. They're smiling on the edge of their seats as he talks, arms moving back and forth in a big circle. When he suddenly freezes—on the punch line probably—they all burst out laughing. Totally regular kids, doing totally regular things. They'll help us. I know they will.

"Actually, I could use a cup of coffee myself," Doug says as he turns off the car. "No offense, but this little detour is going to add some driving time." It almost sounds like it could be the truth, like he really just wants coffee. But truth or not, it'll be a lot harder to talk to Jasper if we're not alone.

"Well, I'm not staying out here by myself," Lexi says as she undoes her seat belt and starts to get out. She's forgotten about the baby they're supposed to have. I watch Doug catch her eye, see her hesitate as she remembers. "Let me just grab the baby?"

My feet feel heavy as I make my way up the diner's rickety metal steps. I'm almost at the top when the door swings open and there's a burst of shouts and jostling as the kids from the window spill out.

"Oops," the first girl says as they collide into one another. Their voices drop politely as they try to make way for us to pass. "Sorry."

When I take the door from the last girl, it feels weirdly too light. Like none of this is actually real. Like it is a dream I will wake from. *Help,* I want to say to her. But with Doug and Lexi right there, I can't say a word.

"Here you go," the girl calls cheerfully when I hesitate too long. She is cute and petite with long, black hair. I stare at her and think, *Please, don't go.* But all she does is smile a little more before hustling after her friends. At the bottom of the steps, they burst into laughter before they disappear. And just like that, our very best option is gone.

"Now I want a burger, too," Doug says, positively cheerful now.

"Ugh." Lexi sounds disgusted as she makes her way up the steps. She has the car seat in one hand, the top of it pulled low so no one can see that there's actually nothing inside. She's even doing a decent job of supporting herself with the handrail, as if the car seat is actually heavy. "A burger at a place like this?"

As I step into the diner vestibule, a wave of warm, damp air hits me, pumping out loudly from a radiator next to an M&M vending machine. I move on through a second set of doors into the diner, which is much cleaner and busier than I would have expected at nearly ten p.m. The half-dozen booths along the front windows are filled—teenagers, older people, a family with two young, sleepy boys, and it smells like bacon and apple pie, the walls a cheery bright red.

But not everyone in the diner is happy. One long-faced couple in the middle of the room is surrounded by a circle of empty tables and nestled in a zone of gray; their faces, their clothes, even the air around them seems coated in soot. They are utterly silent, almost motionless, their eyes on the tabletop. The woman has a full plate in front of her that she hasn't touched, and the man is chewing slow and hard, like he's trying to gnaw through rubber. They feel like a terrible, terrible omen.

I'm still watching them when a hostess appears in front of us. She has a dirty-blond ponytail and is cute despite her too-big eyes and crooked teeth. She's wearing a red T-shirt with *Trinity* printed in big black letters, a flag on either side.

"Four of you?" she asks, smiling as she grabs up some menus.

"Actually, we're just getting something to go," Doug says.

Did he say that kind of too forcefully? Like he knows something is up? Who knows? It could easily be my imagination.

My heart is beating so hard, I feel like it is rocking my body as I stand there. I pray that Doug and Lexi can't see.

"Where's your bathroom?" I ask the hostess, hoping that Jasper will follow my lead. That he and I can talk privately back by the bathrooms, match notes, come up with a plan. Who knows, maybe he'll even think it's safe for us to be honest with Lexi and Doug, to tell them we know there's no baby. Maybe Jasper will tell me that I'm being paranoid. And maybe I will even get myself to believe him.

"Sure, hon, bathrooms are right back there." The hostess points toward a door at the far end of the counter. "Ladies' is at the end of the hall."

"Okay, thanks." I avoid meeting Doug or Lexi's eyes as I step toward the back. "I'll just be a second."

Lexi smiles. "Take your time, sweetheart."

Did her voice also sound weird? A tremor to it like

she's scared, but trying to hide it? For sure, my racing heart has made the floor spongy underfoot as I make my way to the bathroom. By the time I finally reach the door, my body feels numb. I can see my hand on the knob, the door coming back toward me as I pull it, but I can't feel it. I can't feel anything.

On the other side of the door is a short, wood-paneled hall, the men's room to the left and a ladies' straight ahead. It's colder out here, like the walls are paper-thin. When I put a hand on one to steady myself, I hope it doesn't punch right through. By the time I reach the women's bathroom, Jasper's still not there like I hoped he would be. But I can't just stand there like I'm waiting for him, on the off chance Lexi or Doug comes in behind me instead. It'll look like I'm up to something. I have no choice but to go on inside the women's room. Jasper will knock when he comes, right? He'll know that's where I went. He's not an idiot.

The bathroom itself is filthy—hair all over the sink, stains on the floor, no toilet paper. Like the otherwise squeaky-clean diner saved up all its scum for this one room. It's ten degrees colder yet again in here, and the laminate floor is peeling, the corners lifted and curled. I lock the door behind me, then press an ear to it. I can hear the dining room: voices, the clinking of silverware. I'll definitely be able to hear Jasper when he comes through. *If* he comes through. I wait for a minute longer. Still, nothing. But he has to be coming. He has to be.

And when he gets here, we'll need a way out the back. There's a window high above the toilet, and when I climb up, it opens easily. Big enough for Jasper and me to make it through. But when I poke my head out, it's a long drop to the ground. Hard to see exactly how far in the dark. Probably not so far that we'd be seriously hurt, but even hurt a little would slow us down too much.

I'm still leaning out the window when I finally hear the door to the bathroom hall open, at least I think. Jasper, finally, thank God. I jump off the toilet and head for the door. And really, I am still hoping he won't even think we need to run.

I've already turned the lock. My hand's on the knob when there's a second sound. The hallway door opening and closing again. A second set of footsteps, these ones fast. Then Jasper's voice.

"Dou—"

A hard thud against the wall. Doug. That was Jasper trying to say *Doug*. Wasn't it? I press my hands against the door, heart racing. Do I open it? There are more sounds now, louder, a scrambling against the floor, then someone kicking the wall. Struggling. Jasper struggling with Doug?

I feel around my pockets for my phone, praying that I'll somehow have a signal. That I can call the police, because now I will. I will have no choice. But I don't have a signal, of course. As I shove my phone back into my other pocket, it gets caught on something. My mom's pocketknife. When I dig it out, it's cool and heavy in my palm, stiff as I tug out the short blade. My heart pounds in my ears as I stare down at the small flash of metal.

"St-op." Definitely Jasper this time. Like he's gasping.

I have to be ready to do something when I open the door. Just in case. That stupid little knife is my only option. The way my mom once taught me to split a log with an ax. I'll have to swing with my full weight behind it.

When I yank open the door, my chest seizes. Because there it is. There they are. What I expected and yet still cannot believe. Doug has Jasper up against the wall. His arm on Jasper's neck. Jasper's face red. His eyes wide as he kicks against the wall. Jasper looks so terrified.

Doug's other hand is pressed flat against the wall for leverage. A big enough target. A place to aim. He's choking Jasper. He needs to let go. Now. I need to make him let go.

I lunge forward and swing. When the knife finally comes down, I'm jolted by pain—*my* pain—as the knife and my fist closed around it come down against Doug's knuckles. I would have sworn that I'd hit the wall, if it wasn't for the blood all over me.

"Fuck!" Doug yells, grabbing at his hand as he buckles.

Jasper coughs violently and lurches for the door. But I'm frozen. All I can do is look at the blood on my hand, on Doug. The floor. There's so much already. So much more blood than I ever would have thought. And it's such a bright red.

"Come on!" Jasper pulls me past Doug and toward the door.

We bang too loudly back into the dining room. The noise, our speed, it's enough to make the whole room fall silent, turn to look. The hostess who was so nice a second ago turns, suspicious. I don't see Lexi. She's not near the door. Not at a table. Nowhere in sight, and neither is the car seat.

Jasper and I thread our way through the restaurant, toward the door. Not running, not quite. Pretending not to be two people on the run.

"Whoa, buddy, is that blood?" A voice behind us. When I turn, Doug is leaning against the doorway. There's an older man next to him, a hand on his shoulder. I watch Doug say something to him. "Hey, those kids just tried to rob him!"

He points at us as a waitress rushes over to Doug with a towel. But Doug never takes his eyes off us. Or me. Never even blinks. And that look on his face. Like he wants to kill me. Like he will. The only question is when.

"Watch out!" It's the old man again. "She's got a knife!"

It isn't until then that I look down at my hand. Sure enough, my mom's pocketknife is still gripped in my fist. There's blood on the stubby blade, and all over my fingers. I am no longer just a crazy girl with chopped hair. I am a crazy girl with chopped hair and a knife. A girl who has already proved that she is definitely a danger to others.

And am I? Did I really need to stab Doug? Why didn't I yell for him to stop first? Why didn't I at least try shouting for help?

Jasper tugs me forward again. We're running now through the restaurant, but in a way that feels slow and useless. Like with every step forward the way out is getting farther away.

"You! Stop!" It's the hostess. She's standing in front of the door with a phone in her hand. Pointing at us. "I'm calling the police. Don't you go anywhere." She waves at a couple of big guys in a booth at the back. "Come on. We can't just let them leave!"

"Sorry, but we've got to go." Jasper shoves her politely but firmly to the side.

We pound out one set of doors and then the next. Fly down the rickety steps. When I glance back, I can see a pack forming near the diner doors, maybe around Doug. I can't see him. But who knows what he'll convince them of? He is a really good liar.

"Look," Jasper says as we hit the gravel of the parking lot. "Over there."

Lexi and Doug's car is on the other side of the parking lot. Engine running, pointed at the exit. Whatever Doug's plan, Lexi was his getaway driver. Slowly, she turns in our direction.

"She's looking at us," I say.

But she doesn't jump out of the car like I brace for her to. She just stares at us for a long moment before dropping her face into her hands. Why? It's such a weird, weird thing to do. Is she hiding? Crying? Not because of what I did to Doug. If she knew, she'd be running back inside to help him.

"Let's go," Jasper says, sprinting ahead toward the back of the diner, in the direction of the woods. "They'll be coming."

CHAPTER 12

Branches whip across my face, snapping back against my arms as we rush headlong through the darkness. Soon the forest is so dense that we have to slow. Can't go much faster than a walk, each of us hiking our knees up over fallen trees, tripping into small ditches. Not moving fast enough to outrun anyone.

With each big marching step farther into the pitch-black woods, deeper into the silence, I feel more and more lost. The branches feel more tangled, our path less and less clear. And yet we can do nothing but press on. For us, there is no turning back. Not anymore.

After five, ten minutes—I don't know how long—the trees finally open up a little. But just when the going gets a little easier, lights flicker off the tall trees in front of us. We stop short. But it's not lights up ahead. They're coming from behind us.

Flashlights. Someone following. We knew they would. Probably not the police, not that fast. Doug for sure, assuming he isn't bleeding to death. With some people from the diner, maybe. I think of that truck with the NRA sticker and the dead deer. There were people with guns in that diner. I wonder if it would be legal to shoot us in the back. I *was* the one with the knife. The one who did the hurting first. I am the one who is a danger to others.

Even in the dark, I can see Doug's blood staining my fingers. And I can still feel the way my mom's little knife bounced back when it hit flesh and bone. I shake my head hard. Because I have to focus. They, whoever they are, are closer now, their voices echoing through the trees.

We'll never outrun them. I've done my share of hiking, sure. But no amount of that experience will make the going any easier. The woods are just too dense. We need another plan. Alternatives. Climb? It could be our best chance. Our only one, actually.

I head over to where a log is rested against another tree with a few thick, low-hanging branches. I stare up the length of it, reaching forever into the dark sky. The only thing my mom ever taught me about climbing trees was *not* to do it to escape a bear. But I do know how to adjust my balance. How to test a foothold. I know that my arms are much stronger than I think.

"Hey," I call quietly to Jasper. "Up?"

It's so dark I can't see the look on Jasper's face. Part of me is hoping he'll say no. That he'll have another idea.

"Shit, seriously?" he whispers.

"Do you have a better idea?"

"No. I don't have any ideas at all."

Climbing the tree is way harder than I expected. Not at all like the rock faces with my mom. There we were always sliding over and up, over and up. This is just up, up, up. We aren't far and already my arms have started to shake. Jasper seems to be having no problem, though, and him being right behind pushes me higher, until finally, he reaches up and puts a hand on my calf.

Stop climbing, the touch says. *Don't make a sound.*

Sure enough, there are voices below. Cracking branches and crunching leaves. I pray that the tree holds when I hear Doug's voice, clear as day.

"Isn't there some kind of path somewhere?"

I am relieved I didn't hurt him so bad they had to call an ambulance. And I am also terrified that I left him well enough to come after us.

"There's trails a ways back, up to the right," another man says. "We use 'em to hound the bears. That's where they must be headed. We should cut them off before they get there. On the trails, they'll be off like a shot."

"But they'd have no way of knowing the trails are even there," Doug says quietly. He's almost right beneath our tree. "They're not from here."

"What we need is a warning shot," a third man says. Younger, more jacked up. Like he's looking for any excuse to blow something away.

"Sheriff will beat your ass if he catches you firing again outside—"

Bang! Bang! Bang! So loud, so close to my head. I almost let go of the tree.

"Screw the goddamn sheriff." The young guy laughs stupidly.

"You dumb fucking—" Doug shouts. "If I wanted to get the police up here, I would have called them myself."

No police. Because Lexi and Doug do have something to hide. Of course they do. My arms shaking as I squeeze my eyes shut. I'm gripping the tree so hard it feels like my hands might start to bleed. And the way my heart is racing—if Doug doesn't kill me, passing out from this height surely will.

"Hey, shithead," the young guy laughs at Doug. He sounds high. "You're the one who asked for our help."

"Finding them. Not killing them, you idiot!"

"Listen, you motherfucking—"

"He's right," the older hunter growls. "Knock it off. I'm not getting my ass locked up because of you."

"Now, come on," Doug snaps. "Let's get to that trailhead. Maybe they know this area better than I thought."

After the flashlights bounce away and the voices fade, Jasper starts back down the tree. My whole body is trembly and weak by the time my feet are back on the ground.

"Good call on the tree," Jasper says, brushing himself off. "And thanks, you know, for back there. The diner. That was—" He can't even find words. "No offense, but I wouldn't have thought you had that in you."

Like stabbing someone is a thing to be proud of.

"I don't want to talk about it." And I don't. "I want to pretend it never happened."

"Okay, but he would have killed me. You know that, right?" Jasper asks. "You had no choice."

"Everyone always has a choice." All normal people anyway.

"Okay, whatever, feel bad about it then," Jasper says, sounding annoyed and exhausted. By me. And why would he understand? He doesn't know what my dad said to me. Doesn't know how bad it could be if I am a proven danger to others, even if that "other" is Doug. Jasper steps forward into the darkness. Like we've already decided which way to go. "I saw a light this way when we were up there. Maybe they'll let us use their phone."

We move on, scratching and slipping our way through the rough woods once more. In the darkness, I lose all sense of time. Lose all sense of everything, except the rhythm of the crunching leaves and my shifting feet. Jasper flips on his flashlight app now and then, only long enough to be sure we're not headed off a cliff. Having to focus so hard on not falling down, not tripping, not getting whacked in the eye with a stick has calmed me. In the midst of the very worst, I am once again at my best. So twisted, and so pathetically true.

"Hey," Jasper calls after a while. "We should head more to the right."

When I look up, I can see we have been drifting to the left of the lights. Or *light*. A single house, it looks like now. I don't know what I'd been expecting, a little town, maybe, but I can't help feeling disappointed. We'll just have to hope that they, whoever they are, are actually good people this time. And not just pretending to be.

I don't get far left before there's some kind of dip in front of me. A wide swath of dark that could be a real ditch, a deep one. "Can you flash the light over here? It goes down. I can't tell how far."

Jasper flicks on his phone, shining its metallic yellow haze on the branches before panning to the spot in front of me.

And that's when my eye catches them. At the faded edge of the light. Boots. With someone's feet in them. Someone right there. Close enough to grab me.

"Run, Jasper!" I shout as I leap forward into the shadows, then stumble downhill with a jerk.

Just as fast I'm back up the other side, a slope, not a pit after all. And then I am running. Fast over all those sticks and leaves. I wait for my foot to catch something. For some kind of pain.

But nothing happens, and second by second those lights in the distance are closer. Jasper is right behind me. At least I hope that's him. Feet fast, his breath coming in strong, even puffs. Which one was it in those boots? Can't be the young crazy one. I'm pretty sure he would have shot us on sight. And not Doug. He had on some kind of sneakers or hip, urban shoes. Didn't he? The third one then, maybe. At least that one seemed reasonable.

We don't slow down until we come up on the back of a run-down cabin in a small clearing. Haunted-looking, but not abandoned, apparently. The lights are on. Jasper marches up the steps and pounds on the door. When no one answers, he peers in the windows.

"I don't think they're home," he says, going back to the door to try it. He turns back and shakes his head. Locked. "We could break a window, but I didn't see a phone."

There's a rusted truck parked nearby. Maybe the keys are inside. Amazing how easy it is to consider stealing a truck once you've stabbed someone.

I walk over and push up on my toes to look in the open driver's-side window. In the pale light from the cabin, I can just make out the ignition. No key. I should check under the mat and in the glove box. People who live in the woods always leave their keys in their cars. Don't they? I press the stiff button on the door handle, but it takes a few pulls to finally get the heavy rusted door open. I'm looking in the glove box when Jasper calls my name.

His voice sounds weird. He's not judging my trying to take the truck, is he? Because we are way past caring about that. *Ignore him, keep on looking for the keys.* "Wylie, come out of the truck."

This time Jasper sounds scared. And not about the truck.

"Wylie," he says again. "You should come out. Right now."

When I finally slide back out, I see the boots first. Someone close enough to grab me again. Between me and Jasper, too. I suck in some air as I look up to see who's wearing them. But the man himself is not nearly as scary as I'd been bracing for. Creepy, to be sure. He's superthin and really old with wild, white hair and a gnarled beard. Not one of the guys from the woods, though. He's much older than they sounded. The owner of the cabin, probably. It would explain why he's got one hand resting on his chin, the other on the back of his neck, like he's contemplating what to do with a trespasser. He's breathing hard, too; definitely the one who was chasing us. At least he is small. Jasper could definitely take him. *I* could probably take him.

And so why does Jasper look so worried? Eyes wide, color all gone. That's when the man moves his hand. The one I thought was resting on his neck. It's not. I can see that now. He's holding something, resting it against his shoulder. Something long and thin, with a handle. And a big, curved blade.

"Tourist trapping is still illegal round here," the man barks at me finally, like the last shot in a long argument we've been having. "So is trespassing."

"Tourist trapping?" I ask. Better to focus on the part I know for sure we haven't done. Might make him think less about our trespassing.

"The damn hounds? The doughnuts? I know how you people do it." The man points his huge knife toward the woods, then swings around and points it right at me. Its long blade is so close I could lean forward and touch the tip with my nose. "It's shooting fish in a goddamn barrel."

I have no idea what he's talking about. None. Though that seems to matter much less than his big knife.

"We're just trying to find our friend." I hold up my hands. "We didn't mean to bother you."

I look over at Jasper and he nods. *Good, keep talking*, the look says. But the man's not even listening.

"I didn't give a shit about those damn animals before. That's the damn honest truth. Kill 'em, don't kill 'em, makes no difference to me. I sure as hell didn't care how they did it." He's having a totally different conversation. Not even with me. "But if it wasn't for the goddamn doughnuts, the bears never would have even been over here. 'Oh, I'm sorry,' that's what Sarah said, when she come up on them. Like she'd just walked in on someone pissing. You know the sound someone makes when they're being eaten alive?" He shakes his head, the anger twisting his face.

"We aren't bear hunters. Look at us," I say. "We're kids from Boston. We don't know anything about hunting or guns. But there are some bear hunters in the woods right now."

I have no idea whether those men hunt bear, much less whether they trap them with doughnuts. But they did almost shoot us. Doesn't seem totally unfair to send this guy their way. I feel confident he will have the upper hand even without a gun.

"Where?" he snaps, eyes flashing toward the dark woods.

"Behind the diner," I say. "They were headed for the hounding trails."

"Goddamn assholes," he mutters angrily as he starts toward the woods, knife gripped at his side.

"Wait," I call after him.

"Wait?" Jasper snaps at me. "Are you insane?"

"Can we use your phone?"

"No phone," the wild man shouts back without slowing down.

"Then your truck, please. Can we borrow it?"

Now he does stop.

"Ha!" he barks, then shakes his head angrily, before starting again for the woods. "My truck. Fuck off."

"Wylie," Jasper hisses. "Just let him go."

But we need the truck, and for some insane reason I feel like there is a chance he'll give it to us. Maybe because he is crazy and paranoid and it takes one to know one, but it's still worth a try.

"Listen, my mom is dead and now my best friend—these people have her and they might hurt her. I haven't left my house in three weeks because I'm so messed up, but I came all this way because my best friend is all I have left. If I lose her, I don't know what will happen to me."

The old man stops again. But this time he spins and starts back toward me, fast. Head tilted down like a charging bull. Not the response I had hoped for. Not at all. And the knife is gripped tight in his fist now like he's getting ready to swing for maximum effect. The only small mercy is that he's headed toward me and not Jasper. If someone is going to pay for my gamble, it should be me. I press back against the cold truck as he gets closer. Pull my chin in when he shoves his face in close to mine. His breath smells sour, his clothes ripe. *This is how it ends?* I think as I close my eyes and wait for the pain.

"Hey," he barks then, right in my face. And when I finally squint open my eyes, I do not see the knife. Just his dirty fingernails cupped around a set of keys. "Now, get the fuck out of here before I change my mind."

CHAPTER 13

Jasper drives away from the cabin fast. So fast, down the dark and bumpy dirt road cutting through the woods in front of the cabin that it feels like the old man's truck might fly apart. After we've made it a safe distance from the cabin, Jasper pulls to a stop so hard that I have to brace myself against the dashboard.

"Okay, what the fuck now?" he asks, like everything so far has been of my design.

"Why are you asking me? How would I know?"

I pull out my phone, hope for a signal, to call who, I'm not sure—my dad, Karen, the police? All of them and none of them feel like options. Definitely, we can't just keep going anymore. But can we stop? Go home? And what will I even be going home to? What's going to happen when they find out I stabbed someone? How can I expect anyone to believe that it was necessary, when *I'm* not even sure?

"I mean, who the hell was he?" Jasper asks.

"Some crazy, sad old guy whose wife or girlfriend or somebody got eaten by a bear." It's amazing how ordinary that seems to me. "I bet he was a real jerk even before that happened, though."

"Not him!" Jasper shouts. "Doug. Who the hell was he? He tried to *kill* me. You seriously think that has nothing to do with Cassie?"

"We asked them for a ride," I say, because that's what I've been relying on to keep myself from connecting Doug and Lexi to Cassie. Because that would be the only thing worse than them being random bad luck.

"And so it's just a coincidence that we're trying to find Cassie and we run across this guy who tries to choke me for no reason outside the bathroom?"

"No," I say quietly as my stomach starts to churn. "Probably not a coincidence. There's somebody who doesn't want us to find her, but why?" I stare at the side of Jasper's face as he stares at the bright patch of rocky dirt road in our headlights. "Is there anything else about Cassie you're not telling me? Something else she was mixed up in?"

"I don't know." Jasper turns and looks straight at me. "I swear. She got arrested, that's the only thing I know about, and that was months ago." He's telling the truth, at least it seems like he is. Or I have no way of knowing if he isn't. "But like I said, I think there was something else going on that she was hiding. Or maybe somebody did kidnap her and they don't want us to find out where they have her."

"Kidnap her?" It just sounds ridiculous. "For what? It's not like her parents are rich or something."

"Sex slavery." Jasper shrugs. "They sell girls into prostitution. I heard about it on NPR." He shoots me a look. "And yeah, I've listened to NPR. *All Things Considered*. And no, not on purpose. One of the cooks at the IHOP is some kind of writer."

"I guess it could be that," I say, even though that does not feel at all right. And also, I do not want it to be true. "Listen, we know we have to call somebody, right?" I say, and it makes me feel a tiny bit better just to admit it. To start there and get that out on the table. "The police, Cassie's mom, somebody. Or we can text Cassie and make her call them. Either way we're going to need a cell signal. Why don't we start with that? We drive until we get a signal."

Jasper stares out at the road for a minute longer, until finally he nods.

"Okay," he says without looking at me. Like he's trying to convince himself. He puts his hand on the truck's long gearshift, tugs it back into drive. "Okay."

We drive on until the dirt road T's back into Route 203, the diner and Seneca to our left, home to our right. To the right we know for sure we will have a signal, and soon even. If we go left we'll be headed onward toward Cassie, but who knows how long we will have to drive in that direction before we have a signal again? Not to mention what other messed-up things might lie in store.

"So?" Jasper asks, knowing the question is much, much bigger than it sounds. "Which way?"

Neither option feels right or good. Jasper stares at the steering wheel like he's considering. *We should go home,* that is what I think. Even if the police are waiting there for me. Even if they make me go to a hospital. Too much bad has already happened. We've gotten too lucky. We should call it quits while we're ahead, or at least, still alive.

I'm about to say that—let's go home—when Jasper pulls ahead and turns left. Onward and toward Cassie.

"Just until we get a signal," he says, like it's a thing we've agreed on. And I nod, even though I still feel like we should probably do the opposite. They are all bad choices now.

But going on toward Cassie and Seneca does mean we have to drive right past the diner. I hold my breath as we pull back onto Route 203 and I see that big sign for *Trinity's Diner* floating again way too high in the distance. I brace myself for police cars. Sink lower in the seat, out of sight. But there are no flashing lights like Doug had said, no police. Maybe it should be a relief. No police means they're not out looking for me.

But it is not a relief. Not at all.

"Do you see Lexi or Doug?" I ask.

"No, I don't think so." Jasper looks around some more. "I don't even see their car."

This too makes me feel worse. And I can tell from the way he says it that it doesn't make Jasper feel better either. Because if Lexi and Doug are not in that parking lot, they could be anywhere.

"Do you really think Doug was trying to keep us from getting to Cassie?" I ask, as we roll on past and I push myself back up in the seat.

"Yes," Jasper says without hesitating.

"And you really think it has something to do with a sex slavery ring?"

"No," he says, just as fast.

"Oh, then what do you think it does have to do with?"

Jasper keeps his eyes on the road. "I have no idea."

We're quiet as we drive on, like we're both trying to come up with some better, less frightening explanation for what has happened to Cassie and how it might connect to Lexi and Doug. But both of us are coming up empty.

"You know, I wanted to kill you back there when you yelled after that old guy," Jasper says finally. "Pretty crazy how you got him to give us the keys."

"Yeah, crazy," I say, because that is the operative word. "It takes one to know one, I guess."

"I don't know," Jasper says. "You had the right call with Lexi and Doug, too. If I'd noticed the empty car seat I might have been suspicious or whatever, but not enough to get out of the car. Imagine what would have happened if Doug had gotten us out in the middle of nowhere. I'm pretty sure I'd be dead right now. You're two for two."

"When you're freaked out by everything, you'll eventually be right about something," I say, but I feel aggravated. Does he actually think all I need is one pep talk from him and I'll be all sorted out?

"Maybe you should try to be more positive." Now Jasper is annoyed that I'm annoyed. Because I guess I'm supposed to be honored or something that he is trying to help me. "You'd probably be less stressed all the time."

My nostrils flare. And here I'd almost forgotten

completely why I didn't like him.

"Now, why didn't I think to tell you that when you were trying to rip the steering wheel off back at the gas station?" I say. "How about I'll learn to 'be more positive' when you learn a little anger management."

Jasper glances in my direction and, annoyingly, actually seems hurt. "Just trying to help."

"Yeah, well, I don't need your help," I say. "Cassie does."

I feel embarrassed as I look down at my phone. Why am I even getting into this? Do I actually care what Jasper thinks? I check for a signal as the diner fades into the distance behind us.

"Anything yet?" Jasper asks. His voice is different now, chilly. And maybe I'm even glad. We don't have to be friends, he and I.

"Do you think she's okay?" I ask. If he's going to be honest with me, now would be the time.

"Yes," he says, too quickly for me to believe.

"Why?"

"Because she has to be, right?" and when he looks at

me this time, his eyes are shiny in the dark.

"Yeah," I say, my own throat burning as I turn away from him toward the windows and the darkness beyond.

It isn't until that moment that I realize what I said to that crazy old man was true: I don't know what I'll do if I lose Cassie, too. How will I ever live without her and all her insane manic energy, making me see past my world of worry?

"So, did you ask your dad or what?" Cassie peered at me over the top of her Western Civilization textbook.

For the past hour, she'd been sitting in a beanbag chair in the corner of my room, pretending to study. But I could tell she was mostly texting behind her book. To Jasper, maybe. It was only the beginning of October and they weren't officially dating—yet. I was still hoping something might head it off at the pass. So mostly, I pretended that it—whatever it was—wasn't happening.

"Ask him about what?" I was playing dumb.

Partly because I just didn't want to deal and partly because I wasn't in the mood to be doing Cassie any favors. But I knew she was desperate to take my dad's test. Cassie had a glass slipper complex—forever hoping to discover she was a long-lost princess.

"Ask him about his *test*." Cassie rolled her eyes.

"He's going to say no," I said. "This week especially he's in a really bad mood. He had to fire that assistant guy he was obsessed with."

"I thought he loved that guy," Cassie said, because even she had been treated to one of my dad's endless speeches about how everyone in the world should try to be more like the insightful and dedicated Dr. Caton.

"Thin line between love and hate." I shrugged. "Why do you care so much about taking that stupid test anyway?"

"I feel like there has to be something more."

"To life?"

I watched Cassie's face sink. "To me."

And now I felt bad. I wasn't actually trying to hurt her feelings.

"You don't need some dumb test to prove that you matter," I said. "You matter to me."

"Yeah, thanks," she said with a wink. "But I still want

to take that test."

Fifteen minutes later, when my whole family was assembled around the dinner table, there Cassie went, asking my dad herself. She was tenacious. I had to give her that.

"Do you think Wylie and I could try your test after dinner, Dr. Lang? Just even like a little part of it?" Cassie asked. Her voice was intentionally high and squeaky like a little girl.

My dad frowned into his beet salad. "I don't think that—"

"Please, please, please," Cassie begged. And it kind of made me love her that she couldn't care less that my dad seemed so displeased. "Knowing our results could be super useful, you know, in school."

"In school?" Gideon asked, staring at Cassie as usual like he both loved and loathed her.

Cassie rolled her eyes at him like he was her brother, too. "Or fine, just for our own personal use. Or whatever."

I could tell from the look on my dad's face that there

was no way he was going to say yes.

"Yes, well, as much as I'd like—"

"Oh, let them, Ben," my mom said, swooping in with one of those smiles of hers. The kind that always made my dad cave. "They're the ones who haven't seen you for months. It will give them a chance to be a part of it, a part of you."

"A part of me?" My dad blinked at her like he had absolutely no idea what she was talking about. He really was becoming more and more like a robot every day.

"Yes, honey, share something of yourself with your kids." My mom was being playful now, but firm. "You know, connect with them. It might help them better understand why your work is so important to you."

"He's never going to say yes," Gideon said to Cassie. "I've already asked him a hundred times."

"Oh, come on. Life is short, Ben." My mom got up and wrapped her arms around my dad's neck, then leaned over to kiss his ear. "Let them have a sneak peek of this thing you love. It'll be fun. You used to have fun with them all the time, remember?"

We did used to have fun with him. He was always the best at making up puzzles or designing family treasure hunts whenever we were on a road trip, and once upon a time he would play Legos with us for hours. He was never the warm and fuzzy type like my mom, but he had his own things with us and I loved them, too. Until for some reason this particular study came along and devoured the part of him that had always belonged to us.

When my mom rested her forehead against his, his whole body softened.

"Okay, fine." He leaned back in his chair and tossed his napkin down. "I surrender. Let's do it."

"What?" I asked, feeling queasy. It had not occurred to me that he could possibly say yes. I was not at all into any kind of mental assessment. I already knew all I needed to about my monkey mind. "Seriously?"

"Yeah!" Cassie pumped her arms in the air.

"What do you mean, 'okay'?" Gideon looked like he'd just been slapped. "All Cassie has to do is ask and all of a sudden you say yes?"

"I am not saying yes to Cassie, Gideon. I am unable

to say no to your mother. Someday you will understand."
My dad stood from the table, seeming brighter than he
had in a long time. "Listen, I'll make it up to you—how
about you go first?"

Downstairs in the basement—my dad's home lab—
Gideon, Cassie, and I sat stiffly on my dad's bright-red
couch and watched him set up. It wasn't bad-looking
down there these days, not since my mom had insisted on
improvements: a shaggy cream carpet, some posters on
the walls, the bright Ikea sofa. With my dad spending so
many hours down there, she'd worried he'd get depressed.

"I'll hook you up to the electrodes to monitor your
heart rate, perspiration, and all that," he said. "We'll run
the test in pairs, two of you having a conversation, while
the third does the reading. That is the bulk of the study.
We'll keep the whole thing shorter than the actual study,
but we'll also do it with the blindfold and with the noise-
canceling headphones and then with both so you can get
a general sense of that part, too."

"A conversation about what?" Gideon asked, probably

nervous that his feelings for Cassie would somehow come out.

And I was a little nervous, too, for what would happen when my dad's test revealed somehow that I was extra insane?

"Don't worry, I'll give you the topics. They are meant to generate some emotion—so there's something for the reader to intuit. But nothing too personal." My dad pulled three chairs into a triangle formation. "Cassie and Wylie can have a conversation first, and Gideon will be the reader." He set about hooking Gideon up to all the wires—electrodes, a pulse monitor. And now he seemed like he was enjoying himself. "The equipment I have here isn't nearly as sophisticated as what I have at my lab on campus. The chairs there read the slightest shift in body temperature and muscle response. Because a piece of this is, of course, about someone reading not just how you *think* you're feeling, but how you *really* feel."

He moved over to hook me up to the same set of wires. But I was so tense already (because I am tense always), I wondered if it was possible I would short out the machines. I wanted to kill Cassie for getting me into this.

But when I looked over at her, she smiled and mouthed, "Thank you." And she had this look in her eyes that felt like love.

And I thought, for the first time in a long time, that maybe she and I would be okay. After all, didn't we have to be?

My phone vibrates in my hand, startling me. Cell coverage again, finally. Probably not for long. All the alerts I've missed come through in a blast. Four calls and one text from my dad. Three new texts from Cassie. My mouth feels dry looking down at all of them.

I read the texts from Cassie first. *Where are you guys?* And then, when I didn't respond, *Is everything okay? How much longer? I'm scared.* And then the last, just minutes ago: *Never mind what I said. Go to the police in Seneca. It's not safe anymore for anyone. I'm sorry I got u mixed up in this. But don't text my mom. Please. She will make it worse.*

I would have sworn all I wanted was for Cassie to

give us permission to make this emergency someone else's problem. But I hadn't counted on how much more worried it would make me once she finally did.

"Cassie says we can go to the police in Seneca." I type the town name quickly into Google Maps, hoping to get some directions or at least how far it is before we lose the signal again. I feel a surge of relief when the pin drops in the center of Seneca. "It's not far, ten more minutes on this road, then Route 4 for thirty miles, then Route 151 for another ten."

"Is she okay?" Jasper asks.

"She didn't say. But she was still texting as of a half hour ago. That's a good sign."

"But her sending us to the police isn't," Jasper says. "Is it?"

I don't answer. Because he's right, of course. Something has gotten worse, bad enough that Cassie doesn't even care about a criminal record. *If* that's even why she said no to the police in the first place.

We're coming, Cassie, I write back. *Just hold on.*

I hit send quickly before the signal is lost again to the

wilderness, then look down at the little number 4 next to my voice mails, all my dad. But I can't bear to hear the sound of his voice. Especially because I'm betting he didn't call to apologize. At least all the calls are from our home number, which means he hasn't come looking for me yet. And his last text came after the calls anyway. That's the very last thing he had to say to me, the only thing I need to read, just in case.

Ironically, it's from his cell number and not *Dad* in my contacts, probably the spotty cell signal. Or like after threatening to have me committed, even my cell phone has turned its back on him. I take a deep breath as I tap open the message.

The police are out looking for you. Dr. Shepard called them. You left us no choice. They will commit you when they find you. After what happened in the diner, I won't be able to stop them. Unless I can get to you first. Tell me where you are, Wylie. And I'll come. We can figure a way out of this together.

CHAPTER 14

Jasper asks me twice on the way to Seneca whether everything is okay. But I'm too ashamed to get into details. To tell him that my dad thinks I should be committed. Though he does have a right to know that somehow my dad already knows about what happened in the diner, which means they've identified me. Maybe identified Jasper, too. We could already be fugitives.

"It's just my dad being my dad," I say, and I silently promise to tell Jasper the rest before we get to the police station. "He's still being a jerk about me leaving."

"You can vent about it if you want. I know about shitty parents, believe me."

"Thanks," I say. "But I'd rather just pretend it didn't happen."

Jasper nods, looks kind of sad. "I get that, too."

When Jasper and I finally pull into Seneca, it's picture-perfect quaint. All the buildings in the little downtown are white with matching green shutters, set out just so around a small town square. There's even a neatly trimmed lawn with a white pagoda in the middle, for concerts, maybe. There's a darkened church with a spiky steeple, too, and a row of shops with their names etched in matching arcs on their front windows. It's past eleven p.m. now, so everything's closed, except for a bar attached to the Fiddler's Inn. A small wooden sign hanging out front says *The Pub*. The only other place lit up is part of what looks like it could be the city hall or something. It's the largest building around, marked off by three flags out front: US, State of Maine, and a third, which might just be about bears.

"Maybe that's the police station," I say, pointing.

I am relieved that we might be getting Cassie real help soon. But it's a risk for me to go inside. After all, I am the crazy girl who stabbed a man in a diner bathroom. The girl whose therapist has already reported her as a danger to herself or others.

"What are we going to tell them?" Jasper asks as he pulls into a parking spot alongside the square, a little distance from the station. Like he's still thinking we can guard Cassie's secrets somehow.

"Everything," I say. But I can't not warn Jasper about the rest because I'm ashamed. Not when it could affect him, too. "But there is something else. They already know about the diner. The knife. Doug."

"Who knows?" Jasper asks. "How?"

"I'm not sure, but my dad mentioned it in his text. I guess the police must have made the connection. He sent them out looking for me because I'm 'unstable.'" And maybe I can just leave it at that. "Anyway, you might get caught up in this—my—you might not want to come in. Just in case these police know about it too. I could tell them about Cassie on my own if you want."

"Unstable?" Jasper looks totally confused. Almost offended, as he turns off the car. "Yeah, I'll take my chances. You weren't in that diner alone."

The police station is brightly lit, but so small—just six metal desks in a single open room. There are three men sitting there, playing cards, when we walk in. Two look on the younger side, maybe late twenties. One is older than my dad, fifties maybe. They turn in our direction when we walk in, not startled or surprised. But also not particularly interested even though you'd think they would be—two teenage kids, walking in at eleven at night.

"We help you?" the older one calls, though he makes no move to get up from his card game. He has salt-and-pepper hair and looks puffy, like a football player whose muscles have gone soft. He makes a big show of squinting up at the clock on the wall. "You lost?"

There's an edge to his voice, too. Like he wants us to *get* lost.

"No—um—we're not lost," I say as Jasper and I make our way up to the counter. I sound nervous and guilty.

I swallow hard, hoping my throat will clear. "We're here, um, looking for our friend?" Like it's a question.

"Missing friend, huh?" says the younger officer who's facing us. He has beady eyes and a pockmarked face, and now that he's talking, I can see that he's *really* young—not that much older than Jasper and me. There's the hint of a smile playing on his lips. "You lose her somewhere?"

This time he smiles wider, like a wolf. I wait for the older guy to shoot him a look telling him to knock it off. But the only one who does anything is the third officer, and he just begins collecting the cards. He hasn't even looked in our direction.

"She texted us and said that she needs our help," Jasper says. "We drove all the way up from Boston."

He adds that part, I think, to make us seem like good, dedicated kids. Loyal. To help make up for the mess that Cassie is in.

The older cop finally heaves himself out of his chair with a grunt, looking officially annoyed as he makes his way over. For sure not concerned about what happened to this friend of ours. Like he's already decided that nothing has. Once he's close, I see his badge: Sergeant Randolph Sternbach. When I look up from it, he's staring at me. Or my hair, to be exact. His eyebrows are scrunched together. His frown is disgusted.

"Let me guess, your friend came up here to party?" he asks, still staring at my hair, and making no attempt to pretend otherwise. I put a hand up like that could hide how crazily hacked it is.

"Party?" I ask. It comes out in a squeak. Already I do not like where this is headed.

The sergeant takes an exasperated breath and looks away from my hair to reach for a pad of paper. He slaps it down on the counter in front of us. "Yeah, you know, meth." His eyes narrow on my face. "And I know, she's never done it before in her entire life and she'll never ever do it again."

He even rolls his eyes a little. *Blah, blah, blah.* He doesn't actually say that, but it's what he means. All I can do is stare at him. It's not very policeman-like.

"Meth?" Jasper asks like he must be hearing things.

"You know, chalk, dust, ice, crank, glass," the pockmarked, weaselly one says, slithering his way over to stand next to his boss. Unlike the sergeant, he seems happy to be talking about it. Excited almost. Like he's taunting us.

"You're kidding, right?" Jasper asks. "We're in high school. We don't shoot up."

I turn to look at him. The way Jasper says "shoot up" sounds so awkward, *too* awkward. Like he's playing up how little he knows about it.

"Lots of ways to take meth, son. Most of them don't require a needle," the sergeant says, and like he's damn sure Jasper already knows that. "And you'd be surprised what 'regular people' do. Trust me, you're not the first to come in here looking for a missing friend. We got a whole damn cottage industry in screwed-up kids making a mess of what used to be—what ought to be—a nice town."

"Pigs is what they are," the weaselly guy says, but with this glint in his eye like it also turns him on a little. "Look at those tweakers from the other day."

"Mmm," the sergeant says without looking at the other officer. Like he doesn't necessarily approve of where this conversation is going, but doesn't disapprove enough to stop it.

"One of them stuck a damn fork right in another one's *eye*." The weasel points two fingers toward his own eye, then jabs them at Jasper's and mine. "Some damn argument about Peeps. You know, those stupid little bunnies? Fork in the eye for a freaking marshmallow. EMTs said the guy was so high he didn't even know there was a fork sticking out of his face." He laughs, full on. Like this is hilarious. "Guy kept on talking the whole time."

The sergeant finally glares at him. "You got somewhere to be, Officer O'Connell?"

"Not really," the weasel says, eyes still on us. "Not unless I can go back to kicking your ass at Bullshit."

"Then go pretend," the sergeant says.

"Okay, boss man." Officer O'Connell holds up his hands and grins some more. And I wonder if he could be high himself. He's having an awful lot of fun. With his hands still raised, he whistles low and long, spinning on a heel and heading for a door at the back of the station. He pauses before he reaches it, grabs a piece of paper off a desk nearby. He crinkles it into a ball before winging it at the head of the other officer, the one who still has his back turned to us.

"Two points!" Officer O'Connell calls.

The paper ball bounces off the other officer's head. But he easily catches it in midair and tosses it into the garbage can at his feet. Like it's something he's done, and that's been done to him, a thousand times before.

The sergeant exhales, loud and annoyed. "You got to excuse Officer O'Connell. He's, well, him." He shakes his head, like that's all the explanation we should need. "But he's not making up the bit about the fork. You may not want to hear this, but if your friend is here, meth is almost surely the reason. Doesn't even mean she's not a nice kid. That garbage has ruined a lot of decent folks."

Meth. This time the word sinks into me. I knew about the drinking, and Cassie being arrested for buying pot isn't even that much of a shocker. But meth? It's like comparing a fender bender to an eighteen-car pileup. But it also doesn't feel totally impossible either. Not nearly as impossible as I wish it did. It would definitely explain her not wanting to tell us what was going on. Would explain someone like Doug wanting to keep us away from whatever crack den they have her in. And meth sure would have kept Cassie skinny.

"It could be meth, I guess," I say quietly.

"What?" Jasper whips in my direction, eyes wide. "Cassie doesn't do *meth*. What's wrong with you?"

"I'm not saying that *is* what's going on. But I can't swear it's not. Can you?"

And in that moment, all I want is for Jasper to say that he does know for sure it's not meth. That he has proof. But instead, he closes his eyes and shakes his head, rests a fist down on the counter.

"I can't say anything for sure anymore," he says quietly.

I look back to the sergeant. The other younger police officer—the one the weasel beaned in the head—has finally gotten up and is making his way over. He's surprisingly good-looking, with thick black hair and deep-set brown eyes. But there's something a little wounded about him. Strange for someone so good-looking and tall. Weird for a policeman.

"This is Officer Kendall," the sergeant says. "He spends a lot of his time cleaning out the users, combing through the mess they leave behind." It's kind of insulting the way the sergeant says it, like Officer Kendall is literally on garbage duty. "Your friend say where she was? There's spots we can check, but there's a lot of them. It would save time to have a place to start."

"Camp Colestah?" I say.

The sergeant glances over at Officer Kendall, who still has not spoken. The two nod knowingly to each other. "Colestah's a popular spot," the sergeant goes on. "Shelter, privacy—what more could a junkie want? They are like rats. We chase 'em off and they keep coming back and coming back. But you and O'Connell did a pass-through earlier today, didn't you? It was clear?"

Officer Kendall frowns and nods, glances back the way O'Connell has gone. *Yeah, but with him, who knows,* the look says.

"Might be worth a second look," the sergeant goes on. "Most of the other camps are pretty well secured. They learned fast, hired people to live on site in the off-season.

Caretaker kind of thing. But the Wynns, who own Camp Colestah, have been gone so long—I warned their lawyer the place will be destroyed soon. They'll never sell it." The sergeant checks his watch. "I've got to head out. But Officer Kendall here will take another ride up there, check for your friend."

But there is still something off about the way he says it to Officer Kendall. Like there's a *you know what to do* under his actual words. Rats or not, why are the meth addicts so sure that Seneca is such a safe place to set up shop? Is somebody—like maybe the meth *dealers*— paying the police to look the other way?

I watch Officer Kendall head back to his desk for his keys. And I'm already thinking about how I'm going to feel afterward, once he reports back that there's nothing up at Camp Colestah. I'm not going to believe he even looked. I don't trust these police officers, period.

"We want to come look for her," I say, my heart racing.

But the sergeant is already shaking his head. "There's no way in hell that—"

"Please." I sound desperate and a little crazy, but what does it matter? "We won't get in the way. We'll do whatever you say and—"

"Absolutely no way, nohow." The sergeant eyes me firmly. "Listen, you seem like decent enough kids. I can see you're real worried about your friend, but we can't take civilians out into the field. Much less a couple kids."

He has common sense on his side. The police don't usually let regular people tag along. Even I know that much. I'm going to need a better argument.

"If there are a bunch of people there, how will you know if she's one of them?"

The sergeant's jaw tightens. He's pissed, maybe because he doesn't have an easy answer for that. Makes me wonder even more whether it's that he doesn't think Cassie's up there or is just invested in not finding out.

"You got a picture of her on your phone?"

"No, we don't," I say, probably too quickly. "We can stay in the car when we get there. We'll do whatever—"

The sergeant holds up a hand, silencing me. "I'd quit while you're ahead, kid." The *don't test me* look on his face is pretty convincing. And if I push too hard, he might demand to see my identification. Might do some kind of search and learn all about what happened in the diner or about the police Dr. Shepard has sent after me. "If there's anybody up there, we'll be bringing them all in for trespassing, at a minimum. Then you can see for yourself whether one of them is your friend." He nods like that's the end of that. Though I can't really see how Officer Kendall is going to bring in a bunch of people in his one car. Probably because the sergeant has already told him not to. "Now, about three miles past town there's a Dunkin' Donuts at a Hess station. It's one of the few places with decent cell coverage. I'm sure Officer Kendall wouldn't mind giving you a call after he's checked out the camp."

The sergeant looks to Officer Kendall for confirmation. Kendall frowns some more, then nods.

"Come on," I hear Jasper say. "Let's go get a doughnut."

"I don't want a doughnut," I say through gritted teeth.

He puts a firm hand on my shoulder. "Yeah, you do."

***

Outside, it feels much colder as we make our way down the steps. And I feel so much worse than before we went into the police station. It's knowing that there's nothing to do now but wait that's getting to me the most. Wait for news on Cassie, wait to see if the Seneca police realize who I am, wait to see if everything is going to be okay. I look over at Jasper as we finally reach the old man's truck. He's swinging the keys in his hand, shoulders loose, looking more relaxed than I've ever seen him.

"What are you so happy about?" I snap.

"Happy?" He looks confused as he heads over to the driver's side. "What are you talking about?"

Good question. What *am* I talking about? And why do I even care if Jasper is feeling better? I don't know why I care. But I do, and it is seriously pissing me off.

"You were awfully quiet back there," I say to him over the back of the truck.

Jasper raises an eyebrow. "What was I supposed to say?"

"Something, *anything*," I say. "It was kind of like you were on their side." That isn't true or wasn't true, at least not until the very end, when I did feel like Jasper was too quick to leave just because they told us to.

"On *their* side?" he asks, and still with the wounded face.

"Even now, all you're doing is repeating what *I'm* saying!" I shout, and so loud that my words echo in the quiet. "Do you ever have an original thought about anything?"

Jasper's jaw tenses as he looks away from me and over the dark center of town. Mission accomplished: he's mad now, but trying to keep his temper in check. "I didn't say anything because you seemed like you knew what you were doing and I didn't want to get in your way. Until the end, when you started losing it and I thought you were going to screw yourself, and us. So excuse the hell out of me for trying to have some respect. If that makes me a dick—whatever, fine," Jasper says, yanking open the truck door. "And I'm not happy, trust me. But do I feel better now? Hell, yes. Going to the police feels like the first good decision we've made."

"Yeah, well, I feel worse."

"Maybe that's because you are so insanely pessimistic," he says, and not in a nice way. "You always feel bad."

I roll my eyes. "Is that supposed to make me feel better?"

"No," he says, glaring at me.

Before I can respond, I see something catch Jasper's eye behind me. When I turn, Officer Kendall is headed our way. He looks left and right like he's checking that the coast is clear. Did they get word about me? Is he here to hold me until someone comes?

"M-m-meet m-m-me around back," he says when he reaches us. "At the c-c-corner."

It's a bad stutter. Maybe why he didn't say much inside? But a stutter for sure doesn't mean he can't arrest me.

"Why?" I ask, trying to sound casual. (I do not. Not in the least.)

"You c-c-can ride along," he says. "I had a g-g-good friend who OD'd. I g-g-get it. J-j-just d-d-don't t-t-tell my boss."

CHAPTER 15

I've never ridden in the back of a police car, but I'm guessing this one is way nicer than most. It's a brand-new Ford Explorer with smooth leather seats. It even has that new-car smell, which unfortunately reminds me of Doug and Lexi's car. The meth problem might be ruining Seneca, but it's sure not ruining their police cars. More proof maybe that they're not doing a whole lot of actual fighting in this drug war.

We're quiet most of the fifteen-minute drive up to Camp Colestah. Jasper looks over at me a couple of times like he's searching for a sign I want him to speak up, which is, of course, my fault. Eventually, he even motions toward Officer Kendall, then himself: *you want me to say something?* Just in case I didn't know what he meant. All our quiet mouthing of words makes Officer Kendall glance in the rearview. I shake my head and turn toward the window in silence.

The farther we go, the darker it gets and the stiffer my lungs become. But I feel a tiny bit better when we finally turn onto a dirt-and-gravel driveway. Soon, at least, we'll know something.

"Th-th-this is it," Officer Kendall says as we pass disintegrating stone columns and a lopsided wood sign, the words *Camp Colestah* barely visible. "Once upon a t-t-time it w-w-was a real nice place. R-r-rich kids from Boston."

"Why did it close?" I ask. Already, I can feel something terrible has happened there. I'm hoping maybe it was a long time ago.

"Owners' s-s-son drowned in the p-p-pool," he says. "Got c-c-caught on the d-d-drain in the d-d-deep end. I knew him. G-g-good kid. Parents c-c-closed up and moved out west after."

The gravel crunches under our tires as we roll on, our headlights flashing across the tall, bare trees as the ragged driveway curves right and then back to the left. We go a couple of hundred more feet before Officer Kendall finally stops.

"S-s-stay here," he says as he puts the car in park, then motions to the dark woods. "G-g-got to sweep each b-b-building as we go. Clear it. Oldest c-c-cabins are d-d-down here. Those are th-th-the ones they like."

I would have thought I'd demand to go along with Officer Kendall, but I'm more than happy to stay safely in the car. Evidently, Jasper isn't as put off by how creepy the place is.

"You sure you don't want us to—"

"S-s-s-stay here," Officer Kendall shoots back with a lot more force the second time. "B-b-be g-g-glad I let you c-c-come."

We sit in silence, watching from the backseat as Officer Kendall's flashlight bounces through the trees, down a slope, then up again. Once my eyes adjust to the darkness,

I can make out where he's headed, four small cabins up on the hill. Officer Kendall—or his flashlight at least—seems headed first to the one on the far right.

"Well, this sucks ass," Jasper says as Officer Kendall's flashlight disappears inside the first cabin. It's the first really negative thing he's said.

"I thought you were all about optimism," I say, and it is a dig for calling me pessimistic before. Even though I know there are much worse things he could have called me. "What happened to your glass half-full?"

"Maybe you drank it." Jasper smiles a little when he turns to me. But it fades once he reaches forward and tries the door. It doesn't open. "We're locked in here, you know."

"It *is* a police car," I say, like that was already obvious to me. It wasn't, and I definitely wish Jasper hadn't mentioned it. Because now all I can think about is what will become of us if something happens to Officer Kendall out there? What if whoever is responsible comes after us, trapped there in the middle of nowhere?

My heart beats harder as I watch Officer Kendall's flashlight bounce around the inside of the second small cabin. When the light shines through the front window, I see something hanging out in front of the window. Screens, maybe? We're too far away to be sure, but that's what it looks like. Like someone tore them up trying to escape. I don't realize how tight I've been holding my body until Officer Kendall has finished searching the last two cabins and his flashlight is finally bouncing back our way.

"We shouldn't have come here," I say before he reaches the car.

"What do you mean?" Jasper asks. "Here where? The camp?"

"I don't know." And that is the truth. I don't know what I mean. But there is no doubt that is exactly the way I feel.

"Hey." Jasper reaches over and gives my hand a quick squeeze. But long enough for me to notice just how stiff and cold my own fingers are. "It's going to be okay. She's going to be okay."

"You don't know that," I say.

"Maybe not," Jasper says. "But that's not going to stop me from believing it."

"N-n-nothing," Officer Kendall says when he finally opens the door and slides into the driver's seat. "Except s-s-s-ome g-g-garbage, wrappers, b-b-beer cans."

"That means someone's been here," I say.

"S-s-someone's always b-b-been here," he says. "They use it, m-m-move on."

We go on like that cabin after cabin. Roll forward, stop. Roll forward, stop. Officer Kendall gets out. Officer Kendall checks the building. Officer Kendall comes back. Shakes his head: *nothing*. Roll forward, stop. Roll forward, stop. All he reports are different kinds of garbage: candy wrappers in some, empty beer cans and cigarette butts in others. One had a huge pile of unraveled Saran wrap, which Officer Kendall can't explain. I don't want him to try.

As we move farther up the driveway, the cabins seem in worse shape; some are too broken down for him to even go inside, one not much more than a pile of boards. Officer Kendall shines his flashlight on even that, like maybe Cassie could be buried somewhere underneath. At least he seems competent, thorough. But it does make me think that I should have called Karen from town. Should have told her what we knew, the name of the town at least. I didn't because Cassie had specifically asked us not to tell her mom, and that was even after she let us go to the police. But the truth is I also didn't call Karen from Seneca because I didn't want to end up talking to my dad. Now that he's tried to get me committed—something I still can't fully believe—I'm not sure I'll ever talk to him again. It's too late now to change my mind anyway. Back here, so deep in the woods, my cell signal is already long gone.

Finally, we pull to where the driveway dead-ends at the top of another hill in a circular parking area. There are three slightly larger cabins and a fourth much larger building, the size of two or three cabins combined. They are all pitch black, like the others, but easier to make out in the brighter clearing. From a distance, they look in much better condition, too.

"These are th-th-the main b-b-buildings," Officer Kendall says. "But p-p-people usually stay down at the others—easier to g-g-get in. G-g-g-get out."

I hear Jasper exhale hard. He shakes his head and turns back to me. "This isn't looking good."

He's right. What will we do when Officer Kendall doesn't find Cassie in any of these buildings either? I don't have an answer for that. I look over at the buildings again. I'm not high on meth, but if I was going to go anywhere at that camp it would be there, the buildings that aren't totally falling apart. This isn't over until we've checked every last place. There's still a chance that Cassie's there.

"I'll s-s-still check," Officer Kendall says. "Th-th-there are the other c-c-camps, t-t-too. We'll head there next. Maybe she g-g-got the n-n-name wrong." He is being kind, staying hopeful. And I'm glad because someone needs to keep looking at the bright side now that Jasper can't bring himself to.

Officer Kendall parks facing the open lawn between the buildings. It's actually legitimately bright with the moon nearly full in the open patch of sky. He leaves the headlights on, too, this time, passing through the two beams of light on his way to check the first building. Lit up gold, Officer Kendall looks even more handsome and genuinely brave. And I try to see that as an encouraging sign until he pauses suddenly in the middle of the lawn to look down at something. His hand moves to his gun.

"What's he looking at?" I ask, narrowing my eyes. But it's impossible to see from where we're parked.

"I don't know." Jasper presses his face in close to the wire cage locking us out of the front seat. Whatever it is, Officer Kendall kicks at it with his foot. "It's a pile of something, maybe logs—wait, is that smoke?"

"Where?" My heart is beating hard as I squint harder. And then I see it, when Officer Kendall kicks again— smoke curling up toward the sky.

"Holy shit," Jasper says. "There is somebody here."

"Or *was*. *Was* somebody here," I say, trying not to let myself feel too relieved. Or too worried. Because the thought of someone really being at that camp fills me with so much hope and even more dread. I pull in a mouthful of air, but already I feel light-headed.

A second later Officer Kendall is back, leaning in to grab his radio.

"Three-zero-six requesting b-b-backup," he says. "Camp Colestah. Possible 207." There's no response. Maybe there never is, or maybe that means the sergeant and Officer O'Connell have closed up for the night. I feel like they might do that in a place like Seneca, close the police station. And what's a 207? I'm too afraid to ask. Officer Kendall looks back at us. "I expect whoever was here is already g-g-gone. But I'm g-g-going to s-s-sweep the b-b-buildings just t-t-to be sure."

It's much worse being locked in the back of the car when Officer Kendall leaves this time. At least, it doesn't take long for him to get through the first building and then the next, but the last of the small cabins he's inside for a while. We can see his flashlight through the window, moving this way and that like he's teasing a cat.

A minute later he's coming back in our direction. But this time, he's moving fast. He's found something. And it isn't good.

"I'm g-g-going to need the two of you to c-c-come with

me," Officer Kendall says when he opens my door. And all I want to do is slam it shut again. "There's s-s-something I need to see if you can identify."

Cassie's body? That's all I can think. "Identify what?"

"Just some c-c-clothing and a b-b-bag. New and expensive, not like an addict would have. I need to know if they belong to your f-f-friend. I'd bring them here, but I d-d-don't want to disturb the scene, in case—" He doesn't finish the thought. In case something horrible has happened to Cassie, that's what he means. What's inside could be evidence of a crime. Officer Kendall looks down the driveway and around the edges of the woods, like he's considering. "Would p-p-prefer to wait for b-b-backup, but they could be a while."

But we might not have that kind of time. *Cassie* might not.

The air is full-on bitter when we get out of the car. The cold burns my lungs, and a white cloud of steam gathers around my face as I exhale. Officer Kendall starts forward quickly across the grass, waving silently for us to follow.

He swivels his head right and left, watching for danger, checking the perimeter as we make our way toward the cabin to the far right. As we pass the other cabins, I can see the screens aren't peeled back and the doors look solidly on their hinges. But it's making me feel worse, not better. Of course, up here at these cabins is where you'd go to hide something or someone. I clench my fists like the pain of my fingernails digging into my palms is going to release some of the pressure in my gut. But what I really need to do is breathe. I know that. For real, I have to. If only that wasn't so much easier said than done.

"I'm scared," I whisper to Jasper.

"Me too," he says.

"L-l-let's pick up the p-p-pace," Officer Kendall says once we're in the middle of the lawn. Like it's a threat, us being out in the open. "Your f-f-friend didn't tell you anything about these people she was with? No details at all?"

He's *really* listening for our answer now. He wasn't before, that's obvious now. They had written Cassie off as just another junkie. Maybe even the kind they had agreed to turn a blind eye to.

"Just that she got herself into something and that her mom would be mad," Jasper says, doing his own nervous survey of the perimeter. "Then all of a sudden she said she was scared that they were going to hurt her."

Which means, of course, that she had her phone. I've known that the whole time but haven't really thought about it until now. Why would they have let her keep her phone? Maybe she really did come up here to "party" like that sergeant said. And it got out of hand.

"Stay to the left inside," Officer Kendall says when we finally reach the steps up to the cabin door. "There's a big hole in the floor to the right. And there's boxes, furniture everywhere. Flashlight will only do so much."

As we start up behind him, I feel more light-headed. I grab the handrail to steady myself. *Breathe.* Something new feels wrong, though. Something more than everything that is already so very bad—Lexi and Doug, the men chasing us through the woods, Cassie's things maybe being on the floor of some meth den. It's like I've left something crucial behind—my backpack, my phone, a piece of my body—and haven't fully realized it yet. *Breathe, in and out to a count of four.* Officer Kendall stands to the right, holding the door open for us, his flashlight pointing us left.

I'm trembling as I step inside, glimpse the outline of a desk along the wall, a filing cabinet in the corner. The camp office, probably. It smells dusty and a little mildewed but not terrible. Not like death. And that seems important. But there is still that other something in the air, something that feels extra off. Something I can't quite put my finger on.

"It's right there on the floor, under the window," Officer Kendall says, drawing a circle on the floor some distance ahead with the beam of his flashlight.

My heart catches when I finally see it: Cassie's floppy hobo bag. The one she always carries. There's her sweatshirt, too, right there on the floor—the red Boston one with the hole in the right sleeve. I rush toward it because if it doesn't have that hole, then it won't be hers after all. And that bag, they are pretty popular these days. It could be anyone's.

"Don't touch anything!" Officer Kendall shouts after me.

And so I fold my hands against myself as I crouch down next to the sweatshirt. Sure enough, there is that stupid hole. It is her sweatshirt. Cassie was here in this cabin and now she's gone. Someone took her. Made her leave her things behind. Because Cassie loved that sweatshirt and she paid for that bag herself—almost a hundred dollars she'd made scooping a lot of ice cream at Holy Cow. Something else catches my eye then, a couple of inches to the side: pink camouflage. I look closer, and sure enough they are boy-style briefs that say *Sleep with Me* across the butt. Cassie's underwear.

I push myself to my feet. Too fast. Way too fast. Fireworks of little lights cascade in front of my eyes. Head rush. But that's okay. Just a little low blood pressure. The edges of the room aren't actually stretching thin. The tingle in my hands is all in my head.

"Do you recognize any of it?" Officer Kendall asks. Not a hiccup, not a twitch. Not a stutter. Officer Kendall's speech is totally even. It's been even, actually. For how long? He was stuttering before in the car, definitely. And when we first stopped here at these buildings, wasn't he?

But for sure he's not stuttering now. That's what was off. That was what was left behind.

I look up from Cassie's underwear to Jasper's reflection in the window. *No stutter*, I think, but am too afraid to say. *We are not safe.* My heart is beating in my ears. The sound is echoey, like we're underwater. And now the room is so narrow and dark, like I'm staring down a paper towel tube.

There's a sound then. Loud. Near the door. A crash? Is that it? Then darkness to my left and then a burning and a tilt and then—

CHAPTER 16

"Wylie? Are you okay?" A voice. I don't know whose.

I try to open my eyes but they are sealed shut. My mouth is, too. Is my jaw broken? No, it's just the insides of my mouth pasted together. Water. I need water. But when I move, pain slices through the side of my head. Squinting my eyes open makes it even worse.

It's dark still. Nighttime, but not pitch black. Pale-gray light comes from the window. Moonlight, maybe. Scratchy fabric under my hands. I'm lying on a couch—dusty, mildewed, lumpy. The cabin, Camp Colestah, Cassie—it all snaps back to me. Her underwear here. Her somewhere else.

"You blacked out." It's Jasper. When I push myself up on my elbow, my head sings. Jasper is sitting on the floor a couple of feet away, back against the wall. He's staring at me. Worried. No, worse than worried. He looks scared. "You hit your head on the side of the bureau." He points to a big piece of furniture not far from the door. "I tried to grab you, but I didn't make it in time. Are you okay?"

"I pass out sometimes when I get really stressed," I say, trying to make it sound like no big deal. "It hasn't happened in a while. Sorry, didn't mean to freak you out."

"Oh." He glances down, away. "I don't think you cut your head or anything." He points to his own scalp. "I, um, checked. But there's a big bump."

My cheeks feel hot thinking of Jasper lifting me onto the couch, his hands inspecting my head. It's humiliating. And, yes, also sweet.

"Okay, thanks," I say, wincing through the throbbing in my head as I roll up to sitting. "Wait, where's the—" I look around. I can't remember his name. I wonder for a minute how bad I hurt my head. "The police guy."

"I don't know," Jasper says quietly. In the pale light,

I see him turn toward the door. "As I was running to you, there was this loud sound behind us. And then the door slammed shut. I guess someone could have maybe grabbed him or—"

"Grabbed him?" The pain in my head is worse with each word. "He's a police officer." Like that alone means nothing bad could ever happen to him. Then I remember Officer Kendall's stutter, how it vanished. I think about telling Jasper this, but I'm afraid saying it aloud will wind me up again. And maybe it was the rush of adrenaline that smoothed out his voice. Officer Kendall could be like me: better in an actual emergency. Except that seems the opposite of likely.

"Maybe they're so high they didn't even realize he was a cop?" Jasper offers, but not like he believes that. Frightening, too, that this is our best option: people so high they can't see straight.

"I think maybe the stuttering was an act," I say. "Did you notice? He stopped right before we came into the cabin."

"Are you sure?" Jasper asks, and like he actually thinks

maybe I imagined it. I wonder if this is how it is going to be now that I've told him about my dad's call to the police. Will Jasper doubt everything I say? "Why would he do that?"

"I have no idea."

He's still looking at me like he's not buying it. "I think we've got a bigger problem at the moment anyway."

"What?" I swallow over the lump trapped in my throat.

"The door is locked."

"Locked?"

I push myself to my feet and lurch for the door. *No, no, no.* We cannot be locked in this dark and terrible place. The knob does turn a little bit, and for a second I think I'm about to prove Jasper wrong. But the door sticks hard when I push, like there's a bolt across the outside. *Bam, bam, bam,* goes my heart as I head over to the window next to where Jasper is still sitting on the floor. Panes of clear glass fill the window frame. I think of all the peeled-back screens in those other cabins as I put my hand flat against the cool glass. Not even cracked or dusty. Actually, the window looks brand-new.

Jasper looks up at me. My hand is still on the glass, his face half-sunk in shadow. I push up on the window, but it doesn't budge. "That one's locked," Jasper says as he gets up to head to the other window on the opposite side of the room. It won't move either when he tries to open it. Neither do the two in back. He peers closer to the last one. "I think they're nailed shut from the outside."

"Then we should break one," I say, as Jasper comes back to stand next to me.

And this does seem like something the emergency-me could actually do. Shatter glass, scramble through broken shards. Run again through the dark and tangled woods.

But Jasper is already shaking his head. "Look."

What I mistook for one of the thin, easily-torn screens on the other side of the window, I can see now, is actually much thicker wire. Like a chain-link fence. We are not just trapped in a cabin. We are locked in a cage.

"What the hell is this?" I whisper.

Jasper takes a deep breath, like he's steeling himself. "Okay, there has got to be another way out," he says, not answering my question. Maybe he is trying to think positive again. And I hope so because every single thought I have is dark and terrible and ends in doom. Our doom.

Jasper heads to the back of the cabin, poking his head into what looks like a closet. When he reaches overhead and pulls a string, a single bulb goes on. It leaves a slanted gold rectangle on the floor around his feet, brightening the cabin a tiny bit. I feel relieved, but only for a second.

"There's electricity?" I ask. Should that make me feel better? Because it does not. "I thought this place was abandoned."

"Yeah, that's for sure weird." Jasper waves me over to the closet. "But not as weird as this."

When I get over to him, I can see what he means. There's a bucket on the floor of the closet with a roll of toilet paper next to it. There's even some hand sanitizer. A makeshift bathroom.

"They knew we were coming," I say.

"Or they knew somebody was," Jasper says, walking back to the front window. I stare at him, but he doesn't look back at me.

"Who are these people?" I ask, though I already know Jasper doesn't have a clue.

"Probably not the same ones who stab each other in the eye over marshmallow Peeps." He turns to look at me when I come to join him at the window. "Right?"

Of course he's right. It's way too organized and well thought out.

"Wait, is that a person over there?" Jasper points to the cabin across the way, but all I can make out are shadows. "I just saw something move."

I lean in and squint but still can't see anything. Instead, something in the opposite direction catches my eye.

"Look," I say, feeling a tiny surge of hope. "The police car is still here."

"Yeah, but someone turned the headlights off," Jasper says, and from his voice I can tell he doesn't think there's anything good about that. We both stare at it for a moment in silence. "Do you really think that Cassie might be doing meth?" he asks, eyes still on Officer Kendall's car. "That meth is what all of this is about?"

"I have no idea." I turn around and slide down the wall until I have taken Jasper's spot on the cold and dirty floor. "Cassie's done a lot of things lately that I never thought she would." I feel annoyed at Jasper all over again. Because the Rainbow Coalition might have been the reason Cassie got started partying. But Jasper was why she kept at it. "I mean, all those parties she went to—maybe she did try meth. Well, you would know. You were with her."

"Wait, you think there was meth at a party *I* was at?" he asks, then shakes his head, disgusted. "You seriously think I was the reason Cassie was doing drugs, don't you?"

"I didn't say it was your fault." I roll my eyes. It is more than a little ridiculous how innocent he's acting. "I'm saying maybe you could handle it better than she could, that's all."

"And by 'it' you mean drugs?" Jasper doesn't wait for me to answer. "Listen, I know you think you know everything about me. That you know everything about everything. But I don't even drink. I never have. No drugs either. And I mean never tried them," he snaps. "My dad was high as shit when he beat the crap out of that guy. Almost killed him. And yeah, he did it. Wasn't the first time, either. Just the first time he hurt someone so bad he ended up in jail because of it. And yeah, I lied about it to Lexi and Doug, because sometimes people don't think the apple falls far from the tree." He eyes me then like he knows I'm one of those apple people. "And sometimes I even worry they're right. So I'm careful. Like staying away from drugs, for one. I've never gotten high and I never will get high. And I never personally saw Cassie get high. She knew how I felt and so she didn't do it around me. But yeah, I knew she smoked pot and I hated it."

"Okay," I say, holding up my hands. "Fine, sorry."

I do feel like a jerk. Because maybe I am one of those apple people. And Jasper's right, it is a terrible way to think.

"But she was acting weird recently." Jasper crosses his arms, eyes still on the window. "Like I said before, I thought she was cheating on me. But maybe she was hiding some kind of drug thing. Meth even. Shit, I don't know. She definitely wouldn't have told me. She would have known I wouldn't be okay with it. But whatever, if you think I'm lying, there's nothing I can do about that."

"I don't," I say. "I didn't mean to—"

"And by the way, while we're on the subject of your shitty opinion of me," Jasper goes on, angry all over again, "Cassie told me you think I did something to Tasha. Not that it's any of your business, but Tasha and I were friends. Sometimes, she liked to pretend we were boyfriend and girlfriend, and I thought fine, what do I care?" He shakes his head. "But I was too much of an ass to think about how she'd feel when I actually got a girlfriend. And it was bad."

"Did you tell Cassie that?" I ask. Surely she would have thrown that right in my face.

"No. She asked about Tasha, but I didn't think it was anybody's business. Listen, I'm not pretending I'm perfect. And in case you're wondering, yeah, I broke that kid's nose. Knocked him flat out. Did I mean to hit him that hard? I don't know, maybe. He said some crap about my dad and I just lost it. I'm not proud of that. It was a mistake. People make them, you know?" Jasper turns back to the window, crosses his arms. "Maybe if you realized that, you'd be a happier person."

My cheeks feel hot as I stare at the side of his handsome-boy face. I hate how right he is.

"Look there!" Jasper points again toward the window.

I jump to my feet quick enough to see—something or someone in the shadows of the large cabin across the way. Then a flashlight goes on and starts bouncing across the dark grass toward us. Officer Kendall. At least, I think—same light, same height. On his way back to us maybe? It's possible he rushed out to investigate and the door slammed shut behind him. It could even be stuck, not locked. Our situation could be bad still—because we haven't found Cassie—but maybe not *as* bad.

Instead of continuing on toward our cabin, though, the flashlight turns toward the car. Not Officer Kendall? But a second later, once the light is no longer shining at us, we can see who is behind it. And there can be no doubt. It is Officer Kendall. Sure enough, he's headed for his car. And away from us.

I close my eyes. Hope that I am seeing things. I have to be. But when I open them, there is Officer Kendall. Still walking calmly toward his car.

Jasper knocks on the window with two of his knuckles. "Hey!" he screams. "Where are you going?"

If Officer Kendall hears, he doesn't even twitch.

"He's leaving us here," I say, barely able to get the words out. My heart is throbbing in my head.

"Hey!" Jasper screams again as Officer Kendall gets into his SUV. He bangs with his whole closed fist this time. So hard I'm afraid he's going to shatter the glass and hurt himself.

"Jasper, stop." I put a hand on his arm.

He rests his fist against the glass as Officer Kendall backs up and drives away. We stand in silence until his taillights disappear down the driveway.

"Fuck," Jasper says quietly. Then sits back down on the floor.

I watch him down there for a minute, looking so defeated. If Jasper's hope is gone, we are truly lost. But he'll rally. He has to. I just need to give him a minute. I turn away from him back toward the window.

And there is a face. Right there. Right on the other side of the glass. A man with terrible dead eyes locked on mine.

"Holy shit!"

Jasper jumps to his feet. "What is it?"

The terrible man, bearded and thin with blotchy skin, looks over at Jasper and holds up his dirty finger again. *Shhh*, that's the sound he'd make if we could hear him. My heart is racing as he lifts something high in front of him. It takes me a minute to realize what it is: a rifle. As he lowers it, his smile sinks and becomes an awful frown before he finally disappears from view.

"Fuck," Jasper says again, his wide, terrified eyes locked on the window. "We have got to get the hell out of here. Now."

We divide the cabin into sections, searching for a way out. At one point, Jasper moves a couple of boxes, creating a little fence around Cassie's stuff, and I'm glad because I'm afraid if I look too close I might spot something terrible on it, like blood.

I check all the windows again, but they are all nailed shut, each covered with that same wire. Jasper scans the walls for a loose board, a crack in the seals. We both scour the floors for any sign of weakness, some corner we could dig our way out from. I find only the hole in the floor

Officer Kendall mentioned, but it's not big enough to be useful.

We do all of this in silence, neither one of us throwing out theories about who exactly these people are or why they locked us in here. Why Officer Kendall has gone. Because there are no explanations anymore that do not make our situation, and Cassie's, seem much, much worse.

"Do you think she's okay?" Jasper does ask at one point. *Alive,* he means, I can tell.

I do not want him to be asking me this. I want him to know that she's going to be fine, the way he did before.

"She's okay," I say finally, the way he told me hours earlier. "She has to be."

I carry a chair over to inspect a vent up near the ceiling that would be too small for us to crawl through anyway.

"Hey, I think maybe there's something behind here," Jasper calls from the back. "Help me pull this bureau out."

The bureau is so heavy it might as well be made of concrete. Even with Jasper using his full strength we don't get it far, only a foot or so from the wall. But enough to see that there is something behind it. A big piece of plywood—two feet by three feet—is attached to the wall like it's sealing up a hole. A hole that might just be big enough for us to escape through. Jasper crouches down, inspecting the edges of the plywood. There is a screw in each corner and a couple more along each side.

"We need to get these out." He motions around the room. *Find a tool to loosen them.* And he's right that we'll need to be quiet, too. Don't want to draw the attention of that man on the door.

Carefully, gently, we pull open one drawer at a time. I find a broken pencil and four pennies in one, a few dirty manila folders in the next. Jasper is at the tall filing cabinet, trying to silently open and close the rattling metal drawers. He looks disgusted by something in the second, poking his head in closer. A moment later he pulls out a giant stuffed owl and sets it on top of the filing cabinet so that it's staring right at me.

"For you." He smiles a little, and I'm glad one of us can still joke. "Hey," Jasper whispers again a second later, and I turn, expecting another absurd discovery. But he's got a metal ruler. The kind of thing that just might work on the screws.

Jasper tries the ruler, and I'm shocked when it actually begins to turn the first screw. When he looks up at me, the hope is back in his eyes. And I pray that he's right. That we are as good as free.

Ten minutes later, though, it's obvious it'll at least be slow going. He's got three screws out along one corner and a couple more loosened, but there are a half dozen more to go.

"Let me," I offer when it seems like Jasper's hands are starting to give out. Even in the dim light from the bulb in our bucket bathroom, his palms are bright red.

"I've got it," he says, brushing me off, even as the ruler starts to slip.

And so I let him struggle on for a couple more minutes, until it really seems like he's slowing down. And we can't afford to do that, no matter what. We don't have the time, and neither does Cassie. Wherever she is.

I reach out and put my hand over his. "Come on. Take a break for a minute."

Finally, Jasper nods and moves out of the way. When I start in on the screws myself, it's even harder than I expected. Still, it *is* working. I get another one out and start on a second. Makes me think: for people who went to all this trouble, with new glass in the windows and wire on top of that, a makeshift bathroom, a sealed-up hole, leaving that ruler behind was a pretty stupid mistake.

"Lucky we found this, huh?" I ask.

The bad feeling I've got could be nothing. All the time it's nothing. But when you're worried about everything, eventually you are going to be right about something.

"I guess," Jasper says, but he's not listening. He's not worried that finding that ruler makes us too lucky. His eyes are still locked on it and the screws like he's about to grab it back from my hands.

"I mean, like suspicious?" I stop working the screw and look up at him.

Jasper nods, shrugs, still staring down at the plywood. When he reaches out a hand, I think maybe he agrees that we should wait a second and think this through. But instead he just takes the ruler and gets back to work on the screws. Even faster this time.

Refreshed from his short break, Jasper gets the next couple screws out quickly. With all of them off on one end he's even able to pull the plywood back a little. Not much, five or six inches. He nods toward it.

"See it if goes all the way through," he whispers. Meaning he wants me to stick my hand through.

I do not want to do this. There are countless reasons why. Mostly, I am convinced something terrible will happen when I do. Best-case scenario is that someone will grab me. But Jasper is waiting. And he worked so hard to get us this far. The least I can do is help. He's pulling back the wood. *You can do this, Wylie*, I try telling myself. *Do it*.

Finally, I nod and step forward. I suck in one last mouthful of air before jamming my hand through. I hold my breath, wait for teeth in my flesh, my hand being sliced in two. But there's just the cold and the damp and something stringy getting caught in my fingers. It takes me a minute to realize that it's probably tall grass growing alongside the cabin.

"It goes all the way through," I say relieved.

There's a sound at the front of the cabin then—the lock sliding, the door opening. I go to yank my arm back inside, but my bunched-up sleeve gets hung up just as Jasper lets go of the plywood. It snaps down hard as I drag my arm the rest of the way out, and Jasper and I lunge toward the center of the room, as far away from the plywood as possible.

My arm is on fire as the door swings open, my eyes filling with tears from the pain. So many tears that it's hard for me to see. Hard for me to believe my eyes, when someone finally steps inside. I blink hard and pray that I'm not seeing things.

Because there she is. In one living, breathing piece. Cassie.

CHAPTER 17

As soon as Cassie shuffles inside, the door slams shut behind her.

She looks terrible. Her skin is chalk white, her dark-brown curls tangled and flecked with twigs and leaves. Like she's been dragged by her feet across the ground. Her hands are filthy and so are her knees, bare in her short skirt. But the worst part is how stunned she seems. And the way she's moving, stiff and awkward, like her entire body is burned.

But she's alive. She is alive. It's not until that moment that I realize how terrified I was that she might not be.

"Cassie!" Jasper rushes over and grabs her up in his arms. "Thank God you're okay."

She doesn't resist him, doesn't yelp when he goes to touch her. But she stays rigid, arms out over his like a crucifix. I think about Cassie's underwear on the floor, about how it might have gotten there. There are no good reasons for a girl and her underwear to be separated.

"Are you okay?" Jasper asks, pulling back to look her in the eye.

I drift closer to look myself. Cassie doesn't have any obvious bruises or cuts. But I wish she would speak. Say something, anything. Instead she just shakes her head. No, not okay? Or no, not hurt? Suddenly she turns and clutches on to me.

"Shhh." I rub a hand over her head as she sobs against me so hard she sounds like some kind of animal dying in my arms. "You're okay now. Everything is going to be okay."

But I feel so ashamed for saying something like that. Something I know is a lie.

"Cassie, what happened?" Jasper asks when her sobbing slows to sniffling. "What is this?"

"I don't know," she says, finally letting me go. She drops herself down on the couch.

Jasper and I turn to look at each other. She doesn't know? Maybe she was slipped something at some party or some bar she never should have been inside in the first place. She could have blacked out and woken up here.

I walk over and move the boxes out of the way so that Cassie's underwear is in plain sight again.

"Are you hurt?" I ask, motioning to it when she looks at me. "Did somebody mess with you?"

"No, no." She sniffles some more and wipes at her face with the back of her hand. "They haven't done anything to me, except not let me leave."

They. I do not like the way she says it. Like we are outnumbered. I go to sit next to her on the couch. "Karen came to our house. She said you guys got into a bad fight and then you left for school. How did you get here?"

Cassie nods, staring down at her hands.

"She brought up sending me off to that 'therapeutic boarding school' again—a.k.a. prison—and I freaked out and called her the *C* word." Cassie nods. "And then she *flipped* out. She was totally screaming at me. And I'd just had it. I took the bus to school, but I didn't go in. I

270

went downtown instead. I was just minding my business, sitting on this bench, when this guy came out of nowhere and said my mom sent him. He wasn't dressed like a cop, but he flashed some badge and I figured maybe he was some kind of undercover truancy officer." She looks at Jasper. "Anyway, I had to go with him because I couldn't risk, well, you know . . ."

She glances from Jasper over to me. *And you know about me and the police, Jasper,* that's the look.

"I told Wylie you got arrested," Jasper says, crossing his arms. It's quick and matter-of-fact, like he's pulling off a Band-Aid. "Sorry, but with everything else—I had to tell her."

"Oh," Cassie flicks her eyes my way, then down into her lap. "Well, once we were in his car, he said that he was actually from the school my mom was shipping me off to, and I had to go with him or he would turn me in to the police." Tears rush into her eyes again. She blinks them back and looks up at the ceiling. "It's not like those places take no for an answer. They'll throw a bag over your head if they have to. And I thought about running, but I was scared it might make things worse for me."

"And so that's what this is?" Jasper asks, looking around at the run-down cage of a cabin. "It's some reform school?"

But that does not seem right to me, not right at all.

"Yeah, I mean, I thought so until we actually got here and they locked me in one of these piece-of-shit cabins." She sounds mad instead of sad, and it's a relief. "I mean, obviously this isn't any kind of school, not even one for crackheads. So I started freaking out, screaming my head off."

Crackheads. Kind of a coincidence after all the talk of meth. And this story still doesn't feel like the truth. Cassie is leaving something out. Like maybe she wasn't just sitting on that bench minding her business when this guy came up to her.

"So this doesn't have anything to do with drugs?" I ask. I can't help it.

"Drugs?" Now Cassie shoots Jasper a look: *see, this is what I meant, she's judgmental.* "Why? Because I bought pot once?"

"That's not why," Jasper says, defending me. But kind of reluctantly. "The police in town said that meth is the only reason people come up here."

"Meth?" Cassie laughs angrily as she looks from Jasper to me, and back again. "So now the two of you think that I—"

"The police thought that," I say. But unlike Jasper, I just sound defensive. "And you wouldn't tell us anything. What were we supposed to think?"

"How about not the worst?" Cassie's voice cracks. "Sometimes, Wylie, you really are just like my mom."

Ouch. The worst part? She's not even totally wrong. Am I really more willing to believe some version of events that includes Cassie using meth than I am this boarding-school/boot camp story? If Karen did get Cassie into this mess with some therapy school gone wrong, she might even lie to my dad about it when she came to ask for help.

"So that's it?" Jasper asks. "They haven't told you anything else?"

"There is this other guy, not the jerk who drove me and not the freak on the door," Cassie says. "He was pretty nice. He said that they didn't want me to worry. That I'm here because I'm in some kind of danger, but not from them, from someone else. I don't understand what that has to do with them being some therapy school . . ." It's obvious she knows this doesn't make much sense. "But it's like they're protecting me."

"Protecting you?" I ask. "From who?"

"Myself, maybe? That's the only thing that makes sense, right?" She shrugs. "I have no idea. He said that was all he could tell me."

"Why wouldn't your mom tell us?" I ask.

"I'm sure she feels like an asshole. There's no way she expected the place to be like this. I saw the brochures."

"Why didn't you tell us any of this when you were texting?" I ask.

"I was afraid you wouldn't come."

I want to say I would have come no matter what, but that would be a lie.

"Also, I didn't really have the time to explain anything. They didn't know I had my phone." Cassie motions to her bra. She's always tucked stuff in there—cash, lipstick, even her phone—in a way that me and my flat chest never could have dreamed of. "And I had to stand on a chair to get a signal. I didn't want you to tell my mom, because on the off chance she did know what this place was like, I figured she would turn around and tell them I had my phone. You know how she'll never admit she's made a mistake. They finally caught me anyway. They said I was putting myself and everyone else 'in danger' by sending texts. After that, they took my phone."

"Did they actually say they would kill you?" I ask, thinking of that text we got from Cassie at the Freshmart.

"What do you mean?" She looks confused.

"The text you sent," I say. "You said not to call the police or they would kill you."

Cassie shakes her head and looks down. "They must have sent that after they took my phone."

"And you didn't tell us to go to Seneca or the police?"

She shakes her head again. "No."

"You keep saying 'they,'" Jasper says. "How many of them are there?"

Cassie looks up like she's considering, then counts on her fingers. "Maybe a dozen?"

"A dozen?" Jasper looks nervously toward the door. Even he can't do anything with those kinds of odds.

"Maybe more. I've only seen most of them through the window. A couple of them are women. They all look so normal, which is maybe even creepier."

"Yeah, okay." Jasper claps his hands together in a go-team-go kind of way. "I think we've heard enough. We are getting the hell out of here, right now."

He strides over to where Cassie is sitting on the couch and reaches down for her hand. She seems so sad and sorry when she finally reaches up.

"Come on," he says quietly. "You're going to be okay. We're going to be okay." Finally, Cassie's body loosens. She even smiles a little.

And I'm amazed at how he does that: makes it better—makes her better—without actually fixing anything. That's love, I guess. And it's something I don't know anything about.

A minute later, Cassie and I are standing behind Jasper as he sets to work on the last couple sets of screws, harder than ever before.

"What is this?" Cassie asks.

"A way out." And Jasper sounds so confident now that I almost feel convinced myself.

"And then what?" Cassie looks toward the windows, worried.

"We run," Jasper says.

"But what if they catch us?" Cassie asks, and now she sounds officially scared. "There is a guy out there with a gun, remember? Or what if they were actually telling the truth about trying to protect me from something? Maybe we're safer in here."

"Protect you from what?" I ask, staring at her hard. "You said you thought they were making that up."

"I don't know that for sure," she says, her eyes still on the window. "What if there is somebody or something out there? These people haven't actually done anything to me. Maybe they're not so bad."

My stomach tightens as I look out the dark window. It is creepy out there, that's for sure.

"Whoever these people are, they have the police or a policeman helping them," Jasper says. "They grabbed you off the street and have us all locked up here. That's enough information for me. We need to go."

Cassie eyes me for a long time, like she's considering whether or not to agree. Instead, she looks down and takes my wrist in her cold fingers. "Wylie, what happened?"

There's blood smeared on my forearm from three deep cuts beneath my bunched-up sleeve at the crook of my elbow and a few thicker pink scratches. I felt the pain when I first pulled my arm out from the plywood, but after that: nothing. I wrap my fingers tight around my arm, like a tourniquet, which only makes it wake up and throb.

"It was the wood." I point to the wall. "I pulled my arm out too fast. It'll be okay."

Cassie is staring at my arm still. "Thank you for coming," she says. "Especially after all our . . ." She reaches down and links her fingers through mine. "After everything."

"Of course I came," I say, turning to look at Jasper as he keeps on working. "What are best friends for?"

***

Cassie and I were lying on the couch, toe to toe, propped up on pillows doing our homework as we had been each day for the nearly two months since the funeral. And each day, I wanted to tell her that she didn't have to keep coming, to keep pretending that we were friends. But a larger part of me was too afraid of what would happen to me if she stopped.

We both ignored the doorbell the first time. For sure, I was never going to answer it. Not if they rang it a thousand times. Not even if it was more flowers or another kindly casserole dropped off by a neighbor. Because there was also a chance it was another reporter. I don't know what it was: the cruel irony of my mom getting the Pulitzer nomination posthumously, the fact that she had survived so much danger in the field only to die a mile from her home. Or that she was so beautiful. But the reporters kept coming no matter how many times or how many ways we told them to go away.

Cassie knew this, too. And by the time the person rang the bell a third time, she couldn't take it anymore. The people with the casseroles were never that insistent.

"I'll get rid of them," she said, pushing herself up off the couch. A minute later, I heard the front door creak open, a beat of silence, followed by Cassie's quiet voice: "What the hell?" Then her stomping outside and down the front steps: "Hey! Come here, you fucking asshole!"

Reluctantly, I forced myself up to investigate. Our front door was hanging wide open when I got out there, and Cassie was nowhere in sight. I stepped into the open doorway, my eyes watering from the March cold blasting in. Finally, I spotted Cassie out in the street, standing in front of a dark-gray sedan in her cropped sweater, short skirt, and bright argyle tights. Her barely-still-curly brown hair was lifted in an arc around her head in the strong wind, making her look like a pissed-off Medusa. She had one hand on the hood of the car, the other high in the air. It took me a minute to realize what she had gripped in her fist: a plastic baby doll. We'd gotten a half dozen in all, but not a single one since my mom's accident.

"But she's dead," I whispered in the empty foyer. "You got what you wanted."

Cassie was shaking the baby over her head now.

"Get out of the car, you asshole!" she shouted. "You think you can fucking do this to them still?"

I'd almost forgotten about the babies altogether. And all I wanted was for my mom to appear next to me. To shrug and shake her head: *you cannot control the world.* I wanted that so bad it felt like my heart was going to burst. Actually, I wished it would. As depressed as I'd been, I hadn't actually thought about killing myself, not seriously, anyway. But did I want to die? Every single second.

Whoever was in the car—I figured it was a he, but I couldn't see from where I was—must have said something super messed-up then. Because Cassie went crazy.

"Get out here! You piece of shit!" she screamed, climbing up on the hood of his car and slamming the baby down.

And I was glad. I wanted her to smash his windshield. To reach in and grab him by the throat. Because it felt like that guy in the car—who was just some idiot who hated what he thought my mom's pictures said—was responsible for my mom being dead. And watching Cassie out there, waving that baby around like a lunatic, I felt this tiny flutter of hope. Like someday all the sadness flooding my insides might be lit up like that—into an unstoppable blaze.

My dad drove up while Cassie was still on the hood. He screeched to a stop and jumped out, looking for a second like he might beat the crap out of that baby-dropper. God did I want him to. But he didn't even look in the driver's direction. Instead, he calmly talked Cassie down. As soon as she was off the car, the driver sped away. And my dad tossed the doll to the curb, where it sat until somebody— the garbageman, a neighbor, a passerby—must have picked it up and carried it away.

"What did that guy say?" I asked Cassie later when we were back inside on the couch.

"Your dad's right, it doesn't matter," she said, waving me off. "He was a nut ball."

"It matters." I stared at her hard.

"Okay," she said finally. "He said, 'Beware false prophets.'" She rolled her eyes. "I don't know how your mom dealt with those people. But trust me, that particular turtle-ish guy isn't going to be coming back. When I got up on his car, I think he might have peed himself."

And I knew Cassie and my dad were right. That man—whoever he was—didn't matter. None of the people who hated my mom and her pictures did. Maybe I should have even been grateful. Because, in a way, them still hating her kept her alive.

"We're close," Jasper whispers. He's already on the last screws—only one corner and a few along the side left to go. "Hold the board so it doesn't fall and make noise once I have them all out. We're going to have to move fast, too. That way, I think." He points to the other side of the cabin, which backs up to the woods. "No stopping, no matter what. Even if we get separated. Everyone has to just keep running."

Are we really doing this? My heart is thumping. My body tensed for flight. Yes. Yes, we are. And I know I can. Jasper and I just did this a few hours ago. I nod, ready to step forward and take the board. But Cassie is just standing there, shaking her head.

"I still don't know if we should—" her voice chokes out.

"Cassie, come on. You're just freaked out," Jasper says. "You're not thinking clearly."

There's a loud noise from the front of the cabin then. The lock again, the door cracking open.

"Move," Jasper says.

We break off in opposite directions, jetting away from the wall and the wood. The scene of our escape in progress. At least the board is still in place. It's our best chance for them not to realize we've found a way out.

I hold my breath as we wait to see who's coming inside. I pray it is not that toothless man from the window. I do not want to see him up close. But it's not him who finally steps tentatively inside. This man is youngish and normal-looking, a couple of years older than us maybe, with shaggy black hair and warm eyes behind square, black-framed glasses. He's wearing dark jeans, lace-up boots, and an orange down vest over a flannel shirt, but even in those clothes he seems more big city than Maine woods.

"Hi," he says, uncomfortable, even nervous. Aware, maybe, that this situation is profoundly messed up. It could be a good sign. "I'm Quentin."

He's got some bottles of water and some granola bars cradled unevenly in his arms. When he goes to put them down on the table, the water bottles immediately roll onto the floor. He scrambles awkwardly to pick them up.

"You know, whatever Cassie's mom agreed to, she definitely didn't sign up for this." Jasper steps forward. His arms are at his sides, but his fists are clenched. "And Wylie and my parents didn't agree to anything. Keeping us here is false imprisonment."

Jasper will make an excellent lawyer someday. It's actually pretty convincing. If only we were in a position to threaten anyone with anything. The guy holds up his hands, eyes wide.

"You're confused, which totally makes sense. And I was just about to—" The light in the bathroom goes off, making us all twitch. "And there goes the generator again. Wait, hold on one second." He ducks his head back out the still-open door and returns with two kerosene lanterns.

They bathe the cabin in warm yellow light. "Okay, that's better. Being trapped in the dark is not going to help anything. Listen, to be clear, having you here is for your safety. If you could just trust—"

"You're kidding, right?" Jasper takes another step forward, his voice rising. He is much bigger than this Quentin guy. "We don't even have any idea who you are. Why the hell would we ever trust you?"

"You okay in there, Quentin?" A nasally voice outside draws out his name like a schoolyard bully. The toothless guy, no doubt, reminding us that he's out there. With a gun.

Quentin shakes his head and rolls his eyes. "Yes, Stuart, we're fine."

"You're not from some reform school, are you?" I ask.

"No," Quentin says quietly, pressing his lips together and shaking his head again. "And everyone feels terrible about all the deception. We were really hoping he'd be here by now so he could explain himself."

"Him, who?" I ask. "Who are you talking about?"

"Oh." Now Quentin looks confused. "Your dad, Wylie."

CHAPTER 18

"My dad," I hear myself say. It's not a question. Just a word that doesn't make any sense.

"Don't worry. He's fine," Quentin hustles to add. "I didn't mean to make it sound like there's a problem. I guess he's just taking the long way around."

"Why is my dad coming here?" My heart is throbbing in my head again. "How do you even know him?"

"Oh," Quentin says again, looking even more confused, and officially nervous. "You don't have any idea what I'm talking about, do you?"

"What is going on?" I shout, and so loud I almost scare myself.

"Okay, okay." Quentin holds up his hands. "Your dad would have preferred if you had stayed home, obviously. But once Cassie"—he motions to her, smiles uncomfortably—"I mean once we knew you were already in Seneca, your dad had us bring you here so that you'd be safe. That's the most important thing."

"No, he did not," I say, my voice quiet and trembling. I can barely force any sound out.

And it cannot be true. Because that would mean my dad knew all along what had happened to Cassie. That he stood there in our living room while Karen freaked out. While I freaked out. Pretending he had no clue. Pretending he was trying to help when really he had something to do with it. What kind of monster does that? And why?

But it feels like some kind of awful key sliding into place. I'm terrified what's going to happen when somebody pops the lock.

"Have you decided what you're going to do, Ben?" my mom asked my dad that last night at dinner, *her* last night.

I didn't know what she was talking about, except that she was launching into another one of their fights—the ones they had all the time now right in front of us, without ever revealing what they were actually fighting about. But from the way my dad's face puckered, he knew what she meant. And he was not happy.

"Do about what?" I asked. This couldn't be about my dad's study. Finally that was finished, about to be published. "What happened?"

My dad eyeballed my mom: *see what you've started*. "There have been some lapses in cybersecurity campus-wide," he said, glancing in my direction. "But Dr. Simons got a colleague from Stanford's computer science department to bolster my study's data security until our university can work out its problem."

My mom crossed her arms. "And so that's it?" she asked him. "You don't have anything else to say."

"Yes, Hope, that's it." Now he was glaring at her.

I'd stopped eating. Whatever they were fighting about, it was not campus data security. I looked over at Gideon, but his eyes were on his chemistry homework.

I was never sure if he didn't notice our parents fighting or if he just didn't care.

"So I guess that means you still didn't talk to Dr. Simons about the Outliers?" my mom pressed on. "I thought you said you were going to mention it the next time you spoke."

My dad took a deep breath and put down his knife and fork to look at her.

"What are the Outliers?" I asked, hoping his explanation might make me less worried about them getting divorced.

"They're the ones who can do Dad's test blindfolded and with the headphones," Gideon said without looking up from his homework. He was an expert on my dad's work, had read every one of his papers, was always peppering him with questions. Partly that had to do with Gideon being interested in science, and partly that had to do with Gideon wanting my dad to be more interested in him. "You know, the ones with ESP."

"It's not ESP, Gideon!" my dad shouted.

Gideon startled, his cheeks flushing a blotchy pink. For a second I thought he might cry.

My dad closed his eyes, took a breath. "I'm sorry, Gideon, but you know how much I hate that comparison. It's inflammatory, and it degrades the real potential of my research." He reached out a hand but didn't actually touch Gideon. "I shouldn't have shouted, though. I'm sorry."

In my dad's defense, even I knew that ESP was not a word anyone was to use in our house. The number of times I'd heard my dad trying to explain to others that ESP was *not* what he studied was too many to count. And whenever he did, I could hear the defeat in his voice.

"Who *are* the Outliers then?" I asked again, because I needed that answer now.

"Outliers are the subjects whose results are outside the normal range. That's all," my dad said. "Outliers occur in all kinds of studies."

"But not every Outlier is created equal," my mom said. "Are they, Ben?"

And there was this way she said his name: like maybe Outlier was another word for mistress or prostitute.

"And ESP is *literally* reading someone's thoughts, Gideon," my dad said, ignoring her and turning back to

Gideon. "In the old tests for ESP, they'd give one subject a picture of a shape to concentrate hard on, to think only of that thing—blue triangle, blue triangle, over and over again. And then they'd ask the other subject to guess what shape that person was thinking about. And no one can do that. That test has nothing to do with emotional intelligence. To an extent, ESP and the perception aspect of emotional intelligence are related: they are both about reading people. The subjects in my study exhibited a range of capacity for perceiving emotions, which did seem heightened when observing live conversation compared to their ability with static images. The Outliers exhibited an exceptional ability unrelated to the actual focus of my study—they could perceive emotions while blindfolded and wearing noise-canceling headphones. It certainly warrants further research."

"Got to keep on studying and studying and studying before you say anything to anyone? Is that it, Ben?"

Again my dad ignored her. But I watched his face tighten.

"If I was you, all I'd want to study would be the Outliers," Gideon said, oblivious still to the tension between them.

"I'd want to know how they do it, so I could learn to do it, too. And then I could rule the world." He shoveled more food into his mouth, then grinned.

"You can't learn to be an Outlier, Gideon. Like with IQ, you can improve your ability to perceive emotion, but only to a very small degree," my dad said, but quietly now. Sad almost. "And inserting yourself into the scientific research is dangerous and unethical. I fired Dr. Caton for becoming too personally invested. What a scientist *wants* is irrelevant. The only thing that matters is the truth."

"Okay, jeez," Gideon said quietly, jabbing at his pasta with his fork. "I was just joking."

"The only thing that matters is the truth?" my mom asked sharply. She got up to refill her water glass. Kept talking with her back to us. "Ironic, don't you think, Ben?"

"Wait, so Wylie's dad had you bring us here to be safe?" I hear Jasper ask, but he sounds really far away. "Safe from what?"

Focus. I need to pull myself together and focus. This answer is important. I am the only one who will know if it makes any sense.

Quentin looks even more uncomfortable. "There are some people at a company, I guess, a defense contractor?" His voice rises at the end like it's a question. "Honestly, I don't know all the details. But I know that they want your dad's research or his help or something. I guess they are prepared to do a lot of bad stuff to get what they want. Even actually hurt people, with their *actual* hands." He looks down at his own hands like he can't imagine that kind of thing. "Or with weapons, maybe. People from a defense contractor must have weapons, right? Like I said, I'm not really an expert."

Did my mom know about this, whatever it is? Is *this* what she and my dad were fighting about? Funny, how you can think that all you want is an answer. Until you realize that to get to the bottom, you'll need to go way deeper and darker than you ever imagined.

"But he acted like he wanted me to come home," I say.

"Because he wanted you to, very much. It wasn't his original plan to have you come here. At least not all of you," he says, flicking his eyes in Cassie's direction. "But then here Jasper and you were, already on your way. And it didn't seem safe to have you out there on your own."

"Wait a second," Jasper says. "What do you mean 'all of you'? And why did you just look at Cassie?"

I'm afraid to hear the answer, but I am glad that I didn't imagine Quentin looking at Cassie. When I look over at her now, she has the weirdest, blankest expression on her face.

"Listen, this is complicated, and I'm already way out of my depth here. I am nobody, really." Quentin waves his hands. Seems glad to be able to say that. "Dr. Simons is really the person—"

"Dr. Simons is here?" I ask.

"Yes, he's up at the main house right now." And Quentin looks so relieved to be letting me know.

But I'm not relieved. Because if Dr. Simons is here, any hope of this being some kind of misunderstanding and my dad not being involved is officially gone.

"You know him?" Jasper asks, and he sounds suspicious of me now. "This Dr. Simons person."

I nod. "He's my dad's friend."

"Then take us up there so this doctor guy can explain what the hell is going on," Jasper says, taking a couple of steps toward the door.

"Definitely," Quentin says, but then seems embarrassed. "And I know this is going to sound ridiculous, but with the power off—I'm not supposed to take all of you at once. The people from that company I mentioned—well, too many of us together on the open lawn. We're kind of a bigger target?"

Everything he says sounds like a question.

"A target?" Jasper asks. And he sounds mostly angry, but a little scared, too. "Are you kidding?"

Quentin shakes his head. "I mean, we don't know if they're here yet, but they're trying to find us. We know that. But Wylie, I can take you up alone. Then I'll come back and get everybody else?"

I'm already shaking my head. *No, No, No.* And I can't get myself to stop shaking it, even though I can feel everyone is staring at me. But I do not want to go to Dr. Simons. I am too afraid of what he might tell me about my dad.

"No?" Jasper asks, like he doesn't understand. And why would he?

"No," I finally say out loud. Part of me actually hopes I'll get away before I ever have to know what's really going on.

"Then I'll go," Jasper offers.

"No," Cassie says, and loud. "I mean, take me. I'm the one you brought here on purpose. I should be the one to talk to Dr. Simons."

"I'd rather go first," Jasper says, stepping back to squeeze Cassie's fingers before heading again toward the door. Just in case he gets picked off crossing the lawn, that's what he means. "Don't worry, I'll be okay."

Cassie and I stare in silence at the closed door for a long time.

"My dad's research?" I ask finally. "No one has ever cared about his research in my entire life. And did you hear that? You were the one they really wanted? Why?"

Cassie shrugs, shakes her head. "Don't look at me," she says. But she doesn't sound angry at my dad. Not nearly as angry as I want her to be.

Because I'm furious. *Your condition.* How fucking dare he? Especially when all this time his bullshit research was the reason for this entire situation. All I want to do is get him back on the phone and tell him again just how much I *really* wish he'd been in the car that night. How can he be the parent I'm left with? A liar, so obsessed with his stupid job that he doesn't even warn us that we might get mixed up in it.

"You know your mom was completely freaking out when she came to see us? My dad acted the whole time like he had no idea what was going on," I say, in case Cassie isn't getting the full picture of why he is a total monster.

"Whatever, my mom deserves to worry." Cassie shrugs again. "Anyway, shouldn't we at least wait until you know the whole story? Maybe your dad can explain."

"That's awfully generous of you," I say, because she's drifted into annoying territory. Cassie would never give Karen the benefit of the doubt about anything.

"I just don't want you to worry, okay?"

And she means *worry,* worry. Like only I can. Her eyes then drift up to my hair. Like it proves her point, which, of course, it kind of does.

"What the hell did you do?" she asks.

"I looked like her," I say. And it's a relief to tell someone that pitiful truth. "In the mirror, she was all I could see. And I just—I couldn't take it anymore."

Cassie nods, still contemplating my hair, more matter-of-fact than concerned.

"Hold on, I have an idea," she says, heading over to her bag on the floor.

I watch Cassie pick up her underwear and tuck it discreetly inside. When she stands up, she's smiling, two hair ties raised in the air as she makes her way back over to me. "These are your only hope. Now, sit."

I do as I'm told as Cassie's hands move over the hacked strands of my hair like they are searching for a foothold.

"What was your underwear doing on top of your bag?" I ask, because I can't shake the image of it sitting there. I mean, is she not wearing any?

And even if this whole thing has something to do with my dad's research, there is still that disgusting guy outside guarding the door. It only makes me more worried when Cassie doesn't answer my question. Instead, she stays quiet, fussing around my hair. I look up at her and put my hand over hers. "Cassie, seriously?"

She bites on her lip for a minute. When she finally looks at me, her eyes are glassy. "I wasn't just downtown to get away from my mom when they picked me up. I went down there to see this guy. Another guy. I was going to go stay with him for a few days, try to freak my mom out. I guess it got pulled out when I grabbed my sweatshirt earlier."

"Oh," I say, trying not to sound disappointed.

"We weren't together long," she says. "A few months, I guess." A few months? She and Jasper hadn't been together much longer than that. "You want to know the most messed-up part?"

No, is what I think. "Sure," is what I say, like nothing could be too messed up for me, her super-awesome, nonjudgmental best friend.

"I think I did it *because* Jasper is so great. At the beginning, I thought he was kind of an asshole, like you do. And even *I* deserve an asshole."

"But he's not an asshole," I say. And even I'm sure of that much now.

"Nope, he's like this exceptionally *good* person. Principled." Cassie wipes at the tears that have filled her eyes. "Do you know he *still* sends the money he makes washing dishes at the IHOP to the guy his dad almost beat to death? Can you imagine washing dishes at an IHOP and not even keeping the money?"

"No," I say. "I can't."

"Yeah, neither can I." Cassie's quiet again, looking at her fingers. "And so what does a guy like that, a really good guy, possibly see in me? Except, you know." She motions to her body. The way she looks, she means. "But I practically had to force him to have sex with me, he was all 'no pressure, no pressure.' It was just too— perfect. So what did I do?" She makes an exploding motion with her hands.

"Everybody makes mistakes," I say, which reminds me of Jasper. And makes me feel even worse for him.

"I didn't go looking to meet somebody, though," she goes on, like that makes anything better. "I was just working my shift at Holy Cow one afternoon, minding my own business, when this guy came in."

"It doesn't make you a bad person if you met someone you like better than Jasper," I say, which is true enough, though it would have been *a lot* better if Cassie had broken up with Jasper before dating this other guy.

She shakes her head and stares down at her balled-up hands. "It's over now anyway. I was totally wrong about him." The tears are flowing down her face now. "He's actually a really, really terrible person. I see that now." She smiles this sad smile, then shakes her head. Disgusted at herself.

"Oh," I say. Because that sounds bad, even factoring in how Cassie exaggerates. She's not faking that she's upset. *Really, really* upset. "Are you okay? I mean, what happened?"

Her eyes search mine for something she seems not to find. She presses her lips together and stares down at the ground.

"I'll tell you, but I just . . . I can't right now," she says, motioning to the cabin like: *with everything else going on.* But there's also this weird tone to her voice. Like I've said the wrong thing or like I'm not really getting it. She scrubs at her damp cheeks. "Anyway, I would have told you about him when it started, but we weren't talking then. And I guess part of me was glad that I didn't have to see that look on your face again. That disappointment."

"I wouldn't have—"

"Come on, you're looking at me that way right now."

She's right. I can feel the look on my face. I can't help it.

"Who cares what I think?" I say. "I mean, look at me: I'm a mess. What do I know about anything?"

"More than you think, Wylie," she says quietly. Then forces a smile. "But obviously, not about cutting hair."

As she clucks and hums her way around my head, it reminds me so much of when she came and braided my hair right after my mom died. Something about her doing it again now makes me want to cry.

"Perfect," she says finally, pulling back to assess her handiwork. "Come, come look."

She waves me over to the window, then holds up the lantern so that I can see my reflection. There was barely enough hair for her to braid, so little to arm me with for battle this time. But she did. My hair is still *very* short and super choppy, but Cassie has put a small French braid on a diagonal across the top of my head, gathering up all the most uneven bits. It looks boho chic, and almost flattering. More flattering maybe than before I cut all my hair off.

"Not bad," Cassie says, though her voice sounds sad.

"Thank you." And it does make me feel better to look normal. Even if I already know it won't make me feel that way. Nothing ever will.

"No, thank you," Cassie says, hugging me tight from behind. "For always coming to my rescue."

CHAPTER 19

Cassie still has her face pressed against mine when the door opens again. Quentin looks embarrassed that he's interrupted.

"Oh, sorry, I—" Just then the light goes back on in the bathroom. Quentin looks relieved. "Excellent, now I can take both of you up at the same time. You guys ready?"

I feel the acid rising in my throat as I try to suck in some air. *No, not ready.*

"Yes," Cassie says.

And who knows? Maybe Cassie is right. Maybe I just need to wait until I know and see before I decide what my dad is guilty of. Finally, I step forward next to her.

"We're ready."

In silence, we follow Quentin. It's the middle of the night still—after midnight definitely, maybe even later—but brighter with the main cabin glowing warmly in the distance. Still, as we make our way across the open grass, I have the uncomfortable feeling of being watched. Dangerous people from some military company looming in the trees seems both totally ridiculous and totally possible. That could even explain Lexi and Doug, maybe. Doug especially could easily be some kind of professional. If there are more like Doug on the way, we will be no match.

But when I glance over my shoulder to see if there is some army headed for us, there is only Stuart and his one gun, pacing back and forth in front of the cabin.

"I'm sorry about Stuart," Quentin says, catching my eye. "Our security measures have been—well, there weren't a lot of options up here. Your dad definitely won't approve when he meets him."

My dad doesn't know about the toothless guy with the gun? Maybe he doesn't know other things. Maybe he didn't know that his friends already had Cassie when Karen came knocking at our door. Or maybe I'm just desperate to find something, anything that makes him less of a liar.

"What about that police guy?" I ask.

"Officer Kendall? Yeah, he's friends with somebody here. I'm not sure exactly who," Quentin says. "But he's a good guy. He helped us clear out the camp, said he would keep people away for a few days. We needed a place off the grid. Until we can get things figured out."

"And so why didn't he just tell us about this once we were in the police car with him?" I ask when we're almost at the steps to the main cabin.

Before Quentin can answer, the door swings open and two young guys in low-hanging jeans step out. The first is short with a white-blond buzz cut, a beaked nose, and dark circles under his eyes. There's a tattoo on the inside of his forearm, a small square grid with some circles in it—like a game board. The second guy, much taller with big cheeks, has the same tattoo, but on the side of his neck. Each of them has a laptop gripped under an arm. They're youngish, but older than Cassie and me. Older than Quentin.

"Oh, hi," Quentin says to them, startled and kind of nervous. But also like he's trying to play it cool, which he's not very good at. "Thanks again for coming all the way up here, guys. I know it's not the kind of thing you usually do."

"Mmm, yeah," the blond guy grunts without slowing down. "Pretty much the fucking opposite."

"Later," the other one mutters, his cheeks quivering as he jogs down the rest of the steps.

We watch them stalk away, lighting cigarettes as they head on foot down the driveway and disappear.

"Who are they?" I ask.

"Um, hacktivists?" Quentin says, his voice rising at the end even more than usual. "But I don't think they like being called that. They don't seem to like a lot of things."

"Hacktivists?" Cassie huffs. Though I'm not sure why this, of all the crazy things we've been told, would suddenly seem so absurd to her.

"Level99," Quentin goes on. "Not that they'll admit that's who they are. They are kind of like the CIA, but with tattoos." He shrugs. "But they did agree to come all the way up here to figure out who breached your dad's data—things are so out of hand we couldn't risk them doing it remotely—and to secure our smartphones. They had all the texting and everything blocked temporarily, which is why Officer Kendall couldn't reach us when you got here. And with the generator out we didn't even know it was Officer Kendall until he came up to the main cabin, so we were staying out of sight. Just in case."

"My dad said something about someone getting into his data." I feel a little relieved to have two tiny dots I can connect, even if it makes my dad more involved, not less. "But he said it was the whole campus."

"It could have been, I guess," Quentin says, though it's obvious he doesn't think so. "There's a lot we still don't know."

Inside, the main cabin is nothing like the one we were kept in. The furniture is old, but the room is brightly lit and sparkling clean, with a dozen long picnic tables and benches set out in two perfect rows. The windows look new, but more than one is open, the filmy faded curtains fluttering on the crisp breeze. A larger table at the back is covered with a green tablecloth, a couple of stainless-steel coffee urns on top, a stack of white mugs next to it. Like for a crowd, except there's not a soul in sight.

We're still standing there next to the door when an old woman, frail but purposeful, comes out from the back carrying a stack of folded towels in her veiny arms.

"Hi, Miriam," Quentin calls, but carefully. Like he doesn't want to scare her.

"Oh my!" She jumps anyway, pressing a hand to her bony chest. "I didn't see you there!"

"Sorry, I didn't mean to startle you. Have you seen Dr. Simons around, maybe with a young guy?"

"They were just here," she says, looking around, her forehead crinkled. When she doesn't spot them, she peers down under the table nearest to her as though they could be hiding under there. "Wait, now I remember. Dr. Simons was going to show the boy something on one of the computers in the back office."

"Okay, thanks, Miriam," Quentin says, smiling gently as she moves on toward the door. "Miriam was a combat nurse in Vietnam. She has crazy stories."

"And she knows my dad?" Because my dad has no friends. Then again maybe knowing all these people is just another of his lies.

"Either him or Dr. Simons, I'm not sure. Everybody here knows one of them, or knows somebody who knows them. These days, Miriam is an archivist at the university library. Maybe that's how she knows your dad?" The library. My dad's favorite place on campus. "Almost everyone is a professor or a researcher, except for me and Miriam. Dr. Simons was my professor at Stanford before they kicked me out."

"Oh," I say, trying not to make my disappointed face.

"Yeah, apparently, they prefer you actually go to class. But Dr. Simons made it so that I could voluntarily withdraw at least. I'm back here, at UMass now. Not as prestigious, but I'll graduate."

Cassie, who's been lingering near the door, finally steps up next to us. "Can we go find Jasper now?" she asks, sounding impatient. "I really need to talk to him."

She's not going to confess her affair in the middle of this mess, is she? It was one thing to tell me, but telling

Jasper is another thing entirely. "Maybe you should wait until we're home *before* you talk to Jasper?"

"That's okay," Quentin says, oblivious. "Come on, we can go in back and find him."

Just then a short, older man with a ring of curly gray hair comes out from the back. He's wearing khakis and a burgundy cable-knit sweater that hugs a big, very round belly. Dr. Simons. All the pictures I've seen are pretty old, but that belly and the ring of hair haven't changed a bit.

"Dr. Simons, this is Wylie," Quentin says, presenting me like a gift.

"Wylie!" Dr. Simons calls, his face lighting up as he makes his way over. "My goodness, your father said you were tall, but you're taller than me!"

My dad loves to talk about my height even though I'm only a little taller than average. Probably because me growing normally is the one thing he can safely report that makes it sound like I'm thriving.

Dr. Simons's handshake is warm and firm. "Please have a seat." He motions to a nearby table. "I apologize for all the cloak-and-dagger nonsense. Your dad and I have been doing our best to manage this, well"—he takes a breath and looks toward the door—"fundamentally unmanageable situation."

"Is Jasper back in the office?" Quentin asks. "Cassie was hoping to see him."

"Oh, yes, of course," Dr. Simons says after hesitating for a second, like he's not exactly sure where he left Jasper. It makes me wonder if he might be a little senile like Miriam. "Adam is showing him the testing material."

"Come on, I'll bring you," Quentin says to Cassie.

Cassie looks back at me, her eyes watery and worried. "Unless you want me to stay, Wylie. I can if you want me to."

"No, that's okay. You can go," I say, even though I would really like for her to stay. For my sake, and for hers. Jasper isn't going to react well to finding out he was right about the other guy. "But think about waiting to tell him if you can. The truth will still be there when we get home."

"Okay," Cassie says, tears making her eyes shine as she reaches forward to squeeze my hand. "I'll think about it."

But I can already see her chewing on her lower lip as she heads toward the back. She's not going to listen to a word I said.

"I just spoke with your father. He is still some distance away," Dr. Simons says, sitting down as he peers hard at his watch. If he is trying to hide that he's concerned, he's failing. When I look up at the clock on the wall, it's past three thirty a.m. I'm afraid to ask what time was he supposed to be here. "He's had to take a slightly more circuitous route for obvious reasons."

"No, not obvious," I say, taking a seat at the long table across from him. "Listen, I'm not trying to be rude, but nothing about this is obvious to me."

"No, of course not. You can call him if you'd like," Dr. Simons says, looking around like he's searching for a phone. "You should have a signal in here. It's boosted. You should know he feels terrible for lying to you when Karen was there. The timing of this—it caught him very much off guard. And then for his later texts, he was genuinely trying to be sure that you didn't get mixed up in this."

"So he pretended to be Cassie texting me she was afraid someone was going to *kill her*?"

"In your father's defense, he wasn't responsible for that specific message; I was." Dr. Simons takes a deep breath and rubs his forehead. "I realize now that it was unnecessarily frightening. But at the time, you were en route and we needed to get you here—and out of harm's way—quickly. I could have done so another way; that's clear to me now. You should ask your father about it. When he heard about that message, he wasn't at all happy."

When I pull out my phone, there is a signal and already a new text from my dad.

I'm sorry, it reads. *For everything.*

And I feel my stupid heart catch. Is it possible I won't hate my dad forever? I guess I'm hoping it is. More than I realized.

Where are you? I write back instead of calling. I'm afraid if I actually talk to him, he'll make me furious all over again. That he'll somehow topple all the excuses that Dr. Simons has been so carefully building in his defense. *How long is it going to take you to get here?*

Still a couple hours, comes the quick response. *I had to pull off for a bit. I promise, I will explain everything when I get there. But you can ask Dr. Simons anything. You can trust him. More soon. I'm so glad you're okay. I love you, Scat. xo Dad.*

Scat. A nickname from the books I'd loved as a kid about a terrified cat who overcomes her fears with a spunky attitude and her trusty friends. My dad hasn't called me that in years. He must feel *really* bad.

OK, I write back. And that's all. Because no matter what cute nickname he calls me, I'm not ready to forgive anything.

"Were you able to reach him?" Dr. Simons asks.

I nod.

"In the past couple of weeks, your father considered warning you and your brother about these people from North Point. But he had no reason to believe that the threat they posed—at least to the two of you—was either credible or imminent. And in your condition, he didn't want to worry you unnecessarily."

In your condition. My dad's words. Because apparently that's the way he talks to his friends about me. Just when I'm thinking there's a chance I could forgive him eventually, he proves yet again what a huge asshole he is.

I cross my arms, trying not to sound pissed off. Because really, I am mad at my dad and not Dr. Simons. And snapping at him isn't going to get me what I want: information. "And who the hell *is* North Point?"

"They are a defense contractor. Deep military ties, even deeper pockets. And apparently boundless determination. They want unfettered access to certain aspects of your father's research."

"So they are the 'threat' that everyone was talking about?" I ask.

Dr. Simons nods. "But to be clear, we have no reason to believe that they have located us yet. Everything we're doing is simply with an abundance of caution."

I picture Doug's red face, the way he looked at me in that diner like he wanted me dead, the way he chased after us in the woods so easily even though he was bleeding so much. The addition of Dr. Simons and Quentin has not made me feel like we're going to be any less screwed if they do find us. And they already have once. Who says they won't be able to do it again?

"Yeah, I think they might be closer than you think."

Dr. Simons's eyes widen. "What do you mean?"

"Our car broke down, so we asked for a ride." I'll have to talk quickly if I'm going to get the story out. "They pretended they had this baby, but when we realized they didn't, we tried to run. The guy, his name was Doug, or that's what he said, jumped Jasper, so I had to—we ended up getting away, but barely." I can't bring myself to say the stabbing part. Especially not if Dr. Simons thinks that I have a "condition."

"That certainly does sound like it could be them. The fear, of course, was that, given the opportunity, they might try to grab you to elicit your father's cooperation," Dr. Simons says quietly, then he looks up at me with these sad brown eyes. "And I wouldn't be so sure that your asking them for a ride was entirely voluntary. These people are terribly clever. And well trained."

I close my eyes, remembering suddenly. "We were both in the market for a couple minutes, and they were out there together alone by the car," I say. They could have easily done something to make it not start. "But they were at the gas station first. How would they even know we were going to stop there?"

"They were probably intercepting the texts from Cassie. Thanks to Level99, that won't be happening again."

Looks like they were right to take Cassie's phone. It was putting *someone* in danger: us.

"But why did you bring Cassie here? And why did he act like he didn't have any idea where Cassie was? He made it seem like *I* was the only one who knew. That I needed to tell him."

"I can promise you that everything your dad did was in an effort to protect you, to keep you out of this— what could be a very dangerous situation. I suspect he thought you were receiving false texts from someone who wasn't Cassie—remember we didn't realize she even had her phone. We had no reason to suspect she could be sending you texts. I'm sure he was also concerned about revealing too much over the phone. We knew that our communications had been hacked and they weren't secured until just now. Your dad couldn't risk giving out too much information over an unsecured line."

"This still doesn't make any sense," I say. And maybe bits and pieces do, but the whole thing together? Not in the least. "And why my dad's research? No one has ever cared about it before."

Dr. Simons frowns. "Did your dad have an opportunity to tell you about the Outliers?"

"Yes, I mean no, not exactly." Because actually it was Gideon who explained them. Why give my dad credit for being honest about anything? "They are the not-normal ones."

Dr. Simons nods. "That's a fair description. The Outliers are the handful of test subjects who demonstrated simultaneous nonvisual and nonauditory emotional perception," he says. "In other words, capable of reading other people's emotions while blindfolded *and* wearing headphones. There weren't many. Really, they were an inadvertent by-product of your dad's research. The combined nonauditory, nonvisual segment of the test was meant to provide a control baseline. Your father was looking at the implications of live discussion on emotional perception. He never imagined that there would be some individuals capable of accurate emotional perception without visual or auditory clues. But their discovery could have profound implications."

"Profound how?" I swallow hard, try to keep my stomach from pushing farther up into my throat.

"Well, for instance, the US Office of Naval Intelligence has been trying for years to use intuition in combat, and a discovery like this could be critical to that research," he says. "I expect North Point's interest in the Outliers is similar. Their ultimate goal would be to use the Outliers' skills to develop some kind of innovative military strategy or technology."

"So why don't these people just redo the study themselves, find their own Outliers?"

"They've been unable to. Because the Outliers were an inadvertent, inappropriate by-product of your father's study, their existence was acknowledged only in a footnote in his data section."

"Meaning?" I ask.

"They were an accident," he says. "We only know of three Outliers thus far. Notably, all of them were younger than the minimum age for study participants. All under eighteen. Two of the three were included because the study parameters were not properly administered by your father's research assistant."

This is all Dr. Caton's fault because of some mistake he made? It would explain why my dad was so angry at him.

"Dr. Caton, you mean?" I ask.

"Precisely," Dr. Simons takes a breath, puts his hands flat on the table like he's trying to make the next point really clear. "And because North Point has been unable to replicate the research, it seems they believe their only option is to find your father. Not only does he know that subject age is the key factor that unites the Outliers—several people know that, including myself—but your father is the only person who knows the actual names of the Outliers."

And I can see from the look on Dr. Simons's face that this is the point he's been bracing himself to deliver. That *this* is the essential detail.

"Wait, so they literally want my dad?"

He nods. "Yes, we believe so. But as I said, we are taking every possible precaution."

"Awesome," I say quietly. Because I do not feel at all comforted. "And what about Gideon? If they want my dad, and they came after me—he's just sitting home by himself."

"Thanks to Level99's work in interrupting North Point's communications, we have no reason to believe there's anyone coming to your home, or that anyone would come after Gideon or you, had you remained there, which is what your dad wanted, of course," Dr. Simons says. "But as an extra precaution, Officer Kendall also has a friend on the Boston police force who is keeping an eye on your house while your dad is gone, just in case."

"Oh," I say, feeling even worse now about having taken off. My dad was right to try to get me home.

"You know, we have met, you and I," Dr. Simons says, changing the subject, probably because I look freaked out. "You and Gideon couldn't have been more than five. Your parents came out to California to visit, and I think you went on to Disneyland afterward?" When I look up, he smiles gently. "Though, I suppose, if you have any memories from the trip, they would probably be of Mickey Mouse and not me."

I do not remember meeting Dr. Simons. But my favorite picture of my mom is from that trip, so young and happy, her hair in two braids, hands tucked into her overalls. I do have one actual memory, too—my mom and me near the cliffs of Carmel, lost in a sea of prairie dogs. Usually so calm and cool, my mom squealed and ran when the little animals started poking all their heads out of their dozens of holes. And there I stood, unable to tear myself away.

"See, Wylie," my mom said afterward, winded and gasping with laughter. "There are all different kinds of brave."

Do I actually remember even that? Or is that just a story I made her repeat so many times that the words became like my own? These days everything important about my mom feels like a memory inside a memory about to collapse in on itself and disappear.

"I don't even remember Disneyland," I say when I notice that Dr. Simons seems to be waiting for a reply.

"Well, it was such a long time ago and you were so young." But he seems a little disappointed. He takes a deep breath and shakes it off, then rests his hands down on the table. His fingers are puffy, like a row of swollen sausages. "I do want to be sure you know that you *are* safe here, Wylie, completely. I don't want you to feel at all concerned about that." Anxious, he means—don't hyperventilate, don't throw up, don't pass out. "As I've said, our precautions have been extensive. Cassie will be safe here, too."

Cassie. Right, I forgot all about that. They brought her here on purpose. "What do you mean, Cassie will be safe?" He said there were *three* Outliers, didn't he? He specifically explained where two of them came from: Dr. Caton's bad instructions. That leaves the third one unexplained.

"Who is the third?" I ask as my heart beats harder.

That stupid test in my dad's basement lab. The way my dad was so quick to tell us afterward that we'd all scored below average. How he got annoyed when Cassie pressed him for details, still hoping against hope that some glass slipper somewhere belongs to her.

"Yes, Cassie is the other Outlier. But under the circumstances, we'll need to be careful how we explain it to her, Wylie," Dr. Simons says, and it's clear this is a confession he'd been dreading. "I don't want to frighten her. It was bad enough that we had to bring her here this way. It would have been much better for your dad to simply drive her himself, but there was evidence that his movements were being monitored, and then that Cassie's cell phone has been compromised. But I am concerned about how Cassie will feel. It would be unexpected for anyone to learn this about themselves, but then to find out it puts you in jeopardy . . . It could be extremely upsetting."

"In jeopardy?" I ask, not much louder than a whisper. "I thought they wanted my dad."

"Yes, but if they can isolate an Outlier directly, that would be preferable." Isolate. Like a disease. Or the weak animal in a herd. "Wylie, I can see that you are upset, and you have every right to be. This would be a great deal of information for anyone to take in," Dr. Simons goes on, looking me straight in the eye. "But you are safe. Cassie is safe. And so is your dad. After what happened to your mom—I can assure you, no one is taking any risks."

After what happened to your mom. There's a rush of heat to my cheeks. A jolt of cold down my spine. *Bang, bang, bang* goes my heart.

"My mom?"

Here. We. Go. All the alarms in my head sounding at once, so loud I want to cover my ears.

"Wylie, sit back down," Dr. Simons says. "Everything is going to be fine. But you need to stay calm."

When did I stand up? Because I did. When I look down, I am standing on the other side of the bench. And now Quentin and Cassie have appeared behind me. Cassie's only a couple of steps away, arms crossed tight. It looks like she's lost another five pounds. Like she's vanishing. Soon she'll be nothing but vapor, a memory. Just like my mom.

"What happened to my mom?" My voice trembles. Or is that me trembling? My feet are still planted on the ground, but I have started to sway with the pounding of my own heart.

"These people will be held accountable for what they did to her, Wylie," Dr. Simons says. "Your dad is going to make sure of it."

CHAPTER 20

What they did to her. What they did to her. What they did to her. It's a piercing howl in my head. And already I am in motion, trying to outrun it.

Air. I need air. And I need away from these people. Away from those words in my head. Words that no one actually said, but that I already know are true. *My mom's death was not an accident.*

A second later, I'm outside in the dark. Racing across the damp grass toward the trees.

"Hey!" Stuart shouts from my left as I pass the cabin where we began. "Where the hell you think you're going?!"

Stuart. Stuart with his gun. But he won't stop me,

won't shoot me. I know that now. Because I am my father's daughter. And no matter how much I hate him right now, these people are his friends. They will protect me. They have to. Protect me from this mess he has created. *What they did to her.* What *he* did to her. That's the truth. Because if what happened to my mom has to do with all of this—with his research—then her dying is actually my dad's fault.

My feet move so fast they barely touch the ground. So fast it feels like I could fly.

"Hey!" Stuart calls once more, but his voice is just an echo on the wind.

Even if no one stops me, where am I going? I can't leave Cassie behind, can't leave Jasper. Nowhere is safe anyway. No place without lies. *Not an accident. Not an accident.*

But as I finally enter the woods, I can't think anymore about that. I don't want to think about anything except the running away, which is the only thing that feels good and right. *Not an accident.* I think it over and over as my feet pound across the damp leaves, crack across the fallen twigs. But I can still hear my dad's voice: *Tragic things sometimes happen to beautiful people.* He actually said that once, sitting on the edge of my bed a couple of weeks after my mom died. Like there was nothing, no one to blame for my mom's death. Except there was: him and his work.

As I race deeper into the woods, my feet slip and catch, on roots and branches and rocks. Like they did back when Jasper and I were running from Doug. But somehow this feels even worse than that, more hopeless. Because wherever I go, the truth will eventually catch me.

But still I keep on, trying to outrun the thoughts of my mom's car spinning on that dark patch of ice. Was there even ice? Or was she pushed into that guardrail by another car? Did she see it coming? Was she scared?

I want to fly through the air the way she did. I want to fall and hit my head. Knock the memories away. Knock me into nothing. So that I don't have to keep replaying every second of it, knowing that she could have been saved.

"That's ridiculous," my mom said. She was halfway up the stairs from my dad's basement lab that last night. "Sticking your head in the sand is not an option this time, Ben."

It was nine p.m. by then, but only an hour after they had last stopped fighting. After dinner, they had retreated briefly to their separate corners. But now they were back at it. A much faster rebound than usual. Like whatever had been bubbling beneath the surface for weeks was finally hitting a fever pitch.

Gideon and I were together in the kitchen, but like always he wasn't listening to their fight. While there I stood breathless, gripping one of my mom's chocolate chip cookies in one hand—the kind she always made first thing when she got home from a work trip—the milk container in the other hand. I was holding my breath, afraid that this time my mom and dad might break so badly that there would be no putting them back together again. There was silence, and then my dad must have said something to my mom. He was too far downstairs for me to hear.

"'All due caution'?" my mom called down the steps. "Are you even listening to yourself, Ben? Do you hear what you sound like? You're not a scientist, you're a robot." Another long beat of silence. "No, this isn't that simple, not anymore. And I don't care if it is your study and you're the one with all the information. What I think still matters."

When I heard my mom stomping up the last of the steps, I tipped the milk carton over my glass, trying to look busy. A small puddle of milk splashed into the bottom of my cup, the carton otherwise empty.

"Oh man, that sucks," Gideon said, appearing next to me at the counter with a full glass of milk in one hand, a cookie in the other. "Looks like someone needs to go buy some more milk."

"I'll go," my mom said, breezing through the kitchen with a totally fake smile. She was furious at my dad now. I could see it in her eyes.

"That's okay," I said. "I don't even want milk."

"I don't mind," my mom said, putting a hand on my arm and smiling. But up close, I could see this sadness buried in her eyes. "I could use a little fresh air. And a couple minutes to myself."

An hour later, she'd be alone forever.

***

"Wylie!" I'm still running, but there's a voice behind me now. Not far behind, either. Letting my mind drift slowed me down. Let someone close the gap.

I try to run harder, faster. But as soon as I pick up speed, my foot catches something—a root, a twig. It stops. And the rest of my body tumbles on, airborne. A second later, there's a sharp pain in my palms, and my left knee is on fire.

"Wylie! Are you okay?"

I grab for my knee, bending myself over the pain. Goddamn it. So stupid. Now I'm stopped. Still alive. Still awake. Still here. Now I will never catch the answers I was running after. I'll never catch her.

"Are you okay?" It's Quentin. He's crouching down next to me.

"I'm fine," I say through gritted teeth. Luckily, there's no blood, only scratches and a lot of dirt. And my shame. How can I have a father who would lie to me this much? "I just needed some air."

"And a good sprint," he says quietly, as he crouches next to me. But not like he wants or needs an explanation. "Are you hurt?"

My hands are still stinging and my knee is throbbing, but there is still no blood.

"I'm fine," I say again, feeling sore and embarrassed.

"I was yelling your name," Quentin says, still crouched on the ground. He looks confused. "It's really not safe to be out here in the woods. We send people out to check once every few hours to see if anybody—but it's not like we're experts in walling a perimeter." He looks around, deeper into the woods. "These people, they are trained."

"Yeah, I know. Believe me," I say. "And you didn't have to run after me."

As nice as Quentin seems, I didn't ask him to rescue me. Part of me even wishes that North Point would just shoot me. Because I might have halfway survived my mom dying in a car accident, but I will not survive if my dad could have prevented it.

"I'm sorry." Quentin looks around, then up at me before finally standing. "About your mom, about all of this. Seems like you're kind of caught in the middle, and that sucks."

"Sucks. That's one word for it," I say, and probably too snidely. None of this is Quentin's fault. But I can't do this right now, pretend that he's making me feel better.

"I guess sucks would be an understatement." He shakes his head. "Listen, my dad died when I ten, and it pretty much killed everything. Or I wished it had. Even now, it's like the color of the world is off." He flicks his eyes toward me, then back down into the leaves. But I know exactly what he means: the world forever shifted off its axis. "Anyway, I'm not saying I know how you feel, because I hate when people do that. But maybe I get it more than most."

There is a loud crack then, some distance off in the woods.

"What was that?" I ask, my heart thumping. Because one thing has jumped to mind: a gunshot.

"Um, I don't know. Hunters, maybe?" But Quentin sounds nervous. "We should probably get out of here just in case." Another crack in the distance, louder this time. "Come on."

Quentin reaches down and helps me to my feet. As I follow him through the trees back toward the main cabin, I brace for another *pop*, but there is only the crunching of leaves beneath our feet.

"That wasn't North Point, though," Quentin says as we finally emerge from the trees.

"How do you know?"

"They don't miss," he says, half smiling. "Also, I should thank you, because this little excursion has taught me something important about myself."

"What's that?"

He turns to look at me. "I do not thrive on danger."

"What happened to your dad?" I ask once we're crossing the open grass toward the cabin.

Because I already know that not all orphans are created equal—an illness, a history of drug use, years of estrangement beforehand. Suffering can be a bomb or a slow burn. Or, in my case, a nuclear winter.

It's not that one is necessarily harder than another. Actually, that's a lie. That's me being polite. I do think what happened to me—out of the blue, no chance for good-bye, no chance to prepare—is worse. And now it looks like I'll have the pleasure of my mom dying twice: first the lie and then the truth.

"He was in this deli around the corner from our walk-up in Dorchester," Quentin says. "Some guy came in to rob the place, started beating up the old man who worked there. My dad stepped in and got shot in the neck." Quentin shakes his head and looks down. "Want to know the worst part?"

"Yes," I say, probably sounding too glad that there is an even worse part.

"He went there to buy orange juice *for me*."

The hairs on my arms stand on end. "What did you just say?"

He looks up from the leaves. "He was buying orange juice for me?"

"My mom died on her way to buy milk for me."

"Seriously?" He looks like he doesn't believe me.

"You didn't know that?" I ask, feeling a little suspicious. "Dr. Simons didn't tell you?"

"No," he says, and like now he thinks I'm the one making up the bit about the milk. "And he doesn't know about the juice anyway. It's not something I ever talk about."

We're both quiet then, as we walk on, trying to process the coincidence that's equal parts creepy and comforting.

"I'm sorry about your dad," I say when we finally reach the steps of the main cabin. "Even though me being sorry doesn't really help. I know that firsthand."

"Usually you'd be right." Quentin looks at me like this is new for him too. "But this time it actually kind of does."

CHAPTER 21

The main cabin is buzzing with activity when we step inside, even though it's past four a.m. Watching them, suddenly all I feel is tired, like my running burned off the coating of panic that was covering up my total exhaustion.

But the people in that cabin seem like sleep is the last thing on their minds, more proof maybe of just how serious this situation is. They are men and women ranging from their twenties to sixties, clustered in small groups—pairs mostly—talking, hovering over papers. There's a tall, thin guy in a maroon Harvard hoodie next to a pretty woman with a smooth bob and a fuzzy purple beret.

Farther back, against the wall, are two other women my mom's age, in matching black running pants and fleeces, and a graying man and woman. And then there's Miriam at the back, organizing the coffee station. Ten people in all, including Quentin and Stuart. Dr. Simons, thankfully, is nowhere in sight. I'm not ready to talk to him again, especially not if he's going to bring up my mom.

"Have you guys been planning this for a long time?" I ask. If so, my dad is even better at hiding things than I ever thought.

"Dr. Simons called me two days ago and asked if I could spare a few days. I don't know about everyone else." Quentin points to the man in the Harvard sweatshirt and the girl in the purple beret. "I think Adam is the one who grew up here and knew Officer Kendall. Adam is getting his PhD in cognitive neuroscience at Harvard. His girlfriend there in the purple hat is named Fiona. I'm pretty sure they came up at least a week ago."

"And who are they?" I point to the two women in fleeces.

"Beatrice and Gladys are on the faculty at Smith and Williams, respectively. I think Beatrice might be an old girlfriend of Dr. Simons, actually." Finally, Quentin points to the slightly older man and woman. "And they are"— he hesitates like he's trying to remember—"Robert and Hillary. He is a psychology professor at"—he pauses again and narrows his eyes—"Boston University, I think, and I'm not sure about her. It's a lot to keep track of."

"What are they all doing?" Everyone seems hard at work—taking notes, studying diagrams. Adam and Fiona have a laptop open in front of them, and so do Robert and Hillary.

"Drafting a research protocol for the next phase of your dad's study, I think," he says. "I know that's part of it. If your dad can figure out the significance of the Outliers and make it public, companies like North Point will be out of luck."

"So all of you were just willing to come up here and hang out with mostly a bunch of strangers and maybe risk your lives?" I ask, and not in the nicest way. I don't know why I am annoyed by them suddenly. But they feel like enablers. Without them, my dad might have had to tell the truth.

"I had questions, don't get me wrong," Quentin says, and now he sounds defensive. "But the way Dr. Simons laid out the whole thing for me, it seemed really important to protect your dad and his research. Especially from people who profit from war."

"So you're here because you're antiwar?" Now I officially sound like an asshole. And maybe I am. I've never had enough space in my crowded head for a cause.

He crosses his arms. "And you're pro-war?"

"No"—I shake my head—"of course not." I really *do* sound like an asshole. "It's just a lot to risk for an idea."

Quentin shrugs. "Something has to matter," he says. "Or nothing will."

I resist the urge to shudder. "My dad says that all the time." Everything is starting to feel like déjà vu.

"Really?" Quentin asks, then smiles. "Bet right now sounding like your dad isn't making you like me more."

"Are you okay?"

When I turn toward the voice, there's Cassie. And for a second, I feel relieved. But then I see that the color is washed from her face again, the way it was back when we first saw her in the cabin. An Outlier. It's possible, I guess. I would never have described Cassie as especially good at reading people, but maybe it would explain why she was such a mess, so much of the time.

"Actually, I should go tell Dr. Simons about those gunshots we heard," Quentin says. "Can I get you guys something to eat? There's nothing fancy, but we have some pretzels and granola bars and stuff like that."

"Sure, thanks," I say, and to my surprise I do actually feel a little hungry.

"Great," Quentin says. "I'll be right back."

"I was so worried when you ran out," Cassie says when he's gone, pulling me into a tight hug. "I am so sorry about all of this."

"You shouldn't be sorry. My dad should be," I say when she finally lets go.

"I'm the one who wanted to take that stupid test." Cassie presses her lips together. Apparently, Dr. Simons has told her she's an Outlier, probably when I was jetting off into the woods. "None of this would have happened if I hadn't talked your dad into it."

"Okay, taking the test *was* your fault." I smile, squeeze her forearm. "But my dad should have told you about your results. He definitely should have mentioned"—I motion to the room instead of stating the obvious: that some psychos might come after her—"all of this."

"Yeah," Cassie says. "I guess."

"Wait, where's Jasper?" I ask, suddenly realizing that he's been gone for a really long time.

Cassie's face trembles when she turns back to me, her eyes flooding with tears. She told him about the other guy. And it did not go well. Of course it didn't.

"What happened?"

"You were right," she manages finally. And the look on her face is so shattered. "I never should have told him. He was so, so angry." She takes a breath and stares up at the ceiling. "And then he took off."

"What do you mean, 'took off'?" I ask. And the dumbest part is that *I* feel abandoned.

"He left," she says, motioning toward the woods.

"Really?" I ask. Do I seriously feel like he had some obligation to say good-bye?

"Yup. Really," she says, and with this look on her face: *he was* my *boyfriend. I'm the one who gets to be upset*, which is totally fair.

Now I look toward the windows. It's still dark out. "On foot?" I ask. "He just walked away?"

"I guess," Cassie snaps, crossing her arms. She's defensive, angry. Upset. "He wasn't so interested in giving me explanations."

A little while ago Quentin didn't want us even walking across the short patch of grass without taking "precautions," and now Jasper has taken off through the woods? We heard those noises that might have been gunshots.

"But it's not safe," I say, even though I can see that Cassie is already annoyed.

"Can Jasper not be something else you obsess about, Wylie?" she says sharply. "Let it go. Where he went—it's not about you."

"Okay." My cheeks flush. Because she's right about me and my obsessing, of course. And Jasper was her boyfriend, not mine.

"It was nice that he ran after you," Cassie says flatly, nodding in Quentin's direction. He's helping Miriam fold towels now, nodding good-naturedly as she bosses him around. Giving Cassie and me space to talk, probably.

"Yeah," I say. "You know, his dad was killed, too."

"Really?" she says, and now she sounds annoyed. Maybe she's jealous? That doesn't exactly seem like what it is. But with everything happening to her at once—grabbed off the street, given a special power, hunted by lunatics for said special power, dumped by Jasper—maybe she's entitled to feel any way she wants to.

And I so want to make things better for her, but I don't even know where to start.

"Jasper will come around, Cassie," I say, even though I'm not sure that's true. "He really loves you."

But there is a downside to Jasper loving Cassie the way he does. Perfect never bends. It snaps clear in two.

She nods, but not like she actually believes me. "Yeah, maybe."

"Hey, on the upside, you were right. You *are* basically psychic."

I say this even though my dad would hate it. Maybe *especially* because he would.

Cassie nods and forces a fake smile. "Yeah, that's me. Totally psychic. Too bad I didn't see any of this coming."

"So you really don't—I don't know—feel anything?" I ask.

"Not a thing." She shrugs, her eyes moving to Quentin as he makes his way over. "But whatever, who knows. I don't feel like I know anything right now."

"Is everything okay?" Quentin asks when he's finally standing in front of us.

He hands me a small bag of trail mix, which I tear open immediately. I'm even hungrier than I realized once I've eaten some.

"Yes, we're fine," Cassie says coolly and without looking at him. "Thanks."

"Yeah, except Jasper left," I say. Cassie shoots me an angry look. It did go without saying that I wasn't supposed to send out a search party. But I'm worried enough about Jasper that I have to say something, even if it makes Cassie mad at me. "Could somebody maybe go look for him? Make sure he's okay?"

"He doesn't want anyone to look for him, Wylie," Cassie says. And sure enough, now she sounds even angrier. "He wanted to leave."

"Someone can at least drive him to town," I say. "It's not safe out there in the woods, right?"

I look to Quentin for support.

"We can definitely go looking for him," he says. "But we can't drive him. We don't have a car nearby."

"You don't have a car?" I ask. That cannot possibly be true.

Quentin shakes his head. "Blame Dr. Simons," he says, motioning toward the back. "It's another security measure, something about aerial surveillance. But don't worry, we can still find Jasper. Stuart is not good for much, but he can track anything or anyone. I'll be right back."

As Quentin heads toward the door, I glance over at Cassie, bracing for her to be glaring at me. Instead, she's just staring in the general direction of where Quentin went. But not really at him.

"I know you and Jasper are in a fight, but I was just worried that—"

"Never mind. It's fine," she says once Quentin has disappeared out the door. "I get it." Finally, she looks in my direction, nods some more, like she might actually agree with me now. "Really, it's okay."

My phone vibrates in my pocket then. My dad, it must be. *Please be okay.* That's my first thought as I pull it out. My second? *You asshole.* Sure enough, it's my dad's number again at the top of my screen.

I think there might be somebody following me. I've had to reroute again. I'll still come as soon as I can. But tell Dr. Simons it may be too late. They're already on their way.

"Your dad?" Cassie asks, stepping closer and reading over my shoulder.

I nod as I write back, *Are you okay?*

And then we wait, and wait. But there's no response.

"He's still coming, though, right?" Cassie steps even closer. Like she's going to grab my phone from me. "You have to tell him. He *needs* to come."

"I'm sure he knows—"

"Is everything okay?" It's Dr. Simons.

I hold up my phone. "My dad said to tell you 'they're already on their way.'" I say it with an edge. I can't help it. "Which doesn't sound so awesome to me."

Dr. Simons takes a deep breath and pushes the air out in a long stream. "It's not ideal, no," he says with calm efficiency. "But we did anticipate this as a possibility. We have a plan in place. I'd been hoping it wouldn't be necessary to put it into motion, but we are thoroughly prepared to."

Suddenly, Cassie drops herself down hard onto one of the long benches. Her shoulders are hunched, head hanging forward.

"Cassie, are you all right?" I rush over to her.

Without saying a word, she leans over and grabs hold of me, pulling me down onto the bench next to her and burying her face in my neck.

"It's going to be okay," I say, stroking her head. I don't know what else to do. "We have all these people to help us. And my dad is going to be here soon. We're going to be fine. You're going to be fine."

"I'm scared," she whispers. "Really, really scared."

And she'd be crazy not to be. Who knows what North Point will do if they get their hands on her? What they'll do to any of us?

"Just make sure your dad comes *now*, okay? Promise me," she says before finally letting me go.

"I will. I promise," I say, even though he basically just told me he wasn't coming anytime soon.

Cassie pulls back and wipes at her tear-slicked face. Then she stares at the ground for a minute like she's considering something. Finally, she starts nodding. I'm afraid to ask what she's decided. "I'll be right back." She motions to her face. "I'm going to the bathroom."

"Will she be okay?" Dr. Simons asks once Cassie is crossing the room away from us.

"I hope so," I say. "She wasn't exactly in the best place before this happened. You should have waited until I was around to tell her about the Outlier thing."

"Oh, yes, of course I should have," Dr. Simons says. But almost too quickly, like he doesn't feel that sorry at all. "I think I was hoping to restore transparency to this situation. There is so much still to make sense of, so many factors and factions at play."

"Factions? What does that mean?" Because it sounds like a war already in progress. Though I don't know why I am surprised that there would be more to the story than they've told me so far. "I thought there was one company."

"North Point is certainly the immediate concern," he says. "But there are other elements at play."

"What 'elements'?" My voice is rising. I can't help it.

"Wylie, it is imperative that you stay calm," Dr. Simons says, and like I've totally lost it. Have I? When I look around, I feel like everyone has stopped what they're doing—Adam and Fiona, Beatrice and Gladys—all have turned to look at me. Could I have been screaming my head off and not even realized it? "As I said before, we know that the government is also aware of and interested in your father's research."

"The government?" I almost laugh. Did Dr. Simons say that before? It feels like news to me, but who knows.

And already the mention of the government has rung a different kind of bell.

It was a month after the funeral and I was still in no shape to be answering the door. I wouldn't have, except the man on the stoop saw me look out the window. And then he flashed a badge. *Department of Homeland Security.* He was hugely tall, his chest puffed out like a steel drum in his cheap gray suit, and his plain gold-rimmed glasses didn't fit him right.

"You're welcome to verify my credentials," he barked when I still didn't answer.

And then he pushed his whole badge through the slot. It fell to the floor with a heavy thud. When I picked it up, it certainly looked real—worn and with a slightly outdated picture. And so specific: Department of Homeland Security. Who goes with that if it was some kind of scam? Regular old police officer would be way less complicated.

"I'd like to speak with Dr. Benjamin Lang, please." Like an order from a drill sergeant, when I finally opened the door.

"He's not here," I managed, immediately wishing I'd lied and said that he was in the shower or something.

"When will he return?" *Return?* It was off—weirdly too fancy or something for even a federal agent.

"I'm, um—" *Say long enough that he doesn't want to come in.* "It could be a really long time." *But don't make it seem like you're alone and unprotected.* "But my brother will be home any second."

He looked confused—because why would he care about my brother?—then nodded once like a salute and handed me a card: Dr. Frederick Mitchell, NIH. Didn't his badge say *Homeland Security*? He did not look like a doctor. But he also didn't look like an officer of any kind. Just like a giant pretending to be a normal person.

"I'll wait out in the car."

When I peeked out the curtain a few minutes later, Dr. Frederick Mitchell was sitting there in the driver's seat—not reading, not looking at his phone. Just sitting there, eyes dead ahead, like a robot.

I texted my dad. *Some freaky doctor from Homeland Security or the NIH is here. Seems sketchy.*

Oh, right. I forgot he was coming. Sorry. Be home soon.

And sure enough, my dad invited that sketchy doctor-robot man right inside and led him downstairs like there was nothing odd about it or him. I tried to listen at the top of the stairs, but the rest of their conversation was lost, muffled by the basement steps. And I already knew my dad wasn't going to fill me in on the actual details afterward. Ever since the accident, he'd stopped telling me anything that could even maybe make me stressed, which, of course, only stressed me out more.

"What was that about?" I asked anyway, once the guy and his barrel chest had strode out our door.

"Routine grant review," my dad said with a disappointed shrug. Like the whole thing had turned out to be a lot less interesting than he'd hoped. "Bureaucracy making the world go round."

I consider telling Dr. Simons about the man who came to our house. But I don't want to. Don't want to multiply the threats, don't want to be expanding the circle of danger.

"Wylie, I am truly sorry that you had to find out about your mother this way," Dr. Simons says. "I had the false impression that your dad had already had the opportunity to explain. But innocent or not, that was an inexcusable mistake. I hope you accept my most sincere apology."

I shrug. "That's okay," I say, even though it's not okay at all. None of this is okay. At least everyone else in the main cabin has returned to their own business. I'm glad to no longer be the center of attention.

"You should also know that your dad only recently started entertaining the possibility himself that your mother's death might not have been accidental. It's not as though he's been keeping it from you."

"Keeping it from me for long, you mean," I say, looking away.

Do I want to press Dr. Simons for details about what happened to her? Before I can even decide, the door to the cabin opens. Quentin is already back? And he's walking fast in our direction. Carrying something too, draped over one arm. I feel sick when I realize it's my dad's coat.

"Jasper was wearing that," I say when he reaches us. Quentin frowns, keeps his eyes on the jacket as he holds it up. It's dirty and flecked with crushed leaves. But the worst part? One of the sleeves is half torn off. I jump to my feet. "Where did you find it?"

"Stuart picked it up in the woods, not far from the driveway." He glances up at me. "It's not that cold out anymore. Maybe Jasper tossed it because he didn't think he needed it." But that's not really true and also wouldn't explain the torn sleeve. I can tell Quentin doesn't believe that anyway.

I think again about the way Doug had Jasper up against the wall. My heart is racing.

"We have to find him. If those people we ran into find him first, they'll kill him." I look from Dr. Simons to Quentin and back again. They're staring back at me like I am blowing things out of proportion. But they didn't see that look on Doug's face when he was bleeding against the wall. "I'm serious. They will kill Jasper."

"Wylie, wait a second," Dr. Simons says, talking to me like I've gone off the deep end. "Jasper did tell Cassie he was leaving. The fact that he is now gone is not at all proof that something has happened to him. And thanks to Level99 and everyone's hard work here, we know several things that make me inclined to counsel calm. First of all, according to their own protocol, North Point rarely moves against targets during daylight hours, and it is practically dawn." But Dr. Simons knows as well as I do that sunrise is still a ways off. "Furthermore, why would North Point alert us to their presence by taking Jasper and then not advance immediately on the rest of us?"

"I don't know, to freak us out? Besides, my dad's text said they were on the way. We know they're coming!" I shout, and it definitely makes me seem kind of nuts. I'm not sure I care. "And what about Cassie? She's the one they really want. We can't just sit here and wait for them to come for her. We should leave. All of us. Right now."

"We can send Stuart to keep an eye on her," Dr. Simons says, then seems to realize how that might sound. "At a respectful distance, of course. But we can't risk exposing ourselves by leaving the camp. The vehicles are parked nearly a mile away."

And whose idiot idea was that? I think, but manage not to say. I don't think I actually believed it about the cars when Quentin told me before.

"It's a risk to sit here and wait," I say, trying to sound calm, reasonable. Because I don't care how many degrees

Dr. Simons has or how much he knows about this North Point company, I looked into Doug's eyes. Waiting anywhere he might show up and finish what he started is the worst idea ever.

"Maybe Wylie is right," Quentin says. "I mean, I'm no expert, but it is harder to hit a moving target."

"And if all of you want to stay here, then Cassie and I can go on our own. I'm good in the woods. Just the two of us could easily stay out of sight even in the daylight." I sound so confident, I almost believe myself.

"As I said before, we have a plan in place to keep everyone secure here. And I cannot let you leave, Wylie. Not without your dad's permission." Dr. Simons looks uncomfortable, but determined. "In his absence, I'm your legal guardian."

We lock eyes for a minute. Dr. Simons isn't going to make more of this threat, unless I force him to. Isn't going to say: *we will stop you by force*. But we both know what he means. And not just him, but all of them, including Stuart.

"Let's ask my dad then," I say. There is the chance he will have the sense to let me go at this point. He owes me that much.

Cassie and I need to leave, I type. *U said yourself they're coming. It's not safe for her here. We can head out on foot. We will be fine.*

No, comes my dad's immediate reply. Is he still stopped? He said he had to pull over earlier, but I feel nervous suddenly, imagining him typing and driving. I'm angry at him, but I don't want his texting with me to be the reason he gets killed in a car crash, too. *You are safe there. You'll be risking Cassie's life if you leave Camp Colestah. We have a plan in place. Please listen to me this time. Do what Dr. Simons says.*

I stare down at my dad's reply for a long time. The last time I ignored him, Doug did try to kill Jasper.

"Wylie?" Dr. Simons asks gently after I've been quiet for too long. "What did he say?"

Already, he knows the answer.

"He said it's safer for us to stay here." I try my best to sound convinced.

Quentin steps forward and puts my dad's jacket on the table, then comes to stand next to me. Like he wants me to know that he's still squarely on my side. Dr. Simons's face has tightened, but he's trying not to look annoyed.

"If you still want to go, I'll go with you," Quentin says. And I am so grateful.

"How about calling the police?" I offer. And I don't know why this didn't occur to me before. I don't even care if that ends up with me being committed anymore.

But again Dr. Simons is shaking his head. "As you've seen for yourself, Officer Kendall is the only reliable local officer. If we alert the others in that department, we could get removed from the property. We are technically trespassing."

"Then call the FBI or something?" I say.

"Yes, federal agents," Dr. Simons says, but regretfully. "The federal authorities are hardly disinterested either." So, despite what my dad had said to me at the time, maybe the visit from that NIH guy hadn't been so routine after all. "Obviously, the entire government isn't involved, but we don't know which agencies have been compromised. Letting anyone know where we are at this point is just too big of a risk. Not to mention that North Point has exceptional resources. Why do you think no one came to the diner to investigate the stabbing? A company like North Point can buy its own version of the truth."

My heart beats harder. My face feels hot. "You know about the stabbing?"

And I don't know why I am surprised. If my dad knows, then of course Dr. Simons would, too. But still I feel so exposed. And so ashamed. I look around the cabin again to see if anyone is staring at me. I meet only Miriam's eyes, and as usual, she just smiles warmly.

"Of course we know, Wylie. In this world, there are no secrets."

CHAPTER 22

It's a little past eight a.m. by the time we are all outside. I'm standing on the front porch of the main cabin. The sun has fully risen. But it's gray, the clouds low. It's damp and much warmer, too. As it turns out, there was a detailed emergency action plan, and my dad's "they're on the way" was enough to set it in motion, even if Jasper's jacket was not.

Without being directed on specifics, everyone has dispersed to their preassigned duties. I consider querying some of the others about the details. But so far I haven't actually exchanged more than hellos with any of them. It seems best to keep it that way, to draw as little attention to myself as possible. Especially now, when all I'm doing is biding my time until we can run.

Because I've decided that these people can do whatever they want; Cassie and I are getting the hell out of there.

I watch Adam and Fiona carry shovels down the driveway. Gladys and Beatrice, Robert and Hillary are walking to and from the woods in the opposite direction behind the cabins, collecting sticks and piling them in the center of the lawn. They are all so calm and purposeful, so ready and accepting. Trusting. They certainly do not seem panicked or afraid, not like they are looking for a way out. It's as though they knew the risks when they came up here to help my dad and are willing to pay the cost, no matter how steep it ends up being.

"What's with all the sticks?" I ask, motioning to Gladys and Beatrice when Dr. Simons comes to stand next to me on the porch.

"Nothing too sophisticated, I'm afraid. Some controlled fires that will give us a chance to leave out the back," he says. "*If* anyone does end up locating us, which—to be clear—is still not a foregone conclusion."

Dr. Simons's face changes as he peers in the direction of the cabin Jasper and I started out in. When I turn, Cassie is headed toward us, across the open grass. She's changed her clothes, jeans now, a sweater, and a longish wool coat. None of it exactly goes together, but on Cassie looks casually chic. All except the weird, bright-orange knit hat on her head. It's like something a hunter might wear, and it looks odd and out of place. There's no way it belongs to her.

"I thought Stuart told you she went to lie down," I say. And it was Dr. Simons who convinced me not to go after her once everyone had headed off to their jobs.

"Yes, well, that is what he told me." Dr. Simons looks confused himself.

As Cassie gets closer, I can see she has an odd look on her face. Then I notice the cigarette in her hand. For once, I'm not judging. If somebody told me I was an Outlier, I might start smoking, too. But the way Cassie drops it is so strange. It's like she wasn't even aware she was holding it in the first place. And past her, I see Stuart. He's out in front of the cabin we started out in. He takes a long drag of his own cigarette and exhales over his head. He's far away, but I feel like it was for our benefit, like he wants us to know they were talking.

Cassie being upset and confused is understandable. Upset enough that she's willing to chat Stuart up just to get a cigarette? That is not good at all.

"Are you okay?" I ask when she finally reaches us. And I wish it didn't sound so much like I was accusing her of something. "Where were you?"

"Taking a walk," Cassie says, crossing her arms and looking away.

She seems much worse. Before, she was upset about being an Outlier and everything with Jasper, but now she seems jittery and angry, too.

"You must be careful, Cassie," Dr. Simons says, and I'm glad it's him instead of me. "It's not safe for you to be off on your own."

Cassie glares up at him, and for a second I think she's going to tell him off. I kind of want her to. But she just bites her lip and looks away.

"Wylie, why don't you help Cassie carry those sticks down the driveway. You should see Fiona down there in the woods. We're using the sticks as the base for the firewall. Obviously, there are some sticks down there, but not enough. So we need to get more from the woods behind the cabins," Dr. Simons says. "It would be helpful if you could both lend a hand. Besides, I think it would be good for everyone to keep busy."

He nods at me: *take care of her,* the look says. Then he pats me on the shoulder in a grandfatherly way before heading back inside. *I will,* I think. *I'm going to take care of her by getting her the hell away from you.*

"Awesome," Cassie mutters, marching off toward the pile of sticks in the center of the lawn without even looking at me.

"This is going to be okay, you know," I say, when I've made my way over to join her. Do I sound like I believe that? I hope so. I glance back to make sure that Dr. Simons has gone, then lean in and lower my voice. "But we need to go, Cassie, now. Take off through the woods. It's not safe to wait."

I consider adding: *It's not safe for you*. But I don't want to scare her that much.

"Grab some sticks, Wylie," Cassie says. "You heard him. We should all stay busy."

"And did you hear *me*?" I ask. She's upset. I get that. But she is going to have to pull it together. "We need to sneak out of here. If we're careful, I'm pretty sure we can get away without them stopping us."

Cassie pauses and turns to look right at me. In her eyes, there's a crazy toxic mix of fear and anger and sadness.

"No," she says through gritted teeth. And then she turns with her sticks and marches away.

"Cassie!" I shout after her, feeling angry, but really more hurt.

I stand there, watching her go. Does she not trust me enough to come?

Finally, I step forward and collect my own armful of sticks. When I finally have them gripped against me, I'm reminded of the way I held so tight to all those pointless camping supplies in the garage back at my house. Which makes me think again of Jasper. If only Cassie had never said anything to him. Because he'd be able to convince her to go. I know he would.

As I start down the driveway with my armful of sticks, I feel someone watching me. I turn, bracing to see Dr. Simons, or worse yet, Stuart's prying eyes on me. But it's Quentin at the far end of the long porch, some kind of tool gripped at his side. My stomach tightens as our eyes meet and he raises a hand in a wave—and then suddenly there's a loud voice from the other side of the yard.

"I know that!" It's Stuart shouting at Dr. Simons, who is shaking his head and staring at the ground. "You think I'm fucking stupid!"

Is Dr. Simons telling Stuart off for giving Cassie that cigarette? Maybe, but it looks like something more. And it definitely feels like Cassie is still hiding something from me.

When I glance back at Quentin, he's still watching me. I turn away. Uncomfortable because there's something between us or because I'm just uncomfortable in general. I'm not sure I'd even know the difference.

By the time I'm finally halfway down the driveway, I've completely lost sight of Cassie. I have to scan the woods a couple of times before I spot a glowing orange dot to the right. That weird hat Cassie had on.

"Oh, there you are."

When I turn, Miriam is next to me. And she seems surprised to see me. But also, weirdly, like I am exactly who she was looking for. Where did she even come from? A second ago she was at the top of the hill organizing food. Wasn't she?

"Were you looking for me?" I ask.

She smiles at me with a twinkle in her eye that's part sweet, part totally checked out. "Oh, no, dear," she says, then puts a papery hand on my elbow and squeezes. "But are you feeling okay?"

"Yeah, I mean, why?" Does she know something I do not? Can she see through to my insides and their slow, toxic unfurling? She was once a nurse.

"You just look tired, dear." She smiles. "And you're important. We need you to keep up your strength."

"Important?" I ask. "Why?"

Because we need you to take care of Cassie, I think.

"Everything is about to change and we'll need so much help with the transition."

She's talking about the Outliers. At least I think she is. And I should probably just nod and smile and leave her be with her maybe-fuzzy brain and all that joy pouring out of her in a beam. But I don't like the way she's talking about this situation like it's the Rapture. Because I'm pretty sure the Rapture starts with everybody being dead.

"The transition?" I ask, because I can't help myself.

"Oh, yes," Miriam says, as if she is surprised that no one has told me. "After Cassie shares her gifts with all of us, and we share them with the others. It'll be a rebirth for all of us. And we have your father to thank."

And who knows? Maybe Cassie is the Second Coming, my dad a king. That would make me a princess, I guess. If only that were a thing I had ever wanted to be. If only that changed the fact that we need to get the hell out.

"Right, yeah," I say, because she is definitely waiting for me to agree.

And with that, Miriam smiles some more and walks away. When I look down, the sticks in my arms are trembling. Because none of that has made me feel better. It's just made me more convinced we have to go. Now. I'll just have to make Cassie see that.

I follow the little orange dot of Cassie's hat through the woods until I finally reach her and Fiona. A red gas can is on the ground between them, and Cassie is brushing at her legs and coat. They look wet, and I can smell the gas from steps away.

"I'm so sorry," Fiona says to her, and obviously not for the first time. Fiona grips her fuzzy purple beret to the top of her head like she's a teakettle about to blow.

Up close, she's much prettier than I realized, with bright hazel eyes and freckles across her nose. Actually, this is the closest I've been to any of the others aside from Miriam and Quentin. All the little twosomes have mostly kept to themselves like islands in an archipelago.

Fiona steps forward, pulling her beret off her head like she's going to try to dry Cassie's jeans and coat with it. "I don't know how I did that, Cassie. I'm such an idiot."

"It's okay, it's okay." Cassie waves Fiona away. But she sounds like she might cry.

"What happened?" I ask, still clutching my sticks.

"I tripped on that rock, and the gas can just went flying," Fiona says. "Of all the stupid things."

"I'm just going to go . . . dry off," Cassie says.

"Cassie, you can borrow some of my clothes," Fiona offers. "I even have an extra coat. They're in the red duffel bag in the cabin we're staying in."

"Yeah, thanks," Cassie says as she starts for the driveway.

"I'll come with you." I smile back at Fiona as I drop my sticks. "Don't worry. It was an accident."

"But she seemed so upset already." Fiona looks pained. "She must be overwhelmed. Excited, but overwhelmed."

"I think more overwhelmed than excited."

Fiona nods, then smiles. It's a beautiful, serene smile. Maybe a tad too serene under the circumstances. "But once we're out of here, done with all this, she'll see how incredible it is. It's going to be a fresh start for everyone."

***

"Cassie, wait," I call as we reach the top of the driveway, but she doesn't turn, doesn't slow down. Actually, it seems like she might even be speeding up. "Cassie, come on. Wait!"

Finally, she stops, her back to me, shoulders hunched in the pale-gray, misty morning. I have to jog to catch up before she takes off again, putting a hand on her arm when I finally reach her so she can't take off again.

"We have to go, Cassie. Right now," I whisper to the side of her face, when she still won't look at me. "I think those people, North Point, might already have Jasper. Quentin found his jacket in the woods." I'm worried what adding that kind of guilt could do to the whirlpool already churning inside her—after all, she's the reason he left. But I'm more worried about what will happen if Cassie doesn't wake up and realize the danger she's in. "They could be coming for you."

She turns to look at me, not shocked by this news about Jasper. More defeated. Like she's already given up.

"We'll have to go through the woods, but it'll be better than just waiting here," I go on, when she still does not speak. At least she's listening. This is my chance to convince her. "I know the woods. My mom took me all the time, remember? I'm actually pretty good in an emergency, too. Much better even than I usually am."

"It's not you," Cassie says, and with that same dead look in her eyes. "I don't want to—I won't go, Wylie. They're right. It's too dangerous."

"Cassie, I don't think we should be listening to—"

"Wylie, did you hear me?" She steps closer, her eyes bright and angry. "Because you need to hear me. We are not going anywhere." And then she turns. "Don't bring it up again. Just get your dad here, okay? I have to go change. I'll be back."

Cassie walks away, headed toward one of the other cabins, where Fiona's clothes would probably be. As I watch her go, my panic blooms, blotting out my hurt feelings. Now what?

When I look over, Quentin is still working on something in front of the main cabin. I cross the grass toward him.

"Everything okay?" he asks when I've made my way over. "That looked tense."

"Cassie is freaked out. It's hard to blame her."

"Ah, well, this thing sucks for her, that's for sure," Quentin says, inspecting a wire inside the black plastic box he's working on. "Being an Outlier could be a cool thing if the world wasn't such a screwed-up place."

A place that needs a restart, it's true. It reminds me of Fiona and Miriam and all their waxing philosophical about some kind of rapture.

"Is Fiona a professor?" I ask, because the way she was talking for sure didn't seem very scientific.

"I think so. Ouch." Quentin snatches his finger back and sucks on it like he just pricked it. "I think she teaches art or something like that, figurative drawing, maybe. Why?"

He looks at me quizzically, pushes his glasses back up his nose. He is definitely nerdy, but not in a bad way.

I shrug. "No reason." It seems stupid now to care about Fiona or Miriam and however they want to talk about this. "I really can't believe that my dad would do all of this without even warning us."

"I'm sure he didn't see it playing out this way." Now it's Quentin who shrugs. "How could he? It's like he's discovered this tiny little tear in the fabric of the world, which maybe isn't even really a tear if you look at it up close," he says. "I probably wouldn't go around advertising it either until I knew for sure what it meant. Look at these lunatics from this company, already trying to get their hands on it. And no one even knows exactly what 'it' is yet, or what it means."

"At least he should have told Cassie about her test," I say. "She would have had time to adjust to the whole idea that she can do this thing before, you know, she had to run for her life."

"Fair enough." Quentin holds up his hands. "To be clear, I'm on your side, not your dad's. And if I was Cassie, I definitely wouldn't sit here and wait. No matter what anyone said."

I'm relieved that he's brought up us leaving again.

"I just told Cassie that." I glance over at him. "But don't tell Dr. Simons, okay?"

He rolls his eyes. "He's my professor, not my priest, okay? I don't have to confess everything to him."

"Sorry, I just—I know Dr. Simons thinks it's too dangerous for us to go, but sitting here waiting seems—"

"Insane?" Quentin nods. "Don't worry, your secret is safe with me."

The way he says it makes me feel a little ridiculous. Like a little girl waiting for permission. I am sixteen, not six. And what is Dr. Simons going to do? Tie us up? They did lock us in a cabin for a little while, but there's got to be a limit to what they're willing to do.

"It doesn't matter anyway." I motion toward where Cassie has gone. "She won't go."

"Really?" Quentin looks confused. "Is it because she doesn't want to leave without Jasper? Because it looks like at least he got away okay."

"How do you know?" My gut churns. And not with relief.

"Officer Kendall called Dr. Simons and told him the truck you guys came in is gone." Quentin rubs his forehead. "Now that I think about it, I guess that's not *proof* Jasper is okay. A good sign, though."

"Oh, yeah," I say. But I do not feel reassured. "I'll tell Cassie, definitely. But I'm not even sure it was because she was worried about Jasper."

"If you can convince her to go, I'll tag along. I mean, if you want me to."

"Thanks." And I do really appreciate the offer. "I think I'll give her a few minutes to calm down. Then I'll try talking to her again." I motion to the small black square Quentin's been working on. "What is that anyway?"

"A car battery that I'm trying to convert into a portable charging station, in case they kill our half-useless generator."

"That's impressive."

"It would be," he says with a smile, "if I could actually do it. I had this accident the summer after my dad died. I was laid up for weeks, so I taught myself all this engineering stuff." Quentin runs a hand over his hair, then rests it on the back of his neck. "Anyway, I forgot that I was only ten, so it's not like any of it was that complicated. Also, I wasn't actually very good at it."

"What kind of accident was it?" I ask. Because, yes, I am especially interested in such things.

Quentin pulls up his pant leg to show me a scar, at least six inches long, running up from his ankle along his calf. "They actually thought I was going to lose my foot. But three surgeries later, it's as good as new, at least for someone who is completely nonathletic."

A car accident. Of course, that's already popped into my head.

"What happened?"

"I, um, well . . ." He doesn't want to tell me. That's obvious. Which just makes me desperate to know. "I had all these phobias when I was a kid, and they got a lot worse after my dad died. Anyway, my grandfather was this super-old-school guy. One day at the mall he decided he was going to 'cure' me of my fear of escalators." Quentin takes a breath and tries to smile a little, like it's kind of a funny story. But already it's not. "And I wasn't going down without a fight. My pants got caught, pulled my leg right in."

I gasp. Out loud, I can't help it. The image is so horrifying.

"Yeah, nothing like your worst fear coming true," he says.

I do a double take when he says it. Déjà vu, for the second time. But this time it was me who said that exact same thing—nothing like your worst fear coming true—in my last session with Dr. Shepard. Because my mom dying was always my greatest fear, and Quentin is right. Your worst fear coming true turns the world a special kind of dark. And I'm pretty sure it stays that way forever.

But standing there in the middle of that broken-down camp, I suddenly feel a tiny bit better. Because for the first time since my mom died, it feels possible that someone might understand me again. Maybe not the way my mom did. And not even Quentin necessarily, not today. But maybe someone, someday.

"So what about you?" Quentin asks. "Any secret childhood talents that are hopefully more real than my ability to build things?"

For a second my mind is a total blank, like I've never done an interesting thing in my entire life. "I used to take pictures," I say finally.

"Used to?" Quentin asks.

"Yeah, well, my mom was a photographer. So . . ."

"I get it." Quentin nods, and I'm grateful that he doesn't make me spell out how picking up a camera has been a total impossibility since she died. "Listen, do you want to go inside and get a drink or something?" He taps the top of the black box in front of him with his pliers. "I could use a break from this."

"Yes," I say, and I could too. A break from everything. "That would be great."

CHAPTER 23

Inside the empty main cabin, Quentin tosses his jacket on one of the tables before heading over to the refrigerator. I drift over to the stacks of papers at the other end: photocopies of different Q&As, Instructions for Testing, Training Protocol. My eyes scan the pages, picking up familiar bits and pieces. Some of it looks like the test my dad gave us, some of it is a little different. My dad definitely never said anything about a training protocol. So maybe Gideon was right, people can be taught after all.

Quentin comes back and stands next to me, holding out a Coke. It's a relief, cold and solid in my hand. Like a relic of a long-lost civilization. Still, as Quentin and I stare down at the stacks of printouts, I can feel my chest slowly tightening.

"What do you think they'll do with Cassie if they get her?"

"I don't know," Quentin says, keeping his eyes on the table. "Maybe Dr. Sim—"

"Come on, what do *you* think?" I ask. "You don't need to be an actual scientist to have an imagination."

Quentin glances at me, then turns away and shrugs. "They'll want to learn everything they can," he says finally. "See if they can figure out how she's reading people. If it's not her eyes or her ears, then what is it? They'd probably do functional MRIs, that kind of thing also. They want to learn how to be Outliers themselves, right?"

"Learn?" I ask.

He shrugs. "You can learn to do anything, right? I mean, not everyone is going to be Yo-Yo Ma, but most people could learn to play the cello pretty well if they tried hard enough. Maybe there are a lot more people who have Cassie's potential, and they just need help accessing it."

"Yeah, maybe," I say. "Or maybe it's more like basketball. No matter how much you practice, most people are never going to dunk the ball."

"Maybe they'll also want to figure out how many others there are like Cassie. Your dad's study had, what, three hundred people? If he found three Outliers, that's one percent of his study. If that relative percentage held true for the rest of the population, it could be tens of millions of people."

The pit in my stomach pulls a little deeper. Because what will happen if North Point's scanning of Cassie's brain doesn't work? I imagine them opening up her skull, attaching monitors to the squishy surface of her brain, her body kept alive by a series of tubes. I shudder hard.

"Hey, this is all going to be okay," Quentin says, putting a hand on my arm. "I promise."

I turn, about to remind him that no one can promise that, when there's a commotion behind us. The doors bang open, a crowd stumbles inside. And they're carrying something. No, someone. Fiona.

"Put her down, put her down!" It's Adam. He's frantic as someone yanks down a tablecloth and they rest her carefully on the floor.

"Gently, gently," Dr. Simons says. He seems so much older and frailer, his curly ring of hair all wild and out of place as he stands off to the side, as though he's too frightened to actually lend a hand. It's not exactly comforting.

"I'm okay, really," Fiona says, trying to push herself up. "It's not that bad."

"Not that bad? It's a bullet, Fiona!" Adam shouts at her. "Don't sit up!"

"What happened?" Quentin rushes over to where Fiona is on the floor.

"Adam," Fiona pants. Her voice is breathy and high. She is in pain, but is pretending not to be. "Really, I'm okay."

"She got fucking shot in the leg!" Adam shouts at Quentin. Like he's the one who did it.

Shot. A bullet. *Cassie.* Where is Cassie?

I look around, but already I know she's not with them. I never should have left her alone, not even for a second. Not even so she could calm down. My heart is pounding as I start for the doors, but I have to be careful. Can't risk them stopping me now. We'll head straight back into the woods behind the cabins. In the opposite direction of where Fiona got shot. And I will lead. And Cassie will survive.

"Where's Miriam?" Adam shouts to no one in particular. "She needs to take a look at Fiona's leg."

It's my chance. I know that it is.

"I saw her outside before." I move fast now for the door. "I'll go get her."

This is technically true. I did see her out there a long time ago.

"I'll look in back," someone else calls.

"Come on, let's move Fiona to the couch in the office," Adam says without looking up. "We can elevate her leg."

My heart is racing as I reach the door. The far cabin, that's where Cassie must be. Where Fiona's clothes are. It's a straight shot across the grass. I hold my breath, but no one stops me at the door.

**

Outside, I look right and left as I make my way down the cabin steps. The clouds have turned an ominous purply-black, and I have the most awful feeling that I'm being watched as I make my way quickly across the grass. Like there are dozens of North Point people out there, looming in the woods. Biding their time until nightfall. But I don't see anyone. Not even Stuart.

"Wylie!" When I turn, Quentin is rushing down the steps after me. "We found Miriam. She's inside."

Caught. Now what?

"Oh," I say. Lie. I am sure I should do that. I like Quentin and he offered before to come, but I can't risk that Fiona getting shot has changed his mind. "I just want to bring Cassie up to the main cabin with the rest of us. She went to change."

"They already moved her. Back to where you all were. It's our safest safe house." He points in the direction of the cabin we started out in. It's dark. Not a soul in sight. "Stuart's standing watch."

I look again. "I don't see him. I don't see anyone."

"Well, that's the point, right?" Quentin says. "For no

one to know they're over there? It's safest for her there. I mean, not so much if we keep standing here drawing attention to it."

And now I am out of lies. I have no choice but to push down all my doubt and trust him.

"Cassie and I need to go," I say. "Now."

"Agreed," Quentin says without hesitating, and I feel so relieved I could cry. He's not even going to make me convince him. "But not alone, okay? Just let me get my jacket and my phone, and then I'll go with you."

I look back toward the dark cabin. I consider running for it, for Cassie. But I will need Quentin to help deal with Stuart. And the truth is, I am worried. What if I drag Cassie out there and fall apart? What if rushing off into the woods with her is more than I can handle in my condition? What if my dad was right all along?

"Can you be really fast?" I ask.

"Yes, as long as you come back inside with me," he says. "Because it's not safe for you to stand out here waiting. And everyone is going to freak out about where you are. Trust me, it'll be less suspicious."

I nod and follow. Get in. Get back to Cassie. Get out. One step at a time.

When we get back inside, there is no one in sight, just the bloody tablecloth bunched on the ground with some stained gauze pads next to it. But there are some raised voices coming from the back. Or one raised voice, actually: Adam's. He's shouting as Miriam comes out gripping a tray with what looks like medical supplies. As usual, she's talking to herself. She doesn't look in our direction, doesn't even seem to notice us standing there. She's got a *tsk-tsk* look on her face. Like she would be wagging a finger if she wasn't holding that tray.

"Is it bad?" Quentin calls to her.

"Oh, I didn't see you!" She startles, as usual.

"Miriam, is Fiona going to be okay?" Quentin understandably has much less patience for her inability to focus now.

"Oh, yes, I think so." Miriam waves a hand. "It's just a graze," she says in a way that only someone who was once a combat nurse could. "A few stitches and she'll be fine."

"Miriam!" Adam shouts from the back. "She's feeling dizzy!"

"They really need you." Another voice now, this one headed our way from the back. A man's voice that I can't identify. "Adam's freaking out."

But a voice I've heard before. My mind spins around trying to place it, the effort vacuuming the air out of my lungs. By the time the man finally steps into view, I am so light-headed that my vision is blurred. But I make out that the size and shape of this man is bigger than the other men. Large in a way I have seen before.

No. I do not want to be seeing him. I close my eyes. Keep my eyes closed long enough, I hope, to clear them. For that man to disappear. But when I open them, he's still there. And I can see him so clearly now. So much clearer than I want him to be.

"Hey, did you hear me?" the man calls to Miriam. He waves a rude hand at her. "Hello?"

It's when he waves his hand that there can truly be no doubt. Because I see it. The bandage. Covering the place where I stabbed him.

Doug.

Bam, bam, bam, goes my heart. When I turn, Quentin is still staring in Miriam's direction. *That's him. The one who attacked us,* I scream silently at the side of his face. *There's no more preparing for North Point. They're here.*

Cassie. What if they already have her? I never should have come back inside. Shouldn't have listened to Quentin, even if he was just trying to help. I should have just—Doug is going to want to hurt me back. Yes. He is going to want to do that first.

"Coming, coming," Miriam calls to Doug, rubbing her bony fingers together. "Just need some hot water to warm up these hands before I do any stitching. Otherwise, who knows what kind of scar she'll end up with?"

"It's him," I finally manage in a whisper. "The one I stabbed. We have to get Cassie. Now."

I hold my breath and wait for Quentin to turn, to grab my hand and run. But his eyes stay locked on Doug. His face tight, and utterly still.

Angry? Is that it? Maybe he's going to charge at Doug instead of running the other way. But I know that Doug is even stronger than he looks. Stronger than Jasper. Definitely stronger than Quentin.

When I look back, it's already too late. Doug is staring right at us. At me. He recognizes me, too. There's no doubt about it. He even takes a few steps forward, stops in the middle of the room. Fists clenched at his sides like he's getting ready to charge.

And in the endless, frozen moments that follow, the last of the oxygen gets sucked from the room. My thoughts flash and disappear like lightning. Too quick for me to get a fix on, too fast to understand.

All I have are questions anyway. What will happen if Quentin goes after Doug? Will Doug choke Quentin like he did Jasper? Will he grab Miriam? Is he armed? He must be. He works for a defense contractor, ex-military. Isn't that what someone said? A gun, maybe two, at least. And if so, how is it possible that any of us will survive?

And Cassie. Too far away to warn. Too far away to save. How long will it take them to find her? To hurt her? To take her brain apart? That is, if they haven't already.

I wonder what it will feel like when Doug drives a knife into my hand or maybe my neck. Because I remember the hate in his eyes back at the diner as he gripped that blood-smeared wall. He is going to want an eye for an eye. But right now, Doug is still frozen there, eyes wide on mine. We are hunter and hunted. Locked in that moment when there's still a chance to survive.

Run. Toward Cassie. But I'm already so light-headed. A single step and I might crash right to the ground.

In the end it's Miriam who cracks the stillness. She peers at Doug, still halfway across the room. Of course, she's confused why this nice new guy is staring that way at Quentin and me. And I know how nice Doug can seem when he tries. Like a totally different person than he actually is. Who knows what he said to convince all of them he wasn't a threat? And to Miriam, already living in a fog of half-formed memories. She probably pretends to know people all the time just because they seem to know her.

Miriam walks up next to Doug, studies the side of his face with a look of playful consternation. *Move away from him, Miriam*, I think. *He is not who you think he is.* But I'm afraid to say a word. To do anything that might make Doug lunge for Miriam. She is so old. It wouldn't take much to hurt her, to kill her even.

"Look there, I was wrong. Wylie isn't outside, she's right here. I could have sworn—" Miriam points one of her bent fingers at me, then waves a hand. "Oh, never mind. Wylie, this is Doug. He and his wife Lexi have been on an errand since you arrived. They've been looking forward to meeting you." And with that, she pats Doug on his big arm and disappears in back with her tray of stitching supplies.

An errand. Miriam knows Doug. He isn't a stranger accidentally invited in. He isn't a stranger at all. The world is bent, the corners dark as I turn toward Quentin: *What? Why?*

And Quentin keeps on staring straight ahead at Doug for these endless, awful seconds.

"Wylie," he says when he finally turns toward me. His eyes are bright, hands raised like I'm an animal he is trying to contain. But Quentin's voice is so terrifyingly calm. "I can explain."

CHAPTER 24

Quentin knows Doug. Doug tried to kill us.

I do not need to know anything else. Get out of that main cabin. Find Cassie. Now.

I spin toward the door. Sprint. Heart racing. In a second, I'm there. But my hand slips on the knob. Once, twice. Finally, I grab hold and pull. But the door won't budge. Then I see a hand high above me pressing it shut. Doug's hand. The bandage is right there. Inches from my face. I close my eyes, brace for pain. For his fist in the back of my neck. A knife in my flesh.

But nothing happens. There is only the pounding of my heart and all that blood rushing to my head.

"Why doesn't everyone take a breath and sit down," Quentin says, not far behind me now. "Especially before the others come back and things get even more complicated."

His voice sounds totally different, more in control. Older. Or is that just in my head? Slowly, I drop my hand from the knob. What choice do I have? When I do, Doug lowers his arm and backs away.

When I finally turn, Quentin looks different, too. The sweet, nerdy boy is gone. And there is this grown man in his place. This man who seems much taller and stronger. Like he has never doubted himself in his entire life. Who the hell is he?

Quentin takes off his apparently unnecessary glasses and lays them on the table. "Doug, maybe you'd like to start by saying something to Wylie."

Doug glares at me for a minute. "I'm sorry," he says finally, crossing his arms. Like a child who is not sorry at all. "Lexi and I." He points to the back of the room, like she is back there somewhere. "We were just trying to get you here safely. Like Quentin asked."

"He doesn't work for North Point?" I ask Quentin, because there is no way I'm talking to Doug.

"No, no. North Point is a legitimate threat that we need to contend with, but Lexi and Doug work for me," Quentin says, and with this look like this should be a huge relief to me. "I hired them to ensure you arrived safely." He shoots a look at Doug. "It was certainly not my intent that you be frightened. That was unfortunate and unacceptable. But in Doug's defense, it's not as though he's had a lot of experience doing this sort of thing. Your dad has always underestimated how much people are motivated by money. No offense." Quentin motions to Doug, who looks like he could easily kill Quentin now. "We paid Officer Kendall, too, though to be completely honest, I'm still not convinced his motivations were purely financial. I always thought there might be something more complex going on where he was concerned."

"I want to see Dr. Simons," I say.

There is no way he would agree with any of this— trying to kill Jasper? No. I do not believe it. And no matter what Doug says, that is exactly what he was trying to do in that diner.

Quentin takes a deep breath and rubs his forehead. "Yes, but I need you to hear me out first, Wylie. Can you do that?" He heads over to one of the tables. "Please, have a seat for a second. The more quickly I can elucidate this situation, the more quickly you and Cassie can be reunited."

My hands are trembling, my pulse racing. But I make my way over. Because I need for them to at least think I am cooperating. That I am listening. Otherwise, they'll never let their guard back down.

I manage to get myself to sit across from Quentin as Doug drifts toward the back of the room, standing guard. He keeps checking over his shoulder to be sure no one is coming. The others must not know about "this situation," whatever it is. Dr. Simons definitely doesn't, and neither does my dad. And is my dad still headed this way? Straight into this? Who knows what they will do to him once he gets here?

"Without question they're nice people." Quentin gestures to the back, the others, he means. "Though I did have to take them as I found them. Miriam, for instance, is not exactly predictable." He sighs. "As a group, they were far too trusting, however. I show up and introduce them to Dr. Simons, who explains how he is your dad's friend. Three short meetings after that—" He snaps his fingers. "People want someone to follow so desperately. They want to believe. It's human nature. Look at all it took for you: Harvard. One mention that Adam is a professor there and his sweatshirt. Two independent data points and most people will accept an otherwise unverifiable conclusion."

"Adam doesn't teach at Harvard," I say.

Quentin shakes his head. "Adam works the help desk at Best Buy, but he is surprisingly adept with computers."

He's right. I just took Quentin's word for everything. I never even asked Adam himself. And once I believed that about Adam, it made me believe everything I heard about everyone.

"Who are they?" I ask. Because they are not my dad's friends. That's obvious now.

"The 'spiritual' part of their group has actually been much less disturbing than I expected. I needed The

Collective to give me some kind of meaningful context," he says. "But it gives you a sense of the groups who will want your father's research, Wylie. The Collective is harmless, but other groups won't be. That's precisely why we need to be prepared."

The Collective. The Collective. The Collective. The Spirituality of Science, I can see it now on the green flyer under our door. But I trusted Quentin because of Dr. Simons. He was the one who knew so much about my dad and even me—our trip to California, my anxiety. But already I can feel the ground beneath my feet giving way. Data breach, Level99. Could they have learned all of this from my dad's emails?

"That man isn't Dr. Simons, is he?" I ask. And how would I know for sure? The last time I saw him I was a kid. Even the pictures of him I've seen were all from years ago. I believed he was Dr. Simons because of what he knew, not the way he looked. And because my dad told me to trust him.

Quentin shakes his head. "His name is Frank Brickchurch. Biggest and best paid acting job of an otherwise fairly spotty career. I gave him a lot of information, of course, but he's had to improvise quite a lot," he says quietly. When he looks up from the table he frowns, regretfully. "I am sorry for the subterfuge, Wylie. But I needed you to take the time to get to know me. Without getting distracted by whatever preconceived notions you might have."

"Who are you?" I ask.

"I am someone who cares deeply about your dad's research," he says, looking at me hopefully now. Like he's glad to get to this part. "I care about your dad as a mentor and a friend. I would have given up everything to see that he was protected, that his research got the recognition it deserves. I did lie about some things, but never that."

And the expression on his face is simultaneously so sincere and so terrifying that it lifts the hair on my arms.

"Who are you?" I ask again. "Where is Cassie?"

"She's fine, I promise," Quentin says. "She's safe in the cabin, like I said."

"And what about my dad?" There's no way he knows about any of this—not The Collective, not Quentin. "Is he even coming?"

"Yes, of course," Quentin says, and he looks pleased to be telling me that. "He should be here very soon, Wylie. And when he does get here, I'm hopeful that he can keep an open mind, too."

"He is not going to go along with this."

"I believe he will," Quentin says calmly. "I warned your dad that his data and his email weren't secure, that there were going to be people who wanted to use his research the wrong way. But he didn't want to hear about practicalities and implications. He wanted his science to be so pure, but that's not the world we live in, Wylie. As his research assistant, I felt like it was my job to make him see that. But he fired me before I got the chance."

His research assistant. The floor rocks hard to the right. Dr. Caton, that's who Quentin is. *Fanatic. Unstable. Irrational.* At one time or another, my dad called him all of those things and more.

"He fired you," I say.

Quentin frowns and nods. "And I was devastated at first. I cared about your father quite a lot on a personal level. My father was not shot buying orange juice for me, but he did die a long time ago. I'll admit I saw your dad as a kind of surrogate. Like he sees Dr. Simons, I think. I thought he felt similarly attached to me. And he did share personal things, stories about you and Gideon. That's how I knew he called you Scat when you were little. We were close, your dad and me. Or so I thought. And so I'll admit I didn't take it well when it became clear he saw me as an *employee*."

I pull in some air and send it out in a shaky exhale. "I want to see Cassie."

"Yes, we'll bring you to her," Quentin says, but he makes no move to get up. "But there is something else you need to know first, Wylie."

And he has this look on his face. Like excitement but harder to identify.

"The things I told you, about my dad being dead, about my fears and the escalator. Those things were all true—not the details, of course. But I have always been anxious, just like you. That is something we share," he says. And I feel sick, because he's right. We did share something. "And now what you and I have struggled with our whole lives can be turned into this incredible gift, Wylie. If your father won't listen, I'll prove it with my own research. But study subjects aren't nearly as easy to come by once you're no longer associated with a university, *any* university—something your father has helped ensure." His jaw clenches, but I watch him shake the anger off. "But none of that will matter if I have your help. You can unlock all of it."

Awe. I realize finally. That's what I see in his eyes. And it is sickening.

"No," I whisper, and put my hands over my ears. Like that could ever be enough to stop the train barreling down my way. Like that could keep Quentin from telling me what he wants me to know.

"There is something else your dad didn't tell you," Quentin goes on, pressing his hands flat against the table as he looks me hard in the eye. As though *this* is the secret. The one I really need to hear. "Cassie isn't the Outlier, Wylie. You are."

Whoosh, whoosh, whoosh, goes all the blood to my head. I grip either side of the bench to stay upright.

"No," I say again, louder. And I'm shaking my head now. So hard. I can't stop.

"It's hard to believe, I know," Quentin says, his voice soft, almost sorry. "But your dad was trying to protect you, Wylie. I believe that. He just didn't realize that it would come at such a cost."

CHAPTER 25

My head is still ringing as Doug walks me across the grass toward the cabin we started out in. They moved me when I stopped responding. Before the others could come out from the back and see that something was so totally wrong. Before somebody in The Collective could intervene. As if I ever could have staged a coup now. Not when in my brain there is only one thing: *Outlier, Outlier, Outlier.*

But somehow I do walk through the gray morning, across the damp grass. Because they are taking me to Cassie. Or so they say. And I keep trying to focus on that. Getting to her. Getting away. We're not far from the cabin we started out in, and Doug still hasn't said anything about me stabbing him. But with his hand clamped so hard on my arm, he doesn't need to.

"Hey!" someone calls to us in a loud whisper when we're halfway across the open lawn.

Doug squeezes my arm harder, hard enough that I wince. But when we turn, it's just Lexi, making her way across the grass toward us.

"Damn it, Lexi," Doug snaps at her, looking around. We are exposed there, out in the wide open in broad daylight. "Quentin doesn't want the rest of them to know we're moving her."

"Oh, sorry," she says to Doug, then notices his hand on me.

She seems uncomfortable. Actually, more than uncomfortable. Do I "feel" that because I have some special extra sense? I don't think so. I have only ever felt one thing more than other people: anxious.

"I'm so glad you're okay, Wylie," Lexi says.

"She stabbed me, remember?" Doug hisses. "You should be worried about me, not her."

"She only stabbed you because she panicked. Because she probably *knew* something wasn't right." Lexi glances at me for confirmation. She thinks that it was just me being an Outlier that made me plunge that knife into Doug's hand. He didn't tell her about his arm on Jasper's throat.

"You sound just like one of them, Lexi," Doug says. "Pull it together."

"*They* are nice people." Lexi sounds offended on their behalf. "Besides, Quentin's not one of them, and he believes in Wylie."

"Please, he's even worse than the rest of them," Doug huffs. "We came here to do a job, Lexi, remember? To cash a check. Don't get confused by this garbage."

"They were going to take the house when Doug met Quentin at a bar." Lexi glances over at me, embarrassed. "Took our life savings for us to realize that people don't actually want energy bars for their dogs. So stupid. We don't even have a dog."

"Do you even have a baby?" I ask.

Lexi wraps her arms around herself and nods. "Delilah.

She's eight months." She even smiles a little, relieved maybe not to be proven a liar about everything. But she's scared, too. Afraid she won't make it back to her baby. Scared of something else, too. *That* I can feel. It's coming off her in waves.

"She's with my parents this weekend. She shouldn't have to deal with our— This isn't a place for a baby."

"She doesn't actually need to know our life story," Doug snaps. "Let's just get this done so we can get out of here *with* what we're owed."

"We knew that *you* knew about the baby when Jasper called Cassie by another name—Victoria, that was it." No matter what Doug says, Lexi can't keep herself from talking to me. From trying to get me to forgive her. She knows that this isn't right. Wishes that she wasn't involved. "But we were afraid you'd take off into the woods and get hurt. That was why Doug went to check on you in the bathroom. And then things got so out of hand."

"Out of hand?" Maybe if I push open the gap between Lexi and Doug, Cassie and I can slip out in between them. "Doug was choking Jasper. That's why I stabbed him."

Lexi turns, wide-eyed, to Doug. Almost stops walking. "You told me he attacked you."

Doug clamps his fingers tighter around my elbow. But there's only so much manhandling he can do. It will only prove my point.

"Lexi, they were trying to run," Doug says, annoyed. "We needed to make sure that Wylie got here, right? By the way, *you* said you could convince Wylie to get into the car without Jasper, remember? That was your job." Doug's voice is raised, and Lexi won't look at him. "Then, guess what? There he was in our car. And one of us had to do something. I was just trying to get Wylie to leave with us alone, taking care of things the way I always do."

"Right," Lexi says quietly, staring down at the ground.

They are not a united front. Do I know that because I'm an Outlier? Is it really possible *that's* the explanation for my overactive dread machine of a mind? That it's the roar of other people's feelings in my head, and not my own monsters?

No.

Yes.

I don't know.

"Welcome back," Stuart says when we finally reach the cabin. He makes a big show of taking his rifle in one hand and unlocking the door with the other to wave me inside. "They'll be glad for the company. Been kind of awkward in there, just the two of them."

The two of who? And the only person I see is Cassie, leaning up against the wall opposite the door, managing somehow to look pretty in the pale glow from the windows. But her arms are wrapped tight around her frail body like she's bracing for a blow. I rush at her.

"I'm so glad you're okay," I say, but when I grab up her tiny body, it's like her clothes are filled mostly with air.

I am still holding Cassie when I hear the door close and the bolt thud shut.

"I'm so sorry, Wylie," she whispers, her voice trembling.

"None of this is your fault," I say. It's Quentin's, or my dad's, or maybe even mine. But not hers.

"I wouldn't go that far." Another voice. This one behind me. We are not alone. When I turn, Jasper is sitting in the shadows along the far wall.

"Jasper!" I feel such a surge of relief. Like we're as good as saved. But then I see his face in the half-light—bruised and swollen, a cut over his eye. "What happened to you?"

"Doug," he says. He motions to his face. "He was more about the fists this time."

"Why didn't they just let you leave?" It's a terrible sign, I know. For all of us. "You didn't even know anything yet."

"Because I *wasn't* leaving," he says. "After Cassie told me—" His voice cuts off like he can't even bring himself to finish the sentence. "I was pissed and I needed some air, but I wasn't going to leave. In the middle of all this? Anyway, Doug just came out of nowhere. Made up for what he didn't finish outside that bathroom."

"Those assholes," I whisper. He winces and pulls away when I reach out toward his face.

"It looks worse than it is," Jasper says, and totally unconvincingly. "Did you seriously think I would just leave without even saying good-bye?"

I look over at Cassie. I don't want to sell her out, but she was the person who told me that. Repeatedly. Maybe she was hoping that Jasper did leave. "I must have—I guess I misunderstood."

"Seems like there's a lot of that going around." Jasper shoots a vicious look in Cassie's direction. "Why don't you tell her, Cassie? Tell Wylie about *all* the misunderstandings."

That does not sound good. It sounds like more than I want to know.

Cassie closes her eyes and rests her head against the wall, then shakes it back and forth. "If I had known—" Her voice cracks.

"There was another guy. I was right about that," Jasper says when Cassie stays silent. "And boy, did she pick a winner."

Okay. I do know about the other guy. Maybe none of this will be news to me. But my stomach is already a fist. And that is not because I am some Outlier. It is because I know Cassie. And with Cassie, there is always something worse.

"What is Jasper talking about?" I ask.

"I met him the way I said," she begins. And her voice is so small. "All of that was true. He came into Holy Cow when I was working, and he ordered a chocolate milk shake and sat at the bar and we talked for a while."

"This was while she and I were dating, by the way," Jasper interjects as he pushes himself to his feet and goes to stare out the window. Lit up in the pale-gray light, his face looks even worse. Cassie closes her eyes and hangs her head, but doesn't argue. "Sorry, continue." He motions to her, then turns and looks at me. "Wait, it gets so much better."

"It wasn't until he—"

"Wait, he who?"

Because it's obvious that this is the essential fact.

Cassie opens her eyes and looks up at me. "Quentin," she whispers, the tears finally sliding down her face. "I met Quentin."

No, I think. But I can't manage to make a sound. *No.*

I want to cover my ears. I want to run.

"Awesome, right?" Jasper says, eyes still on the window. But this time it's his voice, not Cassie's, that catches.

"First, he pretended that it was all a coincidence that we met. And then later he admitted that he came to find me. Quentin said your dad fired him because they disagreed about keeping my test results from me.

Quentin said he wanted your dad to tell me," she says, and she sounds so broken. "I guess—I don't know why I believed him. But it did seem like he knew your dad really well. And he said all these things that I wanted to hear, that I was being underestimated and everything. That I had this gift."

"A gift," Jasper huffs in disgust, his eyes still on the window.

"You can be mad," Cassie says. "You both can hate me. You should hate me. Because I am selfish and stupid and I made a terrible mistake. But I swear the whole time he had me texting you—"

"Wait, what?" I ask, my heart picking up speed. *No, Cassie. No.* "You were *helping* him? He *told* you to text us?"

She nods.

How could she? Risk that—risk *us*, for some guy she didn't even know?

"Wait, even the 'these people will kill me'?"

Cassie nods some more.

"My God, Cassie," I go on, and I am so angry my throat burns. And maybe she's right, maybe I do even hate her a little bit. "How could you? Some random guy tells you all this insane stuff and you just believe him?"

"Didn't you?" She stares at me hard for a second. She takes a breath and lowers her head again. "I mean, Quentin is convincing, isn't he? And he didn't even start talking about needing your dad until we got here. And he didn't mention *you* as a way to get your dad until way after that—and Quentin made it sound the whole time like he was trying to protect your dad." She's quiet for a second, like she's replaying it all in her own head. "He did some little test on me in the car. That's probably when he figured out that your dad had switched our results. He tried to hide it, but the way he was looking at me after that . . . Like I disgusted him a little bit."

"Wait, so you *helped* him get us here? On purpose?" I say, because I still can't really believe it. "You texted us that you were scared and needed help because *he* told you to do that?"

"Yes," she says, the tears making the horror in her eyes glow. She motions to Jasper, the cabin. "This is all my fault. But I swear, Wylie, I didn't know that you were

417

the person he really wanted until it was too late. At first, he said you were just a way to get your dad here. But then once you and Jasper were here in the cabin, everything changed. He told me that you were the Outlier. And he said that he would kill you—both you and Jasper—if you wouldn't help him. He said that I had to convince you."

"Help him what?" I ask.

"Help him do what you do," she says.

"But I don't know how to do anything!"

"I know, I know," Cassie says, and she looks so worried. "But he thinks he's an Outlier, too. He's convinced that he just needs you to 'unlock his potential.' I know because he said that to me when he thought *I* was the Outlier. And not just *an* Outlier, but I was like *the* Outlier. Totally off the charts. And the most messed-up part is how flattered I was." All I feel is heartbreak when she looks at me. "He promised that if you helped him, he would let you go. That he would let us all go. And I thought that was true, or at least I hoped it was. I thought maybe you could do some of his 'training exercises,' the ones he tried with me, which were kind of like your dad's test, and that would be that. But then when I went to borrow some of Fiona's clothes, I was alone in the other cabin. Instead, I decided to look through Quentin's stuff and see if I could figure out what he was really up to. And I saw this set of, like, instruments in this bag under his bed. I don't know for sure what they were for, but as soon as I saw them, I got really scared he wasn't ever going to let you go. Even if you did everything he wanted. But then I was also scared that if I told you and Quentin found out somehow, he might have Stuart shoot all of us or something."

"What do you mean instruments?" Jasper asks.

"Like for a surgeon or something," Cassie says quietly. "Whatever Quentin has in mind, Wylie, it's not just some kind of question or answer. Or if that's how it starts, it's not the way it's going to end."

"But how can I teach him how to do something *I* don't know how to do?"

"You can't," Jasper says. "That's why we have to get out of here."

"What about my dad? What's going to happen when he gets here?" I ask Cassie. "And is North Point even real? Somebody shot Fiona."

"I don't know," Cassie says, hugging herself harder. "Quentin stopped telling me anything as soon as we got here. Maybe he had Stuart shoot Fiona, I don't know. But he seemed worried about someone finding us here. Maybe that was an act, or it could be someone really coming."

"It was so stupid to trust him, Cassie," Jasper says, his voice cold and sharp. He won't even look at her. "Totally fucking stupid."

Cassie looks over at him, her eyes desperate. "You're right, totally right," she says. Then I watch her face change, set with determination. "But I am going to fix this. I promise."

"Awesome," Jasper says. "And I'll be sitting here, holding my breath."

I remember the plywood in the corner then. Did Jasper forget how close we already are? Soon, who was wrong, who lied about what and to who—none of it will matter. Because we will be free.

"Wait, what about . . ." I head to the back of the cabin, heart racing, to the spot where we spent so long turning those screws earlier. But Jasper is already shaking his bruised face. He looks like he feels sorry for me. "What do you mean, no?"

He makes his way over in silence, finally pulling out all the screws and lifting the plywood away.

And all I can do is stare. There is a hole in the cabin wall. The one I put my hand through. It's even as tall as the plywood. But it's much, much narrower. Large enough to have felt like a way out, but not to be anything of the kind.

I look up at Jasper, my eyes wide. "I know," he says. "Messed up, huh?"

"They'll have to come back eventually," I say. "If Quentin thinks he needs me so bad, he's not going to just leave me out here."

"Yeah, and?" Cassie asks. "How are we going to get out with him in here?"

"We'll just have to figure out a way."

Because I don't have to be an Outlier to know that much for sure. That our lives depend on us getting out that door.

***

In the long hours that follow, we discuss plan after plan, none of which have any hope of succeeding. At least we think it's hours. All of our phones have been taken now, so we have no idea what time it is. And the day is gray, so it's not easy to track the sun. But it seems like a long time. And by the end, we are just throwing ideas out so we can watch them drift away into the useless ether. We do search the cabin again for another way out. But Jasper and I have already done that. There is nothing left to find. Jasper hands out the granola bars that Quentin left there when we first arrived and some water. The last thing I want is to eat or drink. But Jasper is right. We should if we have the chance. Just in case we do find a way to run.

And a while after that comes the quiet and then the dread.

Eventually, we all drift off to sleep. Or Jasper and I must have, because we both startle awake when there's a sound at the door. When I look over at Cassie, I can tell from the raw look in her eyes that she hasn't slept a wink.

When the door finally opens, it's Lexi who steps inside, looking sheepish and sad. She has some more water bottles in her hands.

"Hi," she says quietly, hopefully almost. I don't know how long we were asleep, but it's much darker now. Not pitch black yet, but getting there. I reach over and turn on the kerosene lamp, and Jasper does the same for the one near him. "Sorry to wake you. I thought you should at least have some extra water just in case."

But that's not why she's there. She came with questions. She's worried about herself, her baby. Doesn't trust that Doug has any of this under control.

"Quentin is lying to you," I say. There's such a churning mix of feeling coming from Lexi. I try to focus on it, make sense of it. Isn't that what an Outlier should be able to do? "He is going to kill us."

"That's not true," she says, though she doesn't seem sure.

"Yes, it is. That's his actual plan. To get what he wants and then kill us. And do you think he's just going to trust you enough to let you go after that?" I ask. "What happens to your baby if you don't make it home? I know what it's like to grow up without a mother. And my mom had an acc— You have a choice."

Lexi shakes her head, looks warily over her shoulder toward the door. And then I feel a flicker of anguish—hers, not mine. I have to try to use it any way I can.

"You can't just help Quentin because Doug is telling you to. Listening to him got you into this mess in the first place," I say, hoping it will be enough to make her come to her senses. Lexi is a troubled person, but Doug is a bad one. "Are you really willing to risk not getting back to your daughter for him?"

"Oh my—" Lexi puts a hand over her mouth as the color washes from her face. She looks like she's just been startled awake. "I'm sorry, I have to go. Right now." She's already backing toward the door. "I have to get home to my daughter."

"But first you have to help us," I say. "All you have to do is distract Stuart for a minute, make sure the door stays unbolted."

"No, no, I don't think I can—"

"You have to," I say. "Or you'll be responsible for whatever happens to us. And you won't be able to blame that on Doug. If we are killed, it'll be on you. How will you be able to live with yourself, be a mother to your daughter? We are someone's children, too."

"This is never going to work," Cassie says once Lexi has left, giving us her wobbly assurances that she'll do as we asked, that she'll try to get Stuart off the door. "Did you see how nervous she was? She's going to crack. She'll probably tell her husband."

"That's helpful, Cassie," Jasper barks. "And do you have a better idea? Considering that you are the entire reason we are in this fucked-up situation."

Cassie closes her eyes and shakes her head. "No," she says quietly, dropping herself down onto the couch. "I don't have any more ideas."

"Awesome," Jasper goes on, gritting his teeth. "On the upside, at least you feel special."

It's fair that he's angry. I'm angry at Cassie, too. But there's a part of me that feels bad for her. Cassie is who she is. She can't change that any more than I can. Whoever it is I end up being.

There's another sound at the door then. The bolt sliding back open again. Too quick to be Lexi, though.

When the door finally opens, Quentin pokes his head in. He takes a deep breath and blows it out puffed-up cheeks as he walks inside. He is different yet again. Not quite the nervous boy-man we first met, but much closer. He's even put the glasses back on.

Cassie was right, we are significantly more screwed with him in the cabin with us. And there's no way to tell Lexi to wait until he is gone. We are going to have to go anyway, which means we need Quentin far away from the door.

"I'm glad somebody brought you some water." He steps forward and picks up one of the bottles Lexi left, stares down at it in silence. I worry for a minute he's going to tell us that he knows about Lexi agreeing to help. That Doug has already headed her off at the pass.

"Did you leave those dolls on our porch?" I ask, walking toward the back, hoping Quentin will follow, distracted by the conversation. One way or another, we have to get him off that door. And I'm assuming it was him. It started right after he got fired.

"Dolls?" Quentin asks, confused, and it seems genuine. "I'm afraid I don't know anything about any dolls. But I wouldn't be surprised if someone left something unpleasant at your house, Wylie. This situation is so much larger and more complex than two scientists with opposing philosophical perspectives. There are so many forces at play."

"Is my dad even coming here?" I ask, going to lean against the wall like I was just randomly headed to the back. "And those North Point people aren't real, are they?"

"Yes, of course, on both fronts," Quentin says, but not even like he really cares about convincing me. Instead, he walks right past me, even deeper into the cabin. Farther than I could have hoped. "Now, was your dad *always* coming? No. Were we *always* working together? No, obviously not. Otherwise I would have known from the beginning that he'd switched your and Cassie's results." He pauses like he's waiting for me to say something. "Did I have to employ some misdirection to get him here? Yes, I did. But he will be here soon, Wylie. And make no mistake, North Point is very real. And just like The

Collective, they are only the beginning. We stand in the eye of a hurricane."

Quentin heads over to the wall, to where we removed the plywood. With his back turned to us, he stares down at the long, thin hole in the wall. I step then between Quentin and the door. Between him and my friends. Because it's me that he wants. And maybe this is how all of this is—how I am—supposed to end. I have to believe I will find a way to escape somehow. And if I cannot, that feels like it might be okay. Because I may not know who I am anymore. But I do know one thing: I am done being afraid.

"Let Cassie and Jasper go and I'll do whatever you want," I say.

"Wylie." Cassie's voice wavers. She can see what I'm doing now. Can tell that I am planning to sacrifice myself so that they can run.

"I'll teach you whatever you want," I go on, moving closer to Quentin.

I'm amazed at how convincing I sound, like I really might know how to teach anyone anything. But it's harder to keep my composure once Quentin turns around and locks eyes with me. It isn't until then that I feel the full weight of his emptiness. His insides are a hole. His heart a cliff. And I'm about to slip into the abyss.

"I can't let them go, Wylie," he says calmly, like it's just the unfortunate truth. One that he and I must face together. "Not now." He lifts his head, looks vaguely toward the road, the woods. "It wouldn't be safe anyway—not with North Point."

"Oh, come on," Jasper shouts. "There's nobody coming!"

"I wish they weren't, believe me," Quentin says with a calm shake of his head. "Some of them are here already. Fiona has a bullet wound to prove it." But the way he says it makes me feel like Cassie was probably right: Quentin was responsible for that too. He turns then and crouches down in front of that thin hole in the cabin wall. "I've always thought that the only thing worse than having no way out is falsely believing that you do."

I hear a faint sound then near the door, Stuart's voice maybe, talking to Lexi? Jasper coughs to cover the sound. Lexi doing as she promised, getting Stuart off the door.

This is it. We can't wait any longer. This is our chance. Quentin is still crouched down, looking at the carefully cut rectangle in the wall. He is distracted enough to buy a moment. I turn to Jasper and Cassie.

"Go," I mouth at them. "Now."

Maybe I will even be fast enough to follow before Quentin grabs me. Do I believe that? No, not really. But somebody has to get away. And part of me died the day my mom did. Maybe this is a sign that it's finally time for the rest of me to go.

What happens next happens so fast. And none of it is what I intended. None of it is what I wanted.

The cabin door does not fly open. I do not watch Cassie and Jasper disappear out into the night. It's Cassie who moves first, and so fast. But not toward the door like she's supposed to. Instead, she lunges to the side and grabs up one of the lanterns. A second later she swings it high overhead, then smashes it to the ground between Quentin and me.

And I think: *What? Why?*

Quentin seems to think the same as he stands and we all stare down at the small pile of broken glass, and the silly little blue flame sputtering in its midst. "What the hell are you doing?" he asks Cassie, amused almost.

Jasper speaks next. Because he doesn't understand either. "Cassie, what are you—"

But then she spins to face me, puts a hand in the center of my chest, and shoves. Hard. As I stumble back, I catch a whiff of the smell. The jeans and coat she never changed out of are still tinged with gasoline.

Suddenly, I understand everything. "Cassie, no!"

But it's too late. The rest is slow and terrible. Impossible to believe even though I am staring right at it. And her.

"Go!" Cassie screams again, as she steps forward into the flame and the edge of her coat catches fire.

"No!" I rush toward her. But her body is already engulfed in flame. And it's—she's so hot, even from a couple of feet away. I can feel my eyelashes being singed as I move closer. I hold my hands up in front of my face. But it's no use. My palms have already started to burn.

The worst part is the silence. *Her* silence. The only sound the crackle of things bursting into flame. And Cassie doesn't cry out. She doesn't speak. She doesn't move. It's almost as if she's escaped somehow, slipped out into the cloud of smoke above. But then suddenly, she collapses to her knees.

"Stuart!" Quentin shouts as the couch next to him catches fire, and some paper on the other side of him. He is trapped by flames on every side.

"Oh shit!" A voice from behind the door. Stuart rushes past, grabbing up a blanket to smother the fire.

And then I am jerked backward, dragged away from the smoke toward the door. I am kicking, fighting to be let go.

We have to do something. We have to save her, I think, even though I know it's already too late.

"Come on, Wylie!" It's Jasper shouting in my ear. Pulling me out. His voice is high and tight like a terrified little boy. "We have to go!"

CHAPTER 26

Outside, we run. It's cold and dark and the air smells burnt. Of flesh. And of death. Of Cassie on fire. The smell is coming off me. Seeping out of my pores. I gag hard as we rush across the pitch-black, damp grass toward the even darker woods. No moon tonight, no stars. Like the universe has folded in on itself and disappeared. There are tears in my eyes and a burning in my chest as we run. *No,* I think again. *That did not just happen.* None of this is real. And my legs are so heavy suddenly, too heavy to move.

"Come on." Jasper tugs me on as I slow. "We can't stop. She'd want us to go."

And he's right. She died so we could get away. And there is still my dad to warn. I don't know what he believes. What Quentin and the pretend Dr. Simons may have convinced him of. Why he thinks he's coming here. But I feel sure he'll never get back out alive. When we finally reach the trees, I turn back once, hoping I've imagined it. But the cabin glows orange in the distance.

"Don't look," Jasper says, more to himself than anything. "It'll be worse. Come on."

But it's hard to run, to catch a breath when I'm crying so hard. Am I crying? My face is wet and there's a burn in my throat. But I am otherwise completely and totally numb, making it even harder to run through the woods in the dark. But Jasper and I have done this before. We can do it again. We will have to. And he is right about not turning around. There are already the voices behind us again. So many, it sounds like, but it could be an echo of only a few. At that distance, it's impossible to know.

"Look. Over there," Jasper calls after a while of just sticks and branches and more darkness. I can see the outline of his arm, pointing straight ahead. And in the distance there are very small lights, a house maybe. "It has to have a driveway. Driveway has to lead to a road."

Saved again by some lights on the horizon? But they are so much farther away this time. Because we continue on like that, forever it seems, running as fast as we can in the dark, which doesn't feel nearly fast enough. And doesn't really seem to be getting us anywhere. Not any closer to the lights, which at one point seem to vanish entirely. And the whole time, I brace for a voice behind us. For someone's hand on my arm. For gunfire. But there is nothing in that long and awful forever but the hard beating of my own heart.

Finally—hours later, minutes, a lifetime—we come out of the woods at the edge of a road. The house, it turns out, is still some distance on. And the road is dark and narrow. Dead quiet. I look right and then left. Not a car in sight. Nothing. No one. Anywhere. But Jasper is right. We need to keep moving. Just pausing there for a minute, my chest already feels like it is going to explode.

And later there will be so much time to be sad for Cassie. Later, I will be sad forever. Right now, though, I need to move. I need to keep going. *We* need to keep going before they catch us. We need to warn my dad.

I look left and right again down the dark and silent road. Which way to go? Which way is fastest to a phone, someplace we can call my dad? Or the police. Some police other than Officer Kendall. The FBI? How does one even call them?

"Holy shit," Jasper whispers suddenly, his eyes wide on mine. "She's dead, isn't she?"

Like someone has only just told him what happened. Like he is only just realizing it.

"Yeah," I say. "But you were right. We had to go. There was nothing we could do to save her."

"Holy shit—what the fuck," he says, wrapping his arms around his stomach like he might vomit. "Did you hear what I said to her? I was so mean. That is going to be the last thing I ever say to her. The last thing anyone says."

"She knew how much you loved her," I say. And he has to keep it together. If Jasper crashes to pieces too close to me, I will be swept up in his collapse.

Suddenly, there is a flicker in the distance up the road. Like a shooting star. Gone so fast I think I've imagined it. Seeing things that I want to see. But then it appears again. Small, but slowly and steadily growing. Headlights. A minute later there is no doubt.

"Somebody's coming," I say.

Jasper takes a deep breath, crossing his arms as he steps around me to look. "It could be them, though."

"They'd be coming from the other way. Wouldn't they?"

I hold my breath as the lights get closer, praying that I'm right. Because all I can picture is Stuart's gun. And what my dad might look like with it pressed to the back of his skull.

"It's a truck," Jasper says. "But he's going too fast. He'll never see us."

Jasper is right, the truck is coming so fast, the headlights bigger and bigger by the second. When just an instant ago, they seemed miles away. *He'll stop. He'll see me.* A guess, a hope, an instinct. Intuition. If I am who they say I am, I will be right, won't I?

"Wylie!" I hear Jasper yell as I make my way out into the road. "What the hell are you doing?"

It's okay. This is not how I die. And I don't think that it is. But as I stand there in the middle of the road, waving my arms over my head, part of me wishes that it would be. And Jasper is right, the truck isn't slowing down. The lights are closer now. Bright on the road and the trees. Blinding me as I wave my arms. *This is not how I die.* It's a memory and a wish.

"Wylie!" Jasper screams again.

When I turn, his face is lit up as he sprints toward me at full speed like the athlete he is. But I already know, there isn't enough time for him to do anything but die with me. And so I close my eyes and face the oncoming lights. And I pray that I am right. That I am everything Quentin said. And that if I am not, that this is at least not how Jasper dies.

The insides of my eyelids glow. So bright for a second I wonder if I might not already be dead. But then comes a deafening screech. The smell, too, rubber burning against asphalt. When I open my eyes, there's Jasper at my side, his face turned away, shoulders up, bracing himself for impact. I close my eyes once more. Until finally there is only silence.

When I look, the truck has rolled past us and come to a stop, almost in the woods on the opposite side of the road. I blink down at my hands. They are still there. I am still in one piece. We are still alive. I swallow down a mouthful of air as Jasper and I stare at each other, wide-eyed.

"For fuck's sake!" the driver shouts as he comes around the front of his truck. He's a big man with a bushy black beard, wearing a blue flannel shirt and a John Deere baseball cap. He rests one hand on the grille of his truck, the other on his heart. "What the hell are you kids doing in the middle of the goddamn road?! I almost killed you." Then he looks down at himself as if to make sure he's not injured. "I could've been killed myself. Not to mention my truck." He steps back to inspect it. "I'm a foot away from that goddamn tree."

"We need help, please." I sound too frantic. Like someone who's going to cause trouble, somebody already in too much. Someone on meth, maybe. If he knows this area, that is what he'll think. "We just need to use your phone."

"Fuck no!" He's already headed back around to the front of the driver's side. "Now, get the hell out of the road or I swear to Christ I'll roll over you."

He's pissed. But he's nervous too—*him*, not me. Even though a day ago I would have mistaken it for my own nerves, I actually think they are *his* feelings. He's worried about getting in trouble himself. Nothing too bad, not a dead body in his truck. But something he's not supposed to be doing: driving on that road, cheating on his wife, working past shift to make up time. Whatever it is, he's lying to somebody about something.

"Let us use your phone now, or we'll call your company later and tell them we saw you here." I step back and make a show of looking at the company name on the side of the cab door, and then his license plate. Neither of which I will remember. "This size of truck on this size of a road. There's no way you're supposed to be here."

"Oh, yeah?" he says angrily. "Fuck if I care what you do." Except it's obvious that he *does* care, a whole lot. "There's no damn signal here anyway. Even if I gave you my phone, it wouldn't do shit for you."

But he hasn't gotten back in his truck. He's worried enough that he doesn't want to leave with my threat hanging in the air.

"Then give us a ride. Just to the nearest gas station. We'll use someone else's phone when we get there."

"No fucking way I'm going to—"

"Or we'll make that call," I say. "And everyone will know what you've been doing."

And I know I'm on seriously thin ice here. But the driver grinds his jaw down and narrows his eyes some more, like he is actually buying my stab in the dark.

"Fine," he says. "But your asses are riding in the trailer."

Jasper and I sit in silence inside the dark, freezing-cold trailer. Backs against the wall, feet jammed against a tall stack of plastic pallets filled with boxes of crackers and pretzels, we can hear them creak right and then left every time we hit a bump. We drive for longer than I expect. Much, much longer than would seem necessary. An hour maybe. With the dark and cold and the rocking crackers, eventually, I start to wonder if he's taking us to a gas station at all. And who's to say this truck driver isn't some friend of Quentin's, the way that Officer Kendall was? Or if what he has to hide is so much worse than I thought? Something worth getting rid of us for. I still don't feel like my thoughts are much more than guesses.

And even if I'm right that he's doing something he's not supposed to be, it's one thing to know enough to threaten someone, it's another thing to know what will happen after you do. I'm not breathing much by the time the truck finally jerks to a stop, and Jasper reaches over and takes my hand.

"We're going to make it," he says when he squeezes my fingers. His voice is quiet and calm, but it's too dark to see his face. "And your dad's going to be okay. We'll warn him in time. I know we will."

We couldn't save Cassie, and so we'll save him. Jasper doesn't say that, but that's what he means. It's what he wants to believe. Except he doesn't, not really. I can feel that he doesn't. Jasper is afraid that my dad is walking into a trap, that maybe he already has. And so am I. I'm terrified, actually. But I am trying so hard to stay above it, not to let my panic overwhelm me. Because my dad needs me right now. He needs me not to be afraid.

Jasper and I are still holding hands when there's a sound at the back of the trailer, the lock being flipped open. A second later, the door rolls up loudly.

Dark still. I was hoping for light, even though I know that would be impossible. We're still hours from dawn, a whole nighttime stretching between here and tomorrow. But morning would have felt like such proof everything was going to be okay. Even if another part of me knows that it's already too late for okay. Cassie is dead. Nothing can change that.

"Now get your asses out of there before somebody sees you," the driver says, waving us out. At least we are at a truck stop like we asked. "And you better not have taken any goddamn crackers."

I climb out of the truck to the ordinary hum of the nearby, late evening, highway traffic. The parking lot is mostly quiet. A few drivers are filling up their cars, truckers chatting with coffee in hand. Businesspeople, a few families in and out of the building. Life. As if nothing has changed. And I wonder for a second whether it really has, whether we might have imagined everything.

No, I shouldn't let myself do that. Pretend that Cassie is alive. It will be worse to have to remember that *she* really is gone. That all of it really did happen. I know that. Cassie and my mom are both gone and I am all alone. I don't know what I will do without them. Can't imagine how I will survive. But I have to focus on the here and the now: my dad. We need to warn him. Need to make sure that he doesn't go to Camp Colestah. Doesn't go where his supposedly dear old friend Dr. Simons has convinced him he needs to be. Because maybe I should be angry enough not to care what happens to him, but all I can think about is how badly I need for him to survive.

Inside the rest stop, there's a woman at a table near a McDonald's holding a sleeping baby in her arms while trying to get the tired little girl across from her to eat some more of her chicken nuggets. She looks right up at me when I step inside. Like I've tripped some kind of alarm. Concerned in that motherly way. For her own children. For me. It's hard to tell.

But she will say yes about the phone. I feel sure of it. She will do her best to help. Still, she grips her baby a little tighter when I head her way. Leans in closer to the little girl. It's hard to blame her. I can only imagine what I look like. Exhausted, filthy, covered in soot. Like a liar. Because that's the reality: my truth has become the sum of so many lies.

"Do you think I could borrow your phone?" I ask her. "It's an emergency. I lost my cell phone and I need to call my dad."

"Um, sure," she says. Definitely nervous, though, as she pushes her phone quickly across the table to me, flicks her eyes toward her daughter, who is sitting just inches away from me.

"Thank you." I step away, which seems to make the woman relax a little. "I'll be quick."

I hope she doesn't notice my hands, trembling as I dial my dad's cell phone number. I take a couple more steps. Not so far that she thinks I'm taking her phone, but far enough that she won't overhear every insane word I'm about to say. But my heart catches when the call goes straight to my dad's voice mail. Not even a single ring. Is he close to the camp? Is he already on borrowed time?

"Are you okay?" the woman asks, so much like Lexi. "Do you need help?"

When I look up, she's staring at me. *Yes*, I want to say. *I need so much help.*

"Can I just make one more call?" I ask, moving back to her. "To my house. My dad's cell phone is off."

"Sure." She shifts the baby to her other leg, glances in the direction of Jasper, and then over to a security guard near the door. She knows there's a lot I'm not saying. She can tell. Maybe because she's just a nice person. Or maybe because she's an Outlier. And maybe she'll never even know. "Go ahead."

I've only got one more chance—one more call before she'll at least insist on getting "help." Gideon is my only option. My face feels hot as I dial his cell number, hope that I can get through to him. Hope that he'll do exactly what needs to be done.

"Hello?" Gideon answers before I can move out of earshot again.

"Gideon, it's Wylie. You have to listen to me," I say, and my voice cracks. But I can't fall apart, not yet. "You have to call the police in Boston. Tell them something has happened to Dad. That he's in trouble. Someone—" What can I say that won't sound insane? That Gideon can tell the police so they go looking for a grown man gone only a few hours? "Dad was carjacked, in Boston. Some man with a gun came and took him and his car. He called me once. He said they were near Camp Colestah in Maine."

It doesn't make a lot of sense, but it's not a terrible lie, either. When I look down, the woman with the baby is staring at me with her mouth open—the talk of guns, the police. I can't blame her. But I need to finish before she can have her phone back. Before she can be rid of me.

"What the hell are you talking about?" Gideon asks. "And where are you?" Now he sounds actually worried.

"You can't just take off without telling anybody. Whose phone is this? And what do you mean that Da—"

"Gideon!" I shout, and too loud. I can't even bring myself to look at the woman now. I grip the phone hard so no one can rip it away. "Please, just listen to me. I have to get off this phone now. Just call the police. The *Boston* police. Tell them to look in Maine for Dad's car, somewhere on the highway between Newton and Camp Colestah in Maine. Or something really bad could happen to him. It already has happened, I mean."

"Why don't you just talk to Dad *yourself*?"

"I *can't* talk to Dad, Gideon. That's the whole point. He's not answering his phone. He needs our help."

"Um, yeah, except you *can* talk to him. He's sitting right here next to me."

CHAPTER 27

They send the police. All sorts of police, to all sorts of places. To the camp. To us. Even to Officer Kendall, not that they can find him. State police. The FBI, too, because Quentin took Cassie across state lines. I don't explain all the details to my dad on the phone, just enough for him to understand. To know that something terrible has happened and Cassie is gone. And that the local police near the camp can't be trusted. And he says enough for me to know that he didn't send any of the texts I got after our argument when I was at the Freshmart. The fact that they'd come from his phone number instead of his name in my contacts was a sign, just not the one

I thought it was. And the texts he did send, the voice mails he left, had—without my dad knowing—been blocked from ever making their way to my phone. Level99 might not have known who they were really helping or why, but apparently they were very good at their job.

It takes much more convincing to get my dad to stay at home. All he wants to do is to rush up and be sure that I'm okay. To see for himself. And I am much more grateful for that than I ever could have imagined. But I'm still afraid that Quentin might be looking for him. When my voice cracks as I beg him not to come, he finally listens.

Karen, though, has no choice. She is already on her way.

Jasper and I don't talk much on the ride home, once again in the backseat of a police car. This one is older, though, and more cramped, but feels so much safer. We were at the rest stop overnight answering question after question from officer after officer—patrolmen, detectives, and eventually the FBI. An hour into the drive back to Newton, the sun finally begins to rise, the sky above the trees a swirl of pinks and purples. I fall asleep for a few minutes, though I would have sworn I would never sleep again. I dream of fire, Cassie on fire, jolting awake with a gasp that wakes Jasper. The female police officer riding in the passenger seat turns her head a little toward me, but doesn't actually look at me.

"You're okay," she says, flat and firm. Official. "You're safe now."

It's not comforting. Because I don't feel safe. Maybe I never will.

"Do you think you're really an Outlier?" Jasper asks then.

"I don't know," I say, and that's the truth. There have been things I seemed to know somehow, even since Jasper and I left the house: Lexi and Doug's missing baby, the old man being willing to hand over his keys, that truck driver caving to my threat. But there is so much else that I missed—who Quentin was, what Cassie would do. "Maybe I'm an Outlier. Maybe not."

"Are you going to be okay?" he asks.

"I don't know," I say again, forcing a little smile. "Maybe. Maybe not."

Because that's the truth also. But it's also true that I've felt much less panicked for hours now. Is that because I have this explanation now for how I am? Freed from anxiety Alcatraz because of this secret? I don't know. I don't feel like I know anything anymore, except that I need to get home, and I need to see my dad.

Jasper reaches over again to squeeze my hand. But this time he doesn't let go. Instead, he falls back asleep, fingers wrapped tight around mine.

"I'll call you," he says when we finally pull to a stop at my house at a little past seven a.m. It sounds awkward and strange, like the bad end of an even worse first date. He knows it, too. But it's a thing to say, much better than the truth: *see you at Cassie's funeral*. Neither of us wants to think about that.

"Thank you," I say to Jasper as the police officer opens the back door to let me out. And that sounds just as weird. But it is the truth, too. If it weren't for Jasper, I would have stayed there in that cabin with Cassie. Would have let it engulf me in flames.

***

"Thank God you're okay," my dad says, grabbing me up on the front porch and dragging me inside. Hugging me just as hard as I've been needing him to ever since my mom's accident. I had expected to feel more angry when I saw him. To be furious about what he kept from me. But in this moment none of that matters as much as the fact that he's okay. That I didn't lose him, too.

I try to speak, but instead I start to cry, huge wet sobs. I didn't even know I was holding them in. I can feel Gideon staring at me, leaning against the door to the kitchen. He looks worried when I finally pull back from my dad, wiping at my face.

"What happened?" he asks, and there's this little edge to his voice, like maybe I'm the person to blame for Cassie not coming home.

"Hey, Gideon," my dad says. "Let's take it easy with the questions, okay? Let's give Wylie a chance to get her bearings."

"I did everything I could," I say to my dad as Gideon disappears into the living room. I say it even though it feels like a lie. Maybe especially because it does.

"I know you did, sweetheart." My dad wraps an arm around me again, and it feels so natural and right. "Everyone knows that."

It isn't until much later, after I've washed my face and changed my clothes and tried again and again to scrub that awful smell of smoke and death out of my hair, after my dad has made me toast and tea and had me drink two glasses of water, that I finally begin to tell him everything. Or what I know, which is perhaps—no, surely—much, much less than everything.

"I shouldn't have—" He shakes his head, looks pained. For a second, I'm afraid I'm finally going to see him cry. "You had a right to know about your test results. It was wrong to keep them from you. I see that now. But please know I wanted to protect you. Whatever happens, I just—I wanted you to have a choice."

"A choice about what?"

"Who knows where all of this will lead? But you've seen the reaction so far—Quentin and that Collective. And there is so much more that people don't know. I can't control what will happen once it is out of my hands."

"It already is out of your hands. Quentin—Dr. Caton, whatever his name is, he knew everything. I think he's the one who hacked into your computer system."

My dad shakes his head. "He didn't know everything. I realized some of the data had been compromised, and that my personal email had been, too. What I didn't realize was that my cell phone had been hacked as well, probably using some kind of improvised IMSI device to listen in on my actual calls, too. And I certainly didn't realize that they were sending you all those texts after we spoke at the gas station, manipulating what I had said and using it against you in an even worse way. They must have blocked my subsequent texts and calls to you somehow by accessing either your phone or the central servers, because on my end they all seemed to be going through. Because I never stopped trying to find you." He shakes his head. "In any case, I've done additional research since my study that Dr. Caton certainly doesn't know about. That's all I've been doing since then, actually, looking exclusively at the Outliers."

"And?" I ask. "Because you seem worried, Dad, you honestly do. And worried, as you know, is not actually the best for me."

"I'm not worried, but I am concerned. And I want to be honest with you now—as honest as I possibly can be."

"Okay, but if this is you trying to calm me down—it's not working."

"Well, as you know, there were only the three Outliers that were among the first group of participants—actually two and then you. Of course, you weren't a part of the actual study. And I suspected right away that it was likely the phenomenon was somehow tied to age. You were all younger than the other participants."

"Yeah, Dr. Simons—or whoever he was—said it was all an age thing and those three—or two, and me, I guess—were all under eighteen."

"Well, that's not exactly true. Eighteen wouldn't be some bright-line cutoff in any case—changes with age are fluid and individual specific. Perhaps it's something related to brain structure or connectivity. Both are so dynamic in the teenage years. And it could be that whatever aspect of the brain is enabling this nonvisual, nonauditory emotional perception disappears in adulthood because it has been allowed to lie fallow."

"'Lie fallow'? You're beginning to lose me."

"It atrophies, dries up, dies," he says. "From lack of use. This is all just speculation at this point. I don't know what's causing the phenomenon, only that it exists. There is so much work left to do. But I think there is a chance, if the Outliers could learn to use these heightened perceptive abilities, to cultivate them as a legitimate skill, then perhaps they could subsist into adulthood. And could possibly become even stronger and broader. That it could lead to a genuine, scientifically verifiable intuition of some kind."

"Right, well, that sounds good," I say. "So back to that concerning part?"

"I'll need to do proper, full-scale trials, with a much more substantial study group. And as I said, we don't know the cause. It could be something other than brain structures—genetics, for instance. She never wanted to be tested, but your mother had heightened emotional intelligence. And then there's your grandmother..."

"You think she—"

"I don't know," he says firmly, realizing probably that he never should have brought her up in the first place. It's not like my grandmother's story has a happy ending. "Socialization could be the central factor. Or there could even be some kind of viral mutation at play, I suppose, though that would not seem to account for everything in this circumstance. Also, we haven't included sexual orientation or gender identity as a factor, and as I said, the sample size is far too small in any case to draw any definitive conclus—"

"Dad, stop," I say. "Please. Spit it out. *What* is it? Because whatever is freaking you out, I can tell you are circling around it."

"There appears to be a significant gender disparity, Wylie."

"English, please?" I ask.

"The Outliers—so far they are all girls," he says. "Even in the subsequent trials."

"Okay," I say slowly. "Sounds good. Score one for the ladies."

"But if this skill really does belong exclusively to women, men—all men—will be left standing on the sidelines."

"Then that will suck for them," I say, and I am not trying to blow this thing off. But I still don't see what he is getting at, or maybe I don't want to. But it's that look on my dad's face that's gnawing at me. The fear. I just want him to stop looking so worried. "It's not like all those men get to decide what's true."

"You'd be surprised what some people think they have the right to decide," he says. "For generations, men claimed what made women different also made them inferior. And now I'm going to give them ammunition?"

"We are weaker because we can do something extra that they *can't*?" I ask. "That makes no sense."

"So much of what people believe makes no sense, Wylie." He shakes his head. "That's what can make the world such a terrifyingly tragic place."

Tragic. *Not an accident*. It pops into my head. I've been trying to write Quentin's talk of my mom's accident off as yet another one of his lies, but now it's all I can think about.

"Dr. Caton and fake Dr. Simons said that what happened to Mom wasn't an accident." I clasp my hands together in my lap so I don't have to watch them start to tremble. "They lied about so many things, so I'm not sure that . . ."

But already my dad's eyes are glassy. "If you'd asked me a few weeks ago, I would have said it was definitely an accident. Now, I'm not so sure." He smiles, but it's such a terrible smile. And for the first time actual tears make it out of his eyes. "She was driving my car that night. Maybe someone even thought she was me."

"Who? Dr. Caton?" I ask.

He shakes his head and wipes at his face. "I don't think so. Only because there were things that Dr. Caton still wanted, that he would have needed to know from me."

"Then who?"

He looks at me, uncomfortable. Like this is the very last thing he wants to tell me. "I honestly don't know."

"So this whole 'other people' thing that Quentin kept talking about?"

"I want to tell you that he made that up. Believe me, I do. But this research has broad implications. Just what will the Outliers be able to do if they are given the opportunity to perfect their skills? It could be much greater than we realize, and valuable to a whole range of people. Good and bad." He looks down for a minute. "You know, your mom wanted me to tell you about your test results. She thought you deserved to know. That you had a right." He takes a deep breath. "I didn't even tell her about your results until a month later, after Thanksgiving. And then we fought about it nonstop right up until the accident. Six wasted weeks. One of my greatest regrets will always be that I didn't listen to her. She was right. She was always right about everything. Obviously, I shouldn't have recorded your results at all. But the scientist in me . . ." He shakes his head again. "I was hesitant enough that I switched them with Cassie's, then came to my senses and pulled them down altogether. But by then it was too late—the data had already been hacked."

"Did you know when Cassie was gone that it had something to do with this?"

He shakes his head some more. "I didn't know. But then, when Dr. Simons called that evening when Karen was here to tell me that his friend who'd been helping us with cybersecurity had reported another attempted data breach, I was concerned," he said. "It seemed like a significant coincidence. But I also couldn't see how they were actually connected. I certainly never considered Dr. Caton an actual threat."

I think then of the last time my dad and I spoke. When I was on the phone with him at the gas station. How I had shouted at him that I wished he'd been in the car that night instead of my mom. That I wished he was dead basically. I wince, remembering.

"I didn't mean it. What I said about you and the accident. Really I didn't."

"I know. And I'm sorry for threatening to call Dr. Shepard. But as soon as you said you'd heard from Cassie and were going to get her—I knew something was very, very wrong. I figured she must have told you something very serious for you to go, and then you wouldn't tell me where she was."

"Because I didn't know yet," I say. "I just—I wanted to be a good friend." I shake my head as the tears flood back.

My dad reaches forward and puts his hand over mine. "I know you did, and this isn't your fault, Wylie. It's mine.

I did try everything I could think of to find you. I called the police, but they dismissed me even faster than they had Karen. There was no doubt you'd left on your own, and they made it clear they weren't chasing after you, period. So my mind jumped to my only other alternative, Dr. Shepard. Obviously, those texts that said I *had* called her and that she'd reported you a danger weren't from me. I promise I never would have actually done it. But I shouldn't have even suggested it," he says, looking sad. "It's not an excuse, but I was terrified that something would happen to you. You should have seen me here trying to track your phone. For a moment, I thought I had it. But the signal up there was weak. I had it at one point while you were somewhere in New Hampshire, so I knew you were far away already, but then I lost it for good right after that. They must have had it scrambled up at the camp, too." My dad reaches forward with his other hand and wraps it around the back of my neck, eyes glistening as he rests his forehead against mine. "I'm just so glad that you're okay."

His forehead is still resting against mine when the doorbell rings. I think of how the doorbell rang when Karen showed up at our door. Only two days earlier, but it feels like a lifetime ago.

"Wait here," my dad says. "I'll get it."

I listen as he goes out to the foyer and opens the door. There's a voice I can't make out. Then my dad speaks.

"Yes, can I help you?" He does not at all sound like he actually wants to help. The other person must say something else, something I still can't hear. "Can't this wait?" my dad asks, sharp now, for sure. "She's exhausted."

"She" would be me, obviously. Now I'm up, headed to see who's there, what's going on. Because I am worried. And not because I am an Outlier—my dad and I have a lot more talking to do before I will believe that is true—but because anybody in my position would be.

"Afraid it can't wait, Dr. Lang," a gruff, official-sounding voice says as I get into the foyer. "We have some questions we need to ask your daughter. Unfortunately, time is of the essence."

"She's already told the police everything she knows," my dad says, as I try to see past the door. Still not entirely sure that I even want to.

"I understand that and I'm sorry, sir," another voice says, polite but firm. "But she's going to have to go through it one more time with the Department of Homeland Security."

When I finally look around my dad's arm, which is gripped hard on the door, there are six officers of some kind standing on our front porch. All large, plain-faced, white men. They have on matching Windbreakers with big gold emblems over the right side of their chests. They somehow look identical despite big differences in body type.

"Wylie Lang?" one of them asks. The tallest of the group. He's smiling at me now, but his teeth are too big and too bright.

"Did you find Cassie?" I ask. Because yes, there is still a small part of me that is hoping she could somehow be alive.

"I'm afraid so, miss," another one answers. He is the most muscular, more like a marine. "Deceased at the scene as you described. Along with all the other members of this group: The Collective."

"What? They're *all* dead?" I ask, my heart picking up speed. I think of Fiona and Miriam. And Lexi with her baby waiting for her at home. Maybe not innocent, not completely. But none of them deserved to die. "Dead how?"

"Dr. Quentin Caton," a third agent says. "We believe him to be the perpetrator."

"Perpetrator of what?" Because there are so many options.

"Multiple gunshot wounds, looks like an automatic weapon," he says, like I should know this already. "We have no specific reason to believe that any of the members of The Collective or Dr. Caton were able to flee. In fact, it appears to be a murder-suicide scenario. But we will need to wait for an official identification of the bodies to be sure, as well as medical examiners' reports."

"But that doesn't make any sense. They only had one gun. And it was an old rifle."

"Well, perhaps there was an arms cache you were unaware of?" the skinny one offers, like I'm an idiot to think I'd know about all their guns, and maybe I am. And yet, none of this feels right.

Unless they really came, that's what I think next. *They came and killed them all.*

"North Point, the defense contractors? Maybe it was them?"

"North Point, miss?" the short one asks, his hair so light it's almost white. He's got a tone, *goddamn stupid kid*.

"They're defense contractors," I say, already wishing that I hadn't said that part. Because it sounds stupid. But also like the only explanation that makes sense. "They want my dad's research."

The officers all look at one another with these scrunched-up eyebrows. The pudgy one is already typing the name into his phone. "North Point, huh?" he says out loud. "Well, we've got a church, a glass door company, and digital solutions—whatever that is. No defense-related anything."

"And we're all pretty familiar with the various defense contractors," the skinny one says. He looks around at the others, who nod. "We've never heard of North Point."

"But we'll look into it, of course. We'd be happy to discuss all of this further, Ms. Lang." It's the tall one again. The one with all the teeth. He takes a step closer. "We'd be happy to give you a full briefing and look into any theories you might have. We'll just need you to come with us and answer a few more questions first. I can promise it won't take long."

Before I can answer, my phone vibrates once, then again in my back pocket—two different messages, one after another. Then a third before I can even get it out of my pocket. When I pull it out, there are three texts in a row from Jasper. All asking the same question.

Are there some kind of agents at your house?

I turn my back to the door as I type out a reply.

Yes. Why?

Jasper's response comes instantly. And it's only a single word.

Run.

Acknowledgments

Thank you to my tireless and tenacious editor, Jennifer Klonsky, for taking a chance and then having superhuman faith and patience. Your contributions to this book have been legion. I am grateful not only for your exceptional editorial skills, but also for your sound judgment and sharp sense of humor. Thanks also to Catherine Wallace and Elizabeth Lynch for all your endless help.

My deepest thanks to Suzanne Murphy and Susan Katz for granting this series liftoff and to Kate Jackson for helping keep it aloft.

Thank you to the dedicated and talented HarperTeen marketing team: Diane Naughton, Elizabeth Ward, Kara Brammer, and Sabrina Abballe, as well as to the incredibly creative people in integrated marketing: Colleen O'Connell, Margot Wood, Nina Mehta, and school and library marketing: Patty Rosati and Molly Motch. Thank you also to my fantastic publicists: Cindy Hamilton and Gina Rizzo.

Many thanks to all those who created such amazing

visuals: Barb Fitzsimmons, Alison Donalty, Alison Klapthor, and especially, Sarah Kaufman.

Thank you to the endlessly clever and adept HarperTeen sales team: Andrea Pappenheimer, Kerry Moynagh, and Kathy Faber. Thanks also to: Jen Wygand, Jenny Sheridan, Heather Doss, Deb Murphy, Fran Olson, Susan Yeager, Jess Malone, and Jess Abel, as well as Samantha Hagerbaumer, Andrea Rosen, and Jean McGinley.

Thank you to all the committed people in HarperTeen managing editorial: Josh Weiss, Bethany Reis, and my copy editor, Valerie Shea.

Many thanks to my fabulous agent Marly Rusoff, Michael Radulescu, and Julie Mosow. And so much gratitude to the indefatigable marvel that is Gina Laquinta. Thank you also to Shari Smiley, Lizzy Kremer, Michael Taeckens and Harriet Moore. And to the always wonderful Claire Wachtel.

Many thanks to the experts who so generously lent me their wisdom: Dr. Marc Brackett, Dr. Cassandra Gould, Dr. Allyson Hobbs, Dr. John D. Mayer, Dr. Rebecca

Prentice, Dr. Matt Wall, Wendy Green, and Leslie Lewin. I am indebted also to the incredible work of Roxane Gay.

Endless thanks to my fantastic friends and family: Martin and Claire Prentice, Mike Blom, Catherine and David Bohigian, Cindy Buzzeo, Cara Cragan and Michael Moroney, the Cragan Family, the Crane Family, Joe and Naomi Daniels, Larry and Suzy Daniels, Bob Daniels and Craig Leslie, Diane and Stanley Dohm, Elena Evangelo and Dan Panosian, Dave Fischer, Heather and Michael Frattone, Tania Garcia, Sonya Glazer, Jeff Johnson, David Kear, Merrie Koehlert, Hallie Levin, John McCreight and Kim Healey, Brian McCreight, the Metzger Family, Jason Miller, Tara and Frank Pometti, Stephen Prentice, Motoko Rich and Mark Topping, Jon Reinish, Bronwen Stine, the Thomatos Family, Meg Yonts, Denise Young Farrell, and Christine Yu. Thank you to the baristas at the Park Slope Starbucks for treating me like an honorary employee. And a very special thank-you to the wonderful Kate Eschelbach for so steadily holding down the fort.

Much gratitude to my first reader, Megan Crane, to Nicole Kear, in charge of daily vetting, and to Victoria

Cook, who fanned the flames of a tiny spark years ago.

Thank you to my daughter Emerson for inspiring me daily with your grit and determination. And to my daughter Harper for the living reminder of what it means to be equal parts kind and courageous. Many thanks to my husband, Tony, for the months of way-more-than-your-fair-share of child care and for always making me smile, after making them smile. Couldn't have done it without you, wouldn't ever want to. And to all three of you, thank you for always welcoming me home.

LOOK OUT FOR MORE

THE OUTLIERS

COMING SOON...